RELUCTANT CHEMISTRY

FRANCES COWIE

BLUE BUTTERFLY PRESS

Reluctant Chemistry

Published by Blue Butterfly Press, New Zealand.
www.francescowie.com
Copyright © 2021 by Frances Cowie.
The moral right of the author has been asserted.

ISBN: 978-0-473-57675-2 (paperback)
ISBN: 978-0-473-57676-9 (e-book)

A catalog record of this book is available from the National Library of New Zealand.

Cover Design: Steven Novak - www.novakillustration.com
Editor: The Error Eliminator - www.theerroreliminator.wordpress.com
Developmental Editor: Samantha Burton

250311

To Grant.

May you rest in peace among the flowers and butterflies you so loved.
Your enthusiasm for our lifelong friendship was greatly appreciated.
Much love xx.

RELUCTANT CHEMISTRY

TULLOCH POINT

PART I

1

RABBIT HOLE

Keeping to the grass verge, CeCe headed along Old Cemetery Road, illuminating the way with her phone as the moon slipped behind a cloud. Attending the Christmas party had been her cousin Molly's idea. *Come*, she'd pleaded. *It's about time you let those curls down again.* So CeCe had gone with her.

Restless, she'd nursed a half-size bottle of sparkling rosé until she could no longer stand the same old crowd, the boring small talk, or the sight of her ex, Travis.

She checked her phone for service. Coverage stopped about five miles out of town and didn't start again until you reached the junction of the coastal highway. But even if she had reception, with her parents away for the evening and her brother, Mitch, in town with friends, who would she call?

The beat of the music from the party competed with the roll of the surf, confusing her senses. And as CeCe stood on the side of the road, trying to get her bearings, the sound of an approaching car startled her. Although not unusual for locals to use the back road, her gut clenched and her stride quickened. Maybe Travis had realized she'd bailed and come after her, but his souped-up Impreza had a distinctive throaty roar, and this one sounded quieter.

CeCe hurried across the road and headed toward a shelter-belt dividing one field from the other. Her heartbeat racing, she clambered over the fence in front of her. Pine needles softened the impact on landing, but as she glanced over her shoulder at the looming headlights, her foot caught in a rabbit hole, and she hit the ground with a thud.

"Ow! Shit."

The vehicle passed at speed, dust billowing in its wake before it slowed. Her eyes welling with tears from the pain, CeCe remained frozen in place as its taillights turned from red to white.

The driver reversed, stopped to her left, and lowered the window. She dropped her gaze and kept her head down, knowing she couldn't make a run for it even if she tried.

"Are you all right?" A man's voice, deep and filled with concern, boomed through the night air.

CeCe scooted backward on her butt, pine needles stabbing the skin through her skimpy summer dress.

He opened the door, rounded the front of the SUV, and stepped toward her, his headlights illuminating their surround-ings. "What are you doing out here?"

"Nothing. Walking home."

Keeping to the far side of the fence, the man crouched in front of her. Although darkness shadowed his features, CeCe could tell by his stance and the sound of his voice that he was tall and youngish. "Are you hurt?"

She shuffled backward a fraction, wincing from the pain. "I'm fine. My boyfriend's on his way to collect me. He'll be here any minute."

The guy glanced up and down the road then looked back at

her. "My name's Luka. I work with Search and Rescue as a paramedic. Do you need help?"

"Next you'll tell me you live on the second floor."

He chuckled. "Ah, the girl has a sense of humor! So, how did you become separated?"

"What?"

"From your boyfriend? You said he was coming back for you."

"Look, I said I'm fine. Please just leave me alone."

Luka jumped the fence with ease. "You think I'm going to leave you out here at the intersection of 'Nowhere' and 'I Don't Give a Shit'?"

"I'm not getting into a car with a stranger."

"So you'd rather stay here and wait for your elusive boyfriend? Who, by the way, must be a prize jerk for leaving you alone out here in the first place." He leaned toward her as if waiting for a response, his hair flopping over his forehead. "Do you think you can stand?"

She shook her head.

"What's your name?"

She didn't want to tell him her name, didn't want to get in his car. A female hitchhiker had been murdered in the area when CeCe was a child, and that story had stuck in her head.

"Look, I know you don't know me, but I'm not going to try anything, okay?"

"But you're not a local?"

"No, I'm here on an exchange program with the flight school."

CeCe was familiar with the flight school. Everyone in Tulloch Point was. She took a deep breath. "CeCe."

"Right then, CeCe. Let's get you over that fence."

Bracing herself with her good leg, CeCe reluctantly grasped

hold of Luka's outstretched hand. Once upright, she hopped on her left foot and gingerly lowered her right. "Ouch." She went to grab hold of the fence but lost her balance.

Strong arms broke her fall. "Just take it slowly."

Tears threatening, she gritted her teeth against the pain. "It hurts."

"Okay, don't weight-bear in case it's broken. What happened anyway?"

CeCe hesitated. "I had an Alice moment."

Luka chuckled again. "Those rabbit holes have a lot to answer for."

She almost smiled. Most guys she knew wouldn't have understood the *Alice in Wonderland* reference.

"Right, lean on me."

She took his offered arm again as they stood at the fence line.

"You okay for me to lift you over?"

"Do I have a choice?"

"Sure." Luka glanced upward. "But by the sound of that thunder, it's about to bucket down. So, you either stay here and freeze your wet ass off or get in a car with a complete stranger who just might be a perverted serial killer posing as a Search and Rescue volunteer." Luka shone his phone light in her general direction.

"You're not helping here."

"Sorry, that wasn't funny." He waited. "So what do you want to do?"

CeCe checked out the fence, frowning at the logistics.

"Promise I won't try anything," he repeated. "Okay?"

She nodded. Without giving her time to protest, Luka picked her up, carefully lifted her over the top wire, and set her down.

"Hold on to the post for support, and remember, don't

weight-bear." He followed CeCe over the fence and opened the rear passenger door of his SUV before returning for her. "You'll be more comfortable in the back. You can rest your leg along the seat."

As she took his arm once again, she noticed the SAR logo on the front passenger door and relaxed a little. A small spark fired in her core. Luka the Search and Rescue Guy smelled like infatuation and warm summer nights spent cuddling beside a beach bonfire.

Get a grip.

When they reached his SUV, he lifted her inside, making sure to keep her foot elevated. His arm brushed her torso as he clicked the seat belt into place, and she stared straight ahead, holding her breath steady as she worried the blue butterfly necklace at the hollow of her neck.

"All set?"

"Thanks," she mumbled, her unease returning. What was she thinking, accepting a ride from a stranger?

Luka started the engine, and as the lights from the dash illuminated his face, CeCe studied his angular features. With short hair that hung down over one side of his forehead, he had the lean but broad physique of a swimmer.

Throwing a glance in his rearview mirror, he pulled onto the gravel road and headed back toward town. Eminem's 'Love the Way You Lie' streamed through the stereo as he hit the speed limit, and as Rihanna sang the chorus, CeCe closed her eyes and prayed Luka was who he claimed to be.

At the junction with the coastal highway, he pulled over and turned to look at her. She stiffened and inhaled deeply, struggling to control her racing heartbeat.

"I'll just call you in." He grabbed his phone from the center console and unlocked it.

Who was he calling?

"Hi. You on duty? Okay, I have a patient for you." Luka listened. Chuckled. He had an unusual accent, like a universal melting pot with a distinct British undertone. "Yeah, that's good. We'll be there in ten." Pause. "Ankle sprain of the rabbit-hole variety."

After one final chuckle, Luka ended the call and looked back at her. "You're in luck. That was Drew, a friend of mine. They're having a quiet night at the hospital." He motioned to her phone, still clenched in her hand. "We have service now if you want to contact your boyfriend."

She checked it for missed calls or messages. Nothing. "I'm good."

He held her gaze and tilted his head to the side, and as a faint smile lit up his face, she leaned back and closed her eyes.

Under the harsh lights of the emergency department, Luka looked different. Taller, broader, and much younger than she first thought, with the most intriguing moody brown eyes.

Forms filled in, they sat in the waiting room, CeCe in a wheelchair and Luka beside her. His sight on his phone screen and one hand to his forehead, he scrolled through some app.

Uncomfortable by the silence, she went to speak but didn't know what to say. So instead, she looked around the room, reading posters for flu jabs and hand-washing guides.

"You don't have to stay." CeCe briefly glanced his way, then back to the posters, struggling to keep her hands still in her lap.

He looked up. "It's fine. I'll wait and give you a ride home."

"Thanks, but I live miles away. I can call my brother."

Luka brushed aside her concerns with a gesture. "Well, I'll

stay a bit longer. What were you doing out there all alone, anyway?"

"I'd been to a party. It got boring, so I decided to walk home."

"And the boyfriend?"

She folded her arms across her chest but said nothing, cringing at the memory of Travis, drunk and inappropriate as he'd stared at her over the shoulder of some scantily clad girl in his arms, and mouthed, 'Call me.'

A doctor entered the waiting room and motioned to Luka, who stood and pushed CeCe down the corridor to the treatment area, her reply now redundant. After the introductions, the two men exchanged pleasantries for a moment before Luka excused himself with a brief goodbye.

While she hadn't wanted or expected him to stay, the overwhelming sense of loss when he left surprised her. She'd not forget the kindness of her knight in tight jeans and Henley stretched across broad shoulders.

Dr. Drew checked the form. "Right, CeCe, let's see what we're dealing with, shall we? I just need you to transfer from the chair to the bed."

By the time she returned to the waiting room, bandaged but not broken, Luka had left. CeCe longed to do the same—go home. She didn't want to stay in town at Molly's as planned. She wanted to wake up in her own bed tomorrow morning and eat oatmeal with blueberries. Wanted to have her mum ask about her night and her father disapprove of her choices. She wanted to relax in their care.

With Molly not answering her phone, CeCe flicked her a short text, saying she was going home. Next, she pulled up the contact details for her brother, Mitch, and hit the call button.

"Hey, it's CeCe. Are you still in town?"

"Yeah, why?"

"I'm at the hospital, with a sprained ankle. Can you pick me up?"

"Shit. Are you okay?" The background noise of a rowdy bar competed with her brother's reply.

"A bit sore, but I'm fine. Are you sober enough to drive?"

"Yeah, I'm good. I'll be there soon."

Reclined on the sofa the next day, CeCe realized she'd left her favorite boot in Luka's car. Maybe she could contact him through the SAR office, leave a thank you box of chocolates or bottle of wine with an attached note asking him to drop it off at the library where she worked.

She closed her eyes briefly, thinking of the man who'd come to her rescue. Did Luka read? Possibly. There was something overtly sexy about a guy who enjoyed a good novel, and CeCe loved those social media posts of hot guys reading books on trains or in cafés.

Her phone pinged with a text alert, and CeCe grabbed it off the sofa table beside her.

Molly: How's the ankle?

CeCe: Painful and annoying.

Molly: Sorry, I was outside with Jesse and didn't realize you'd left. Travis was on my case all night, kept asking where you were. He reckons he's still in love with you.

Travis. CeCe had lost count of how many times she'd excused his behavior. How often he'd failed to turn up when he'd said he would. The days of no replies to her texts. She could visualize their future: Packing his lunch and doing his laundry, just as his mother did now. Friday night drinks with the girls. Saturday nights hanging out at the rugby pavilion. Lying awake next to him in the early hours, never feeling he truly 'got' her. Never getting to experience that all-consuming passion she craved.

CeCe: Was that before or after he called me morbid and boring?
Molly: What? He's a dick.
CeCe: Yep!
Molly: When can you go back to work?
CeCe: In a few days. Mum's been fussing over me, bless her.
Molly: Okay. Keep me posted. xx

CeCe dropped her phone on the sofa. With the aid of a crutch, she maneuvered herself over to the window and stared out toward the western hills. The sky had brightened, the sun sitting high overhead. She checked the clock on the wall. Almost one, but her parents had gone out for lunch, and she couldn't be bothered fixing herself anything.

As was often the case when alone, thoughts of Anna drifted into her mind. What would she be doing if she were still here? Would they be on better terms, best friends again?

She returned to the sofa, picked up her phone, opened her Favorites, and hit the Call icon. The usual eight rings before it clicked to answer.

"Hey, it's Anna. Please don't leave a message. Text me. We'll talk later."

"Hi, it's me. I..." As always, CeCe struggled to find the right words. "I guess I just wanted to hear your voice. I know it's been a while, but the truth is, I miss you. More than yesterday or the day before. I miss you so much, and I want... want you back."

It was the first message she'd left in quite some time. Usually, she'd listen to Anna's recorded greeting then hang up. But she'd visited a clairvoyant the week before, a woman named Rita with wild auburn hair and a welcoming smile. Rita had told her Anna was desperate for contact and to look for butterflies because that's how her spirit would present itself.

Skeptical by nature, CeCe still couldn't decide whether the reading had been a profound step forward, a coincidence, or a load of garbage. Didn't most clairvoyants use butterflies as their medium of choice? Were millions of past souls truly floating around summer gardens, all delicately beautiful and having a marvelous time?

CeCe limped out onto the veranda and watched a monarch butterfly flit from plant to plant, wondering why butterflies morphed into their most exquisite incarnation at the end of their life cycle.

Was Anna floating on updrafts and sunbeams? Could she hear CeCe's voice? Feel her pain?

No. She couldn't.

Because Anna was dead.

2

CONSTRAINED

Luka glanced up from the map on his phone screen as his boss, Brad Jones, walked into the office. "Morning."

"It's hot out there already." Brad sank into his chair and booted up his computer, his armpits soaked with sweat. "Any word on the missing hunter?"

Luka stood and crossed the small space to drop a pod into the coffee machine. Before moving to Tulloch Point, he'd thought the exchange program would be a waste of time, but he'd certainly seen plenty of action over the past month. "Nothing as yet."

"I hear you had a rescue of your own last night."

Obviously, news traveled fast in this part of the country, much faster than in Clifton Falls. But then, small towns were known for their robust rumor mills. "I did. CeCe Dobson. I found her by Old Cemetery Road with a sprained ankle. How did you know about that?"

"Her father called, wanting the details."

Luka motioned to the coffee. "You want one?"

"Thanks." Brad accepted the offered coffee and blew across

the rim of the mug. "No doubt he'll pay us a visit sometime soon to find out what went down. Frank's one tough nut." He set the mug down on his desk as Luka added another pod into the machine. "Mind you, with three daughters, he's had to be. Not easy keeping tabs on them, especially that CeCe. She's a wild child, that's for sure. Or was, anyway."

Luka frowned. He'd not got that impression in the short time he'd spent with her. In fact, she seemed rather cautious and timid. "Where does she work?"

"At the library, I think. What happened to her, anyway?"

"She was wandering down the side of the road in the dark and tripped in a rabbit hole. I picked her up, dropped her off at the hospital, and left."

"What time was that?"

Luka cast his mind back. He'd been called out to a false alarm around eight thirty, and by the time they'd arrived at the hospital, it had been after nine. "About nine thirty."

"What was she doing out there on her own?"

"She said something about her boyfriend coming back for her, but he never showed."

Brad sipped his coffee. "Maybe you should log it, you know, just to keep everything aboveboard."

Luka shrugged. He hadn't been on duty by then, and to him, CeCe Dobson was someone who'd needed a lift rather than a rescue, but Brad was the boss. "Okay."

Tulloch Point Public Library annexed a cluster of municipal buildings on the edge of the tree-lined town square. Today was Luka's second visit within the space of a week. The first was when he'd dropped off CeCe's boot a few days earlier. She hadn't been working that day; however the receptionist, an older woman, had assured him she'd take care of it.

He seldom used the library at home, but he loved the ambiance of this one. The nineteenth-century architecture, the smell of the countless pages—bound in such a way as to make perfect sense to those who read them—and the murmurs of staff as they paced through their day with determined efficiency.

And then there was CeCe. For some reason, Luka struggled to imagine her as a librarian—she seemed more of an outdoors type to him. He had no idea how he'd come to that conclusion. Perhaps it was the smattering of tiny freckles across the bridge of her nose or the light tan of her skin.

As he entered the building, the same receptionist greeted him with a smile. Luka perused the crime section, searching for the latest Grisham or Childs. However, new releases appeared thin on the ground in Tulloch Point Public Library, so he strolled along the aisles, coming to a halt when he reached the aviation section. Again, there seemed little on offer, but as he leafed through his first pick, he detected movement out of the corner of his eye. Luka didn't need to look up to know it was her. But he did anyway.

Wow!

Her hair tumbling about her shoulders in a mass of soft curls rather than tied back, CeCe looked different from what he remembered. She stepped in front of the book cart she was pushing, a shy smile lighting up her face. "Excuse me. Are you Luka, the guy who dropped me off at the hospital?"

He couldn't stop staring. In a high-necked ribbed top, a black pencil skirt, and ballet flats, she was wildly beautiful but constrained. He wondered how old she was. The night they met, she'd been a mess—agitated and fearful—but today she seemed amiable and had the cutest dimples he'd ever seen. "That's me." He offered his hand. "Luka O'Leary."

The heat of her palm and the strength of her handshake surprised him. She straightened the already straight books on her cart. "Thank you for the ride into town. I was in pain, so probably wasn't as gracious as I should have been."

"No problem. I was only doing my job."

CeCe motioned to the book in his hand. "Are you into helicopters?"

"Yeah. I'm trying to get enough hours to complete my license, so…"

She turned back to the cart, pulled a book free, and held it out to him. "This one's popular with the chopper guys."

He flipped the book over to scan the blurb, then glanced up. "Thanks. Looks like what I'm after."

"Well, guess I'd better get back to work. Have a nice day."

Luka watched her walk away, surprised by a spark he hadn't felt in a long time. After his last breakup, he'd vowed to keep his four months in Tulloch Point female free.

But CeCe…*Shit*!

As she pushed the cart into the next row and slotted books into place, CeCe fought to calm her racing heart. Luka was a chopper guy! A tall, lean, golden-tanned chopper guy. She stood at the end of the mountaineering section and watched him stroll over to the desk. He pulled his card from his wallet and handed it to Miss Libby, an avid reader in her seventies who'd volunteered as receptionist off and on for the past twenty years. Smiling at each other, the two chatted for a few minutes, and as he turned to leave, CeCe ducked into the row beside her, holding her breath as her hand calmed her chest.

She grinned.

Some men wore their threads well. Their shirts hung impeccably from the shoulder while jeans hugged their butt without compromise. That was him—Hot Chopper Guy: rescuer of girls who tumbled down rabbit holes.

Slowly making her way over to the desk, she stared after him as he crossed the foyer. Miss Libby cleared her throat, and when CeCe met her gaze, she winked. "Nice, eh?"

CeCe chuckled. "Very nice."

"Not the right age for either of us, but I sure could get lost in those gorgeous brown eyes."

CeCe picked up another load of returns and stacked them on her cart. She'd noticed Luka's eyes too, and the word *brown* didn't do them justice. They were more of a cognac. "Plenty of young guys go for older women like you."

"So they say. I saw a documentary on the TV about it once. But I've had my cougar experience. Fun while it lasted, but these days, I get all the romance I need from reading."

"Cougar experience? Tell me more!"

Miss Libby leaned back in her chair and looked up as if replaying the scene in her head. "I was in my late forties, and the guy must have been just shy of thirty. He came to deal to the grass grub in my lawn. Said my décolletage fascinated him." She laughed. "I was fascinated by his stamina."

CeCe tried to imagine Miss Libby as a younger woman but failed. She wondered if women still felt sexual in their seventies, the thought making her shudder. "Did you ever marry?"

"No, not me. I had a couple of proposals, but I preferred having the freedom to come and go as I pleased, to see whoever I wanted on my terms. I had no interest in losing myself in a man's world, and that's what happened in my day. It worked for some, but not for me. Now I'm alone. No kids either, of course."

CeCe already knew Miss Libby had no children and sometimes contemplated what it must be like to be in your seventies with no one to call your own. "No regrets?"

"We all have regrets, but it's best not to dwell on them. Mind you, if I were thirty years younger, that Luka fella could slot his boots under my bed any day of the week. I like them tall with a tight butt."

CeCe snorted a laugh. She seldom experienced an intense physical reaction to guys, especially not older ones. Travis, a year younger than her at seventeen, had worked hard to pique her interest. Luka wouldn't have to work hard. Her interest was already well and truly piqued.

It seemed Travis had been wrong. She wasn't boring; she was bored.

3

TENNESSEE WHISKEY

The Burger Shack's decor had remained unchanged for many years. But the new owners had recently spruced up the place, replacing the original Formica tables and orange chairs, and lining the walls with a mix of corrugated iron sheeting and honed concrete. They'd even added vegetarian options to their menu.

Other than that, they still had the same jukebox—albeit with an updated playlist and a jar of coins for those who didn't carry small change—still served their shakes in ice-cold soda glasses, and still made the best hand-cut fries in town.

CeCe strolled up to the counter and ordered two black bear and mushroom burgers, a large fries, and a couple of strawberry shakes. Seated at a table by the front window, Molly checked her texts. The two cousins were complete opposites. Molly—all makeup, designer clothes, and flat-ironed hair—loved fashion, social media, and high heels. CeCe, who was more of a tomboy, preferred jeans to dresses and considered a lick of mascara and some natural lip gloss a made-up face.

Her change clutched in her hand, CeCe crossed to the jukebox and pushed a couple of coins into the slot. Meghan Trainor's voice filled the room as she returned to the table.

She took a seat next to Molly, so she could watch the world go by while checking her texts. "You know when I twisted my ankle the night of the party?"

Molly's gaze remained glued to her phone, her manicured fingers flicking across the keypad. "Yeah."

"Well, that guy came into the library yesterday."

Molly looked up as the server delivered their order. "What, to see you?"

"No, to get a book. But he's seriously cute—well, when he smiles. Otherwise, he looks kinda moody."

Molly grinned and raised a questioning brow. She didn't need words to make her point—her expression talked for her.

"What?" CeCe asked.

"That's the first time you've used the words *cute* and *guy* in the same conversation since Anna died. You really must be over Travis."

CeCe shrugged. Months ago, the universe had kicked her into a cold, dark place, and her life had ceased to be an endless merry-go-round of cool beer, bonfires, and make-out sessions in the back seat. There seemed little she could do about it at the time, but that didn't mean she had to stay trapped there forever. "I figure I have two options. Live my best life for both of us or stay home and dwell on the whys."

"Living your best life sounds like a plan." Molly picked up her milkshake, twirled the straw in the glass, and took a sip. "What did Travis actually say to you at the party?"

"What, besides telling me I'm morbid and boring? Oh, and I'm obsessive too, it seems. Then he suggested we have sex in the upstairs bathroom."

"You're kidding me. I've said it once and I'll say it again, the guy's a total jerk."

"Yep. I'm beginning to see that."

"Actually, jerk's too good for him. Travis is more of a narcissist, and believe me, they're trouble."

Molly, whose double-D cup size had attracted men's unwanted attention since the age of fourteen, knew how to read the opposite sex in a way CeCe never would. Of course, that didn't mean her love life was perfect. In fact, right now, she was sailing through murky waters with a guy called Jesse, a drummer from a band.

CeCe had no interest in discussing Travis anymore. Her stomach usually clenched at the mere mention of his name, but with her thoughts clearer over the past few weeks, she was finally prying away from his hold. She bit into her burger and groaned. "This is so good."

Molly did the same but pulled a face. "Yeah? I'm not convinced on this whole bean thing."

"Why not? It tastes just like beef."

"Whatever. Anyway, this rabbit-hole guy, have you Googled him yet?"

The jukebox flipped over to 'Tennessee Whiskey.' It had been one of Anna's favorite songs, and CeCe swayed to its slow-tempo beat. "No. Do you think I should?"

"Course. I Google every man I meet. Just in case he has a murky past."

"Good point."

The drive from town to the orchard took fifteen minutes, give or take. Before Anna died, CeCe would sing all the way, but since

July, not so much. The road now seemed longer and more solitary.

She slotted one of her sister's CDs into the player. Ally had been writing music and singing her original songs since she was a child. CeCe wished she could sing like her. She loved the rasp of Ally's voice, and every time she missed her sister, she'd play her CD on repeat.

Will you dance with me? Hold me like I'm precious? Be my only man?
Will you hear me, dare me, catch me when I fall head over heels…?

When CeCe walked through the kitchen door, she found her mum sitting at the island, MacBook open and one hand hovering over her mouse. CeCe hugged her around the shoulders. "I'm home safe."

"So I see. How's Molly?"

Mouth dry, CeCe opened the fridge and pulled out a carton of orange juice. "Okay. Crushing on some guy from a band."

Andrea narrowed her eyes at her daughter and removed her reading glasses. "I saw Hannah at the supermarket this afternoon. She said you left another message on Anna's phone."

CeCe nodded. "Yeah. I just wanted to hear her voice, and some days, I want her to hear mine."

"I know, but they're struggling with their loss, and it's a painful reminder."

"I never thought they'd still be checking her phone."

"They probably just want to hear her voice too."

This she knew. Anna's mother had explained it to CeCe after the first time she'd called and left a message. "I wish I could turn back the clock."

Her mother leaned forward in her chair and rested her hands under her chin. "What would you do differently?"

"Not poke my nose in where it didn't belong. Dillon was, *is* a jerk, but it wasn't my place to tell her."

"Look, that boyfriend of hers isolated her not only from her friends but also from her family as well. So don't be too hard on yourself." Her mother's expression softened. "You know what else Hannah told me?"

"No, what?"

"Anna was at Dillon's place the night she died. She stormed out on them after an argument, and he was waiting for her on his motorcycle at the curb. Hannah and Tom were worried sick. That was the last time they saw her alive."

"But...do they think he had something to do with her death?"

"No. It wasn't his fault, and as a mother, I'm so thankful for that. Imagine how much harder it would be for her parents if he had. It was just her time, I guess."

"I still don't get it. How can sudden death syndrome even be a thing?" CeCe sat at the island, the orange juice sitting forgotten on the counter. "Life's really screwed up at times, don't you think?"

"It can be. Sometimes, it's best not to think too deeply about things."

"But how do you make your mind hush when it doesn't want to listen?"

"Distraction. Remove yourself from one moment and enter another." Andrea stood and walked over to the freezer. She pulled out a carton of ice cream and popped it in the microwave for a few seconds. "Eat ice cream."

"Do you ever miss Mitch's dad?" CeCe knew little about

her mother's first husband, only that he'd died in an accident when Mitch was a toddler.

Her mother slid the carton and a spoon toward CeCe. "It's been over twenty years. Memories fade. But I do still think of him."

"What was he like?" CeCe scooped the spoon around the melted sides.

"Gentle. Handsome. A lot like Mitch, actually. And that's unsettling sometimes, seeing him in our son. After he died, I slept in Mitch's room every night for weeks—too scared to be alone. At the time, I thought I'd never love again."

"So he loved you? Really loved you?"

"He did, and he was very affectionate. Some women hate that, but I loved it. Norman was furious when he found out I was pregnant, but Nicholas stood up to him. He made it clear that if he had to choose, he'd choose me over his father."

CeCe had only met Mitch's grandfather a few times, and she'd never warmed to him. "He was weird, that Norman guy. I hated it when we used to drop Mitch off at Lime Tree Hill."

"Yes, he wasn't exactly the ideal father-in-law. Even so, I had nothing to do with him for years after the accident."

CeCe ate another spoonful of ice cream, savoring the tangy taste of passionfruit and coconut on her tongue. "Do you think souls can hear us when we talk to them?"

"I certainly hope so. Otherwise, I've wasted a whole lot of words and breath speaking to Nicholas." Andrea grabbed another spoon from the drawer, dug into the ice cream, and popped it into her mouth. "Yum. This is good. Anyway, how are you getting on with Travis? Is he leaving you alone?" She helped herself to another spoonful.

"Yeah, and I've deleted our song from my playlist, so that's a start, right?" She returned the lid to the ice cream and slid the carton across the island. "You'd better put this away, or there won't be any left."

"I know you've been through a lot lately, but I'm so proud of you. You're a good kid."

"Thanks. But I'm still making mistakes and gathering regrets."

"Aren't we all." Her mother's expression softened as she opened the freezer. "I miss Anna too. She was a beautiful wee soul."

An unexpected rush of emotion set CeCe's cheeks on fire. "The Burger Shack's jukebox played 'Tennessee Whiskey' tonight. She loved that song." She moved to her mother's side and kissed her on the cheek. "Right, I'm off to bed. See you tomorrow."

"Okay. Night."

In her room, CeCe undressed and lay on her bed, the melody of 'Tennessee Whiskey' playing in her head. The French doors to the veranda stood open, the sheer curtains stilled by the unrelenting heat.

Hot Chopper Guy. He might be a little old for her, but that didn't stop the chemical reaction. And when it came to chemistry, did age matter? Just because she'd never dated an older guy didn't mean she shouldn't. Every time she'd looked at him yesterday, his eyes had held her in suspension—a new and not unwelcome sensation.

She grabbed her iPad from the nightstand and Googled his name. At first, there seemed to be nothing much to see. But as she scrolled down, a Luka O'Leary appeared under a link for the Rata River Equestrian Center. She opened the website and studied their home page. Was this where he worked?

According to the *About Us* page, the Clifton Falls center was a family-run business headed by a Vanessa O'Leary. Although she looked too young to be his mother, the picture might have been photoshopped, as was often the case on promo pages.

CeCe clicked *Gallery* on the menu bar, and as she scrolled down the page, there he was—tight black T-shirt and corded biceps—nuzzling his handsome face into the neck of a chestnut beauty of the equine variety. He looked younger in the shot, maybe around twenty, but there was no mistaking that jawline. And while he'd worn his hair a little longer back then, it still held the same shape, had the same highlighted strands.

Of course, his wasn't the only photo on the site, and in amongst the array of horses, buildings, and random people, an older man smiled back at her. Judging by their similar features, he had to be his father. CeCe studied Luka's picture again. She loved uncovering layers to people's stories; it piqued her interest.

Eyelids heavy, she let the iPad fall to the bed and her thoughts drift. What if she'd had the courage to ask him out for a drink yesterday? Would they be at the pub now, dancing to some country band, constructing the prologue to each other's stories?

On her nightstand, her phone vibrated. She lifted it and read the text.

Molly: Home safe?
CeCe: Yep. Thanks for tonight. It was good to catch up.
Molly: I went to the pub after you left.
CeCe: Good night?
Molly: Night's not over yet!!! I'll fill you in tomorrow. Remember to Google that rabbit hole guy.

CeCe: Done. No murk detected. Stay safe and sweet dreams.
Molly: You too. xoxo

4

SANDWATER BAY

The day was a scorcher, far too hot for clothes, and at the knock on his front door, Luka lowered the David Baldacci novel he'd found in the SAR office and sighed. He'd not had any visitors since arriving in Tulloch Point, but maybe it was a group of kids fundraising for a school project. He grabbed the lavalava from the bed and wrapped it low around his hips as he strode across the room.

When his visitor knocked again, Luka turned the dead bolt and opened the door to find CeCe Dobson standing before him and a classic Kombi van parked in his driveway. Dressed in frayed cutoff denim shorts with a white T-shirt bunched into a knot at the front, she clutched a brown paper bag in one hand and a peace sign key ring in the other. His sight flicked briefly to her long legs and tanned midriff before he could stop himself.

She pushed her sunglasses onto the top of her head, where they disappeared amongst her curls. She smiled, her eyes wide. "Sorry to rock up without calling first, but…"

"Come in." He held the door open, catching a trace of her perfume as she stepped past him and into the hallway. It was the same scent that had been on his mind since the night they met. "How did you know where to find me?"

CeCe shrugged. "Small town and all that." She offered him the bag. "I bought you this—as a thank you."

Luka pulled out the bottle and studied the label.

"Merlot gets a bad rap sometimes," she said, "but this one's from an organic vineyard in Clifton Falls. It's one of my favorites."

"I know it. We lived all over the place when I was growing up, but my family home's in the Rata River Valley. Thank you for this." He put the wine on the counter. Took a deep breath.

"Really? I love that area. How long are you here for?"

"Just until Easter."

CeCe nodded, then glanced around the room, taking in his unmade bed, the book lying face down on the nightstand, and his jeans puddled in a heap on the floor. When she turned her attention to him, he smiled. She seemed young, maybe late teens, but she sure knew how to give off interested vibes.

"Anyway, I should let you get back to your day. I just wanted to thank you for your knight-in-shining-armor gig. It was most gallant of you."

Luka chuckled. "I've been called many things, but never gallant. Would you like a drink?"

A silence ensued. "Actually," she said with a slow smile, "I'm going for a swim. The first of the new year. You want to come?" Hazel eyes held his gaze.

"How old are you?"

"Eighteen. Nineteen in May."

CeCe played with a lock of hair, twisting it around her finger. Feathers fluttered from her earlobes, and leather sandals with beads along the bridge of her foot added a hippy vibe. "If it matters," she continued, "I could lie and say I'm twenty. You?"

"Twenty-six. Twenty-seven in April."

"Perfect." She flashed him a flirty smile. "So, are you coming or not? Because if you are, you'd better ditch that skirt and put on some shorts."

"It's a lavalava, not a skirt. Guys wear them all the time in Samoa."

"Do they? Funny, I was in Samoa last year, and I don't remember seeing any."

"Well, I thought it *might* be better than answering the door naked."

A blush crept up her neck and landed on her cheeks. She had one of those captivating faces: touched by the brush of beauty and a sunny disposition. And as they stood in each other's space, Luka had the strangest feeling that if he got into her VW and they drove away, he was done for.

Eighteen?

CeCe didn't miss a beat. "Come on, go grab your stuff, Chopper Guy. I'll wait in the van."

Still stunned by her invitation, he hesitated before a *why not?* flashed across his mind. "I'll be out in a minute."

Luka waited for her to leave before tugging on his jeans and a fresh T-shirt. *If it matters, I could lie and say I'm twenty.* Did it matter? Maybe it would tomorrow, or in a few days' time, or perhaps months from now when summer's fervor had faded, but right at that moment, he couldn't care less.

Outside, he climbed into her van and clicked his seat belt into place. "Where did you get the Kombi? What is it, a sixty-six?"

She turned the key in the ignition, and the engine sputtered twice before kicking into life. "Yeah, I think so. It was Mum's back in the day, but now I'm the only one who drives it. Has that whole 'summer road trip' vibe about it, don't you think?"

"It does." Luka glanced over his shoulder at the mattress in the back. "I looked at buying a split-window model recently, but I missed out on the auction. They're worth a fortune."

CeCe pulled out onto the street, and as Calvin Harris sung about summer on the radio and the scent of lavender from a small bunch hanging off the rearview mirror filled the air, he relaxed. She swayed in her seat in time to the music, and he did the same.

"Yeah, Dad jokes that whoever I marry can have the Kombi as a dowry, so they can sleep in it when the going gets tough."

Luka stared out the side window, thinking how lucky some guy would be to get both the girl and the van. "Something to keep in mind."

This made her chuckle, and he looked her way. She'd pulled her hair back in a loose ponytail, but with the window down, dancing tendrils brushed her face and neck. He loved a woman with curls. Loved running his hands through the coils and lathering them with shampoo in the shower. "Where are we going?"

"Sandwater Bay, on the other side of the point. Have you been there before?"

"Not to swim, but I've flown over the area a few times, though. Do you surf?"

"I try. You?"

"Every chance I get."

CeCe hung a left and drove a short distance along a gravel road before parking the van behind a bank of sand dunes and cutting the engine.

When they walked the track to the beach, the place was almost deserted.

"Is this where you normally swim?"

"Sometimes. I wouldn't swim here alone but thought you might like it."

He looked across the surf to the horizon, and when he turned to reply, she was already shimmying out of her shorts, her T-shirt lying discarded beside her bag on the sand. Luka took his fill of her through his sunglasses. Nude-colored string bikini, long legs, and flowing dark curls with highlights of copper visible in the sunlight—she was stunning.

"Coming in?"

They waded into the surf, which was warmer than he'd expected. He dived through the breakers and resurfaced to find her watching him as she trod water, rising and falling with the swell.

His heart beating faster than usual, he wanted to swim over and lift her onto his hips. Feel her legs wrap around his waist and her arms around his neck. But instead, he swam toward the horizon, the smooth, even strokes helping to settle his nerves. Luka hadn't felt this way about a woman in ages.

By the time he made it back to shore, CeCe was face down on her towel, her bikini straps undone. He settled beside her on his back and closed his eyes for a moment. As a sudden chill made his skin bump, he turned to look at her. Wild curls framed her face, and a dusting of sand peppered her cheek.

He rolled onto his side and reached out to gently brush the sand from her skin.

She didn't flinch at his touch, just smiled, her expression amused. Knowing. "Hungry?"

"Why, do you have food?" he asked.

"No, but there's a burger place down the road. They make the best burgers on the East Coast. Well, almost."

"Sounds good." He leaned over and retied the straps of her bikini, his hands shaking above the warmth of her back. Gathering her curls to one side, she glanced at him over her shoulder, and they held each other in a still gaze for a moment.

Perhaps he was gallant after all.

The picnic table outside the burger bar was the kind that could give you splinters in your butt if you didn't have your wits about you. They sat side by side, unwrapped their burgers, and both took a bite.

"Great burger." Luka reached for his can of Pepsi and sipped. "So, tell me about yourself."

CeCe dipped a fry in aioli. "Nothing much to tell. I'm a girl. You're a boy. We don't need any more details."

As he opened his mouth to speak, she reached over and placed an index finger to his lips. Luka wanted to suck the salt off it, dip it in the aioli, and suck it some more.

"I'm not trying to be secretive or mysterious, but you're my knight in shining armor, and I could do with a little fairy-tale action in my life right now." She brought her water bottle to her lips and paused. "So, if you don't tell me yours, I won't tell you mine. Agreed?" She took a drink.

"I guess, but—"

"Let's not unpack our baggage. It'll just get in the way."

Their eyes locked. This girl, with her disarming frankness and words drawn from the depths of her soul, could easily get under his skin. "Okay. But am I allowed one question?"

"Depends."

Luka sipped his drink again, the hit of caffeine jarring his stomach. "When we first met, you said you had a boyfriend. Do you still?"

"No. Do you?"

"What? A boyfriend? No."

"Girlfriend?"

Luka shook his head. "A relationship doesn't fit into my

plans right now." He took a bite. Chewed. Grabbed a few fries and grinned. "But that doesn't mean I can't have a bit of fun."

Under the table, CeCe nudged his foot with hers. "I enjoy having fun, don't you?"

He tried to hide his amusement but failed. "I do. As long as there are no strings."

She nodded. "In fact, I have my eye on someone for that exact purpose at the moment."

"And was it lust at first sight?"

"Not straight away, obviously. But the guy sure fit the bill once I got a good look at him."

"So the attraction's purely physical?"

"More chemical. You understand what I mean?"

"Sure." Sensing a shift in the mood, Luka bit into his burger and finished the mouthful while processing her words. Chemistry had always been his strongest subject at university, but when it came to understanding the chemistry between lovers, he knew little. "Are you always this forward with guys you hardly know?"

CeCe placed her burger on the paper in front of her, peered up through her lashes, and then lifted her head, her gaze squarely on his. A slow smile spread to her eyes, and at that moment, he wondered if he would ever have his fill of this girl. Ever be enough for her.

"I'm *never* forward with men," she whispered.

"I'm flattered," he said. And he meant it. Here was a beautiful woman, with the body of a late teen and a mind full of wild possibilities, throwing out her seduction net without an ounce of hesitation.

"Okay," she said. "I have a question for you."

"Shoot."

"Are you a kind man, Luka O'Leary?"

He leaned forward and kissed her lightly on the lips. The touch, although over in a split second, was enough to savor. "Very kind."

She fished in her bag for her keys and pushed them toward him. "In that case, I'll let you drive me back to town."

Amazed that she'd trust him to drive her Kombi, he grabbed the keys off the table. "Really? You want me to drive?"

CeCe's fingers lifted to her lips in contemplation. "I do. It's the first step in a series of preliminary observations."

———

They arrived back at his place just after eight, Amy Winehouse singing on the radio as the last of the day's sun slipped behind a puff of cloud. Luka pulled up to his front door and cut the engine. Without Amy, crickets sang their melody into the twilight air.

They sat in silence, both staring straight ahead, the windows down to take the edge off the heat. CeCe's mind raced. Would he invite her in? Kiss her? Take her in his arms and let his lips find her neck? Was this her new normal, creating an alternative universe?

"Would you like to come inside? There's a hot tub on the deck."

She imagined them in the tub. Stars bright, crickets humming—the trace of her fingertips through the fine hairs on his chest as they kissed. "Thanks, but some other time. I want to visit my friend Anna on the way home."

Luka turned to face her and slid his arm along the seat until his fingers touched her nape. Her breasts tightened in response. "I have a nice bottle of merlot we could share."

"It will keep."

He leaned in for a kiss, then another. Each time she pulled back, he moved closer, his lips soft on hers as he searched her mouth with his tender touch.

Luka sat back, brushed a strand of hair from her cheek, and smiled. "I look forward to opening it." He leaned in again, his lips skimming along her collarbone. Tilting her head to one side, she smiled. He had kind eyes, ones she could lose herself in. Eyes she could trust. But when their lips met again, the urgency behind his touch took her by surprise. His hand slipped beneath her T-shirt, but just as he was about to cup her breast, she pulled away.

"Thanks for the company," she said. "I had a good time."

"Me too." He sighed heavily. "Is that my cue to go inside?"

"Yeah. I think so."

Luka stepped from the van and watched as she scrambled over the seat and slipped behind the wheel. He stood back. "Drive safe."

She shifted into reverse. "I will. Goodnight."

Instead of going to the cemetery as planned, CeCe drove home in silence, the radio's distraction too mundane for the enormity of the sensations coursing through her. This guy was hot. Seriously hot.

Despite the need pooling between her legs, it felt good to carry herself with confidence again. That side of her hadn't gone; it had just lain dormant for a while. She laughed out loud. CeCe had never seduced a guy before, hadn't known she had it in her.

Game on.

5

CASUAL VISITOR

When CeCe parked in the driveway of Luka's studio two days later, the main house lay in darkness. As she stepped from the van and strode toward the deck, the western hill line sat against a deep blue sky, and a scattering of stars were just showing their shine. She knocked on his front door.

Parked down a nearby side street for the past fifteen minutes, she'd agonized over the decision to visit him. This was it. Her moment. If she didn't seize this opportunity, would she be forever afraid to move on?

When her therapist had mentioned how some people feel an insistent need for sexual connection after they've lost someone they love, CeCe had scoffed at the notion, slotting it into the WTH file in her mind.

Until she met Hot Chopper Guy.

A knot gripped her stomach as footsteps approached from inside. The door opened a fraction, then wider, and there he stood—shirtless, worn Levi's sitting low on his hips, and that sexy smile welcoming her. The more CeCe tried to keep her eyes on his face, the more she failed. A smidgen of chest hair curled around each nipple in short tendrils, and the taut skin running from his navel into the waistband of his jeans was one of the sexiest things she'd ever seen. She wanted to touch it so badly.

Luka cleared his throat.

"Here I am again."

His smile softened in amusement. "So I see."

She glanced back at the Kombi: her quick getaway if things didn't go to plan. "Again, I should have called first, but I don't have your number. So…"

"It's not a problem." He stepped aside. "Come in."

The small studio, decorated in various shades of depressing beige, reminded her of a three-star motel she'd stayed at with her parents when she was younger. He'd still not made his bed, but a different novel sat on the nightstand, and no clothes lay discarded on the floor. "Do you enjoy living here?"

"For now. The shower's good, and so's the hot tub. I don't need much else at the moment. The owners are visiting relatives in the States, so I'm keeping an eye on the place until they get back in April."

"So, you're one of those 'no possessions' kind of guys?"

"Guess you could say that. Although I do like books and surfboards and mountain bikes. But those are details, yeah?"

She offered a smile. "Yes, but the odd detail is okay."

Luka picked up the bottle of merlot she'd given him the other day. "Drink?"

CeCe nodded. "Thanks. Just a half glass though—I'm driving." She placed a paper bag on the kitchenette counter. "This is for you. Apple cake."

Luka opened the bag to peek inside, and as he did so, the aroma of fresh baking filled the air. "Thank you. Did you make it?"

"Yes. I enjoy baking. It's so much more satisfying than buying a cake at the supermarket. But I do find it strange how all those ingredients can turn into a delicious cake just by mixing them together and adding heat. It's weird, don't you think?"

"It's all about chemical reaction." He opened a cabinet above the sink and grabbed a couple of wine glasses. "How's your ankle?"

"Still a little weak but fine."

CeCe wasn't sure why she'd come. She'd never chased a guy and had no illusions of this being a long-term thing. Luka didn't seem the type. However, the spark that had ignited at the library refused to be extinguished.

Miss Libby said he'd been asking after her on Thursday, but as she watched him pour the wine, he didn't mention it.

Luka handed her a half-filled glass and raised his in a toast. "To rabbit holes." She clinked. "Let's go outside." He opened the sliding door onto the side deck, where two Cape Cod chairs were draped with a wetsuit and beach towel.

"You've been surfing?"

He grabbed the wetsuit, threw it over the decking rail, and motioned for her to take a seat as he did the same. "Yeah, I went out first thing. The water was freezing after that rain last night."

CeCe sat and sipped her wine, the alcohol's warmth having an instant effect. "I hope you don't mind me just popping in." She looked away, then back. "Some nights, it hurts to be alone."

There was an immediate shift in his expression. "I'm glad you're here," he murmured.

Breaking the unease caused by his intense scrutiny, CeCe placed her wine on the small table between them. "Can we use the tub?"

Luka regarded her with apparent hesitation then nodded slowly. "Sure. I'll go grab you a towel."

When he returned, CeCe averted her eyes as he dropped his jeans and slipped into the tub. He wasn't naked, not completely, but his white boxers molded around his butt, so her imagination didn't have to do any work. Apart from the undeniable appeal of a tight male behind, she'd always been a shoulder girl, and Luka's shoulders didn't disappoint. She'd worn a one-piece underneath her clothes, and as she unbuttoned her shirt and shimmied out of her jeans, his gaze lingered.

He floated backward and nestled into a seat, watching her. And as she slipped into the tub, he took her hand and twined his fingers gently through hers, offering no indication of his intention. Maybe that was the difference between men and teenage boys—no undue pressure or persuasion.

"Tell me...about your hurt."

CeCe inched closer and leaned her head on his shoulder. From their conversations so far, she knew he was a good listener, allowing her the space to speak without interruption. But confiding in Luka about her best friend wasn't part of the plan.

She touched the butterfly at her throat. She'd given Anna the necklace for her sixteenth birthday, and from that day on, her friend had seldom removed it. Several weeks after the funeral, she'd arrived home to find a piece of folded tissue tied with a pink bow on her nightstand. Inside was the butterfly necklace and a hand-written note from Anna's mother about friendship and bonds that couldn't be broken. Perhaps Anna hadn't told her parents that she no longer considered CeCe a friend. "Candor is often overrated, don't you think?"

He shrugged. "Depends."

"Okay"—she glanced up at him—"tell me one thing about yourself."

"Well, I can't stop thinking about this girl I rescued from a rabbit hole."

His admission set her heart on a wild ride. He'd thought about her as she had of him, and that mutual intent made her smile. "Yeah? What's she like, this rabbit-hole girl?"

"Intriguing, if a little wild." He lifted her to face him, so she straddled his legs. "Your turn."

She stared into his eyes, losing herself in the moment. "I'm dreading Easter."

As a slight frown creased his brow, CeCe slid her hands down his chest, surprised by the instant contraction of muscle under her fingertips. Luka leaned forward and kissed her slowly. Another point of difference between him and the younger guys she'd dated. Hot Chopper Guy knew how to execute the perfect lazy kiss. How to cup her face, soften his lips, and keep his tongue gentle. How to pull back and study her before finding her mouth again.

CeCe scooted forward, just a fraction, but enough to feel him stiffen beneath her. And as she returned her head to his shoulder, she smiled.

6

CALLING ALL ANGELS

CeCe floated backward out of reach, and Luka watched as she pulled a hair tie from her wrist to wrangle her curls into a topknot. He looked upward. Stars gazed down from the sky as the waxing moon hid behind a puff of cloud. She'd turned up uninvited, but he didn't care; it wasn't as if she'd find him with someone else. For him, she was that someone for now.

For some reason, he found her one-piece swimsuit sexier than any skimpy bikini he'd ever seen. Black, or perhaps navy blue—he couldn't tell which by the muted light from inside—its straps fastened around the neck and molded cups held her breasts high. Moments before, as she'd straddled him, Luka had stiffened, struggling to stay in control. But she'd set their pace, not him. Because, despite her apparent bravado, he sensed she wasn't quite ready to take things further.

While Luka tried not to imagine having sex with her, as the tension built, he could think of little else. He reached over and turned on the jets, letting the force of water relax him.

CeCe chatted about her day, her hand fiddling with a blue butterfly that hung from a silver chain around her neck. As usual, she failed to mention her family. Maybe they didn't get along. She was eighteen, after all—an age where stepping away from the fold and testing the boundaries was the norm.

Brad had mentioned an overprotective father and two sisters. Then there was her brother, Mitch, who Luka had already met at a pre-Christmas touch rugby game shortly after arriving in Tulloch Point. Otherwise, he knew nothing about her domestic life. Not that it mattered. He wasn't here to meet the parents.

"This has been great, but I have to leave soon." CeCe went to stand.

He reached over and tugged her closer. With her arms wrapped around his neck and those long legs resting between his, he kissed her with increased urgency. She pulled away. Droplets of steam covered her hair, and her lips seemed fuller from his attention. CeCe kissed with skill and finesse, and for the first time since they'd met, he wanted to know everything about her.

"Stay. I have a big bed."

"I can't. Not tonight." As she spoke, she brushed a lock of hair from his forehead—once, twice—then rested her head on his shoulder again, the touch of her breast against his naked chest making Luka even harder.

"Will you at least give me your number so I can text you?"

She kissed him lightly on the lips, a teasing smile coming into play as she cupped his face with one hand. "Maybe someday."

"Why not today?"

"I'm not into the whole texting thing with guys. It makes me anxious."

"But how will I contact you?"

"You'll figure it out. We don't have to be on each other's

screens every minute of the day. That's kind of tedious, don't you think? Besides, it's not fling behavior."

"So that's all you're after? A fling?"

CeCe stood and adjusted her straps, her legs tanned and athletic. And as she stepped from the tub, he wanted to pull her back and hold her until his crazy heart slowed its rapid beat. Watching her, he floated forward and settled his arms on the rim of the tub.

"I wouldn't say no to a brief fling. But it has to be special. I want to anticipate and wonder, to have you flit into my daydreams when least expected." She picked up her towel and kissed him on the forehead. "Do you mind if I jump in the shower real quick? Otherwise, I'll reek of chlorine all night."

"Sure, go for it."

His head resting on his arms, Luka closed his eyes against the unease of separation. He longed to slip into the shower behind her, to run his hands over her breasts, caress her neck and back with his lips and tongue. But if she'd wanted him to join her, she would've said so. Still, that opportunity would come soon enough.

He stepped from the tub and ditched his boxers on the deck before strolling into the studio, naked and relaxed, jeans in hand. Through the wall behind his bed, he could hear CeCe singing Coldplay's 'Yellow' as she showered. It made him smile.

Just as he pulled up his jeans, she walked through the bathroom door. He turned as he zipped up his fly, her round eyes and the flush on her face telling him she'd seen his naked butt.

She looked away, picked up her bag, and slung it over her shoulder. "Thanks for the hot tub. It was fun."

Luka moved toward her and cradled her face in his hands,

the scent of bodywash enveloping them. "Don't go yet—it's still early." He kissed her.

"But I have work tomorrow."

"Me too," he whispered, "but I really want you to stay."

CeCe dropped her bag at her feet. His arms encircled her waist, and she draped hers around his neck as she kissed him. Luka hardened within seconds, so much so that all he could think about was being inside her.

But as he bent to pick her up and carry her to his bed, his beeper started jumping about on the nightstand. "Shit!"

"What's that?"

He let her go and grabbed his phone and keys off the table and a T-shirt from the dresser. "I'm on call. I have to go. But please feel free to stay."

Tingling from the waist down, CeCe stood at the window and watched Luka rush to his SUV and reverse down the driveway. She wanted to stay, to wait for him in his bed, but she'd always thought that a guy respected you more if you held back slightly. Who knew whether or not that was true?

CeCe grabbed a peach from the fruit bowl and took a bite. Juice dripping down her chin, she stood at the sink, smiling at the picture in her head. Luka sliding his jeans over the most perfect naked butt she'd ever seen, its color the same as the rest of his body—warm, golden brown.

Resisting the urge to undress and slip into his bed, she picked up her bag and walked out the door, ensuring it locked behind her.

As she drove out of town toward home, Train's 'Calling All Angels' flowed from her stereo speakers. CeCe sang along, but she didn't need a sign to know Anna was with her. All she needed to do was touch their butterfly.

When she parked in their driveway, the lights were still on in the house. CeCe had texted her mother before leaving town, a habit formed as soon as she'd got her driver's license. Her parents wanted to know when to expect her, and she never took that concern for granted.

As CeCe strolled into the family room, her mother looked up from the paper. "Have you been for a swim?"

"No, I visited a friend who has a hot tub. We should get one. They're so relaxing."

"What friend?" her dad asked with sudden interest.

She shrugged. "Just a guy I met before Christmas."

He sought her gaze. "Are you sleeping with him?"

"Frank," her mother said, "that's none of our business."

CeCe laughed. "I only share my bed with Pixie. Besides, you do realize I'm almost nineteen? Mum was married and pregnant at nineteen."

"That's not the point. Andrea didn't plan that life."

Her mother glared at her father. "Frank!"

"What? It's true, isn't it?"

CeCe smiled to herself as she rummaged through the pantry.

"What are you looking for, sweetheart?" her mother asked. Her parents had called her sweetheart for as long as she could remember. Unless she was in trouble—then it was Sydney Eve Dobson.

"That caramel chocolate."

"Your father ate the last of it after dinner. But there's ice cream in the freezer."

Disappointed, CeCe shook her head. "Nah, think I'll head to bed. I have work in the morning. Only a few weeks until school starts, then I'll be back in that boring uniform every day."

She leaned forward and kissed her father on the forehead. "Anyway, goodnight, Dad."

"Goodnight," he said. "Don't spend all night on that phone to your new *platonic* boyfriend."

CeCe smiled as she wondered how Luka would be on the phone. He seemed a little reserved in person. But when she thought about it, she rather liked that about him. "I won't."

7

MAGICAL MYSTERY TOUR

When Luka walked into a hushed library, CeCe stood at the reception desk, her hands conducting the conversation as she spoke to the older woman, Libby. Dressed in a white blouse and navy skirt and with her hair pulled off her face into a bun, CeCe looked like a businesswoman. An incredibly hot businesswoman. And while she wasn't much older than some of the pupils he'd taught last year at Clifton Falls High, she had a maturity about her that belied her age.

Although he'd returned to Sandwater Bay that morning for a surf, it hadn't held the same appeal without her happy face and the Kombi. Even the burger he'd grabbed for lunch wasn't as delicious as the one he'd eaten the other day.

Luka strode toward reception, smiling when Libby noticed him. CeCe turned. Held his gaze. She walked up to him but didn't enter his personal space. He wanted to sweep her off her feet and swing her around in a fierce hug but resisted the urge. This was, after all, her place of employment.

"Good morning. Are you after something special today?"

He grinned. "Do you mean book-wise, or in general?"

"You are a shameless flirt."

"I've been called worse. Sorry about last night."

"No problem. Was it serious?"

"Not really. Anyway, I'm looking for something good by an author I haven't read before. Any suggestions?"

She tapped her pen to her lips in thought. "I've just the thing." She stepped backward and turned, and he followed the imaginary come-with-me gesture. As she made her way to the fiction area, he couldn't tear his eyes from her rounded butt in that tight skirt.

CeCe stopped at a section on the far wall and ran her finger along the spines. She removed a small paperback and handed it to him.

He glanced down at the couple on the front and frowned. "What's this?"

"A romance, about a chopper pilot working in the Rocky Mountains and the woman who falls madly in love with him. It's a great read. A bit of a tearjerker, but I could throw in a pack of tissues. Are you keen to give it a whirl?"

He studied her joyful face. So full of life and mischief. "No, not really."

"Go on. I'll read one of yours if you read one of mine."

When Luka turned the book over to scan the blurb, the words *hot*, *steamy*, and *summer* jumped out at him. "Challenge accepted."

"But it has to be a novel. I don't want to read a helicopter training manual."

"Of course not. There's nothing much to choose from in the aviation section, anyway. I'll go pick something for you."

"I should get back to work. Just leave it with Libby."

He reached for her hand. "Come over later if you're free."

"Sorry, I'm busy tonight. What about tomorrow? I have the day off."

"Okay. Any time after five."

She withdrew her hand, formed a heart with her fingers, and turned to walk away.

Hearing the Kombi come to a stop in his driveway, Luka smiled. It was almost five thirty, and after spending most of the day with his head in a training manual, he couldn't wait to see her expressive face.

He rushed into the bathroom and ran his fingers through his hair as he checked his reflection in the mirror. Some days, he could almost see his father staring back at him through his mother's eyes.

CeCe's face lit up when he opened the door to her knock. "I'm here."

Her hair cascaded down her back in soft curls, and bracelets jingled on her wrist. Makeup-free and wearing a full-length patterned skirt paired with a fringed top, she looked like she'd spent the day at a seventies rock concert. He pulled her close and kissed her. "Yes, so I see. Are you coming in?"

CeCe motioned toward her van. "Actually, I've packed a picnic. You wanna go on a magical mystery tour?"

"I'd love to. What should I bring?"

"Just yourself, and maybe a T-shirt." As she smiled through her lashes and winged a brow, Luka wanted to scoop her up and throw her on the bed so they could seal the deal that his work had so rudely interrupted the other night. She jingled her keys in front of him. "Keen to drive, Chopper Guy?"

"Sure. I'll just get some stuff." He headed back inside to

grab a T-shit and sweater from his dresser and some cheese and olives from the fridge.

She called out to him, "I didn't pack any meat, so it's BYO if you want to head down that shaky road."

Back outside, Luka opened the side door of the Kombi and packed his food into the cooler, wondering if her 'shaky road' comment meant she was a vegetarian.

The van had a distinctive smell—lavender and aged leather—and Luka knew without a doubt that the aroma would remind him of CeCe from that day forward. Once settled in the driver's seat, he turned the key and guided the gearshift into reverse. "Where are we going?"

"Straight down Coronation Drive and head out of town. I'll tell you when to turn off."

"You realize that's a Beatles album, don't you?"

"What is?"

"*Magical Mystery Tour.*"

"No way. So you're saying I didn't think of it first?"

"Nope. In fact, that album's almost as old as these wheels."

"Guess I've heard the expression but didn't realize what it related to." She shifted in her seat, turning to face him, excitement brightening her expression. "We should seriously download it so we can play it next time we're on an adventure. I don't know much Beatles stuff, but I know about them, obviously. They were kind of a big deal back in the day."

Luka laughed. "Now that's an understatement."

CeCe reached over and turned up the stereo, swaying in her seat as she sang along in a delicate, husky voice. "Okay, take this next left. Then drive until you want to kiss me."

Luka pulled onto the verge and came to an abrupt stop. He leaned over and cupped her face in both hands. "I want to kiss you right now." And he did so before nuzzling into her neck, her soft moan of pleasure making him impossibly hard.

She gently pushed him back, her eyes bright. "You're getting carried away."

"As I tend to when you're around."

"Come on, it's not far now." She pointed up the road. "See that tall pine? Take a right there."

Luka followed her directions, the mellowness of the evening and the fascinating girl riding shotgun making him warm inside. They drove a short distance down a dirt road until they came to a clearing. He stopped the van, shifted into first, and pulled on the handbrake. With water tumbling over rocks and into a small pond surrounded by lush green grass, the sight before them was picture-postcard perfect.

"What is this place?"

CeCe unfastened her seat belt. "Grant's Pond. Isn't it cute?"

"Is this public land?"

"Yeah, I think so, but not many people seem to know about it. Shall we eat?"

Luka slid his arm along the back of the seat and kissed her. "Maybe we should make out while no one's here."

CeCe scraped her teeth over her lower lip. "We could always do both."

8

GRANT'S POND

CeCe climbed from the van and curled her toes into the cool grass. Her brother, Mitch, had introduced her to Grant's Pond years before. CeCe suspected he'd brought his girlfriends here when he was a senior in high school, but they'd also picnicked in the spot as a family when everyone still lived at home.

Luka stood beside her while she opened the van's side door and pulled out the cooler, a rug, and pillows. The shady spot held a slight dampness to the air, and the sound of the water as it skipped over the rocks calmed her. The summer had been hot, the humidity overwhelming, and for a few days around New Year, she'd found herself longing for autumn's softer hues.

But now, autumn meant not only saying goodbye to summer but also farewelling Luka. Easter fell at the start of April, and when Easter arrived, Luka would be leaving. He'd miss the endless blue skies, that settled heat sandwiched between morning and evening coolness she so loved.

"Hey, CeCe?" She looked up. Luka now stood at the water's edge, wearing nothing but his jeans and a smile. He stretched, his finely tuned torso glistening in the early evening sunlight. "Can you swim here?"

"Sure. But it's pretty shallow. And there could be eels."

He strolled back to the van and sat cross-legged on the rug, facing her. Food unpacked, CeCe handed him a pottery plate. Luka turned it over and touched her initials on the back with his forefinger. *SD*. "Interesting plate."

"I made them at school, in art class. This local potter taught us—I'm sure she was stoned half the time. Used to hum Fleetwood Mac songs while she cut the clay. Mum put them in the picnic hamper, so we didn't have to eat off plastic on our adventures, and they've been there ever since."

Luka chuckled. "So, she didn't want them in the house, you mean?"

"Yep. But I've no idea why. They're kinda cool, in a rustic sort of way."

He nodded. "What's the S stand for?"

"I might tell you one day."

"But not today?"

"No, not today."

"When did you finish school?"

CeCe hesitated. This was a detail, one that required an explanation. Her decision to return to school still teetered at the back of her mind, not that she'd told her parents. Sometimes, she struggled to cope with their assumptions. "Last year." She placed the cob loaf on a round wooden board and cut two slices, which she offered to him, then cut another.

Luka appeared not to notice her hesitation. "I left last year too."

She looked up from buttering her bread. "Do you mean uni?"

"No, I taught high school science for a couple of years, but it wasn't really my thing."

"Wow, I can't imagine you as a teacher."

"No? I thought it was what I wanted, but as it turned out, I was just following the crowd. My grandfather passed away during my final year at university, and a week before he died, we talked about fulfilling our dreams. He'd always wanted to be a teacher but never had the chance to go to college. Not that he had a bad life, but… Anyway, I'm letting down my details guard."

She smiled. "I don't mind."

Luka picked up a slice of his bread and spread it with hummus and cheese. He took a bite, closed his eyes, and sighed. "This has to be the best bread I've eaten in a long while."

"I know, right? I bought it from that bakery across the street from the library. When I first started working there, I'd buy one of their wholewheat rolls every lunchtime and eat it with just butter. Libby thought I was crazy, but I love simple food."

"Me too. What about you? Have you always wanted to be a librarian?"

"No. It's not my dream."

"What is?"

"Maybe I'll tell you one day." Reaching for a small container, CeCe lifted the lid, grabbed some carrot and cucumber sticks, then offered it to Luka. "Don't you think it's unrealistic how everyone expects you to know where you're heading in life when you're still in school?"

"Yeah, a bit. But we don't have to be constrained by our initial choices. That dated concept of staying in the same job all your life isn't a reality these days."

"That's true." She thought for a moment. "Do you miss Clifton Falls?"

"Sometimes. Not so much when I'm with you."

CeCe leaned forward and kissed him. "You're so sweet."

He laughed. "Not always."

"By the way, thanks for the book. I look forward to reading it. But it's not from the library?"

"I couldn't find the one I wanted, so I grabbed you a copy from the bookstore by the supermarket. Have you read any of Baldacci's before?"

"No. But the blurb captured my interest. So, can I keep it?"

"Of course."

"Interesting series of numbers on the bookmark."

"Yeah, I thought it was about time you had my number." He smiled. "Just in case you felt the need to text."

With their stomachs full and the shadows lengthening across the glen, CeCe stretched out, her sight fixed lazily on the faded blue sky above. Luka sat beside her, hands resting on his knees as he sipped from a bottle of Corona.

"Are you game for a dip?" he asked.

"I didn't bring my suit. But you go ahead."

"I won't look if you skinny-dip, promise."

"You are a bare-faced liar." CeCe picked up a strawberry, twisted off its stem, and popped it into her mouth. Despite having skinny-dipped many times, it somehow didn't feel right being naked in front of him just yet.

"How is it you know me so well after such a short time?" Luka grinned as he reached for his bag. He pulled out a T-shirt and offered it to her. "Here. You can wear this."

She screwed up her face as she imagined the cotton knit clinging to her breasts.

"What?" he asked. "It's clean."

"Yes, and thin and white. I may as well be naked."

Smiling, he jumped to his feet. "Close your eyes."

CeCe flopped back on the rug and did as instructed but almost opened them again at the sound of his fly unzipping. When she did finally look, he already stood waist-deep in the water, his wet hair slicked back, and his gaze fixed on her.

A soft breeze rippled across the water, and he dipped under, his naked butt on brief display as he dived to touch the bottom. CeCe wanted to go to him, to wrap her legs around his waist and feel him erect as he carried her across the crystal-clear pond. It was a longing lost to her in recent months. But ever since that first day in the library—when her heart had beat a little faster as he'd read the blurb of the book she'd recommended—her lust for this man had grown stronger every time they met.

While Luka swam short lengths back and forth, she swapped her top for his T-shirt, then walked to the edge and dropped her skirt on the grass. Given that it had been such a hot day, the water was chillier than she'd expected, and as CeCe waded into the middle of the pond, the white cotton clung to her every curve like a second skin.

As if sensing her presence, Luka stopped and wiped the water from his face. She stepped back into the shallows and stood before him, his T-shirt tied off-center at her waist, and her pink lace G-string clenched between her thighs.

Luka stared. Longer than he'd ever stared before, and when he caught her slight smile, he slowly shook his head. He offered his hand, not outstretched, but close to his side, so it would be her choice whether she took it.

CeCe stepped forward and swam into his arms. Wrapped her legs around his waist. Kissed him like she'd never let him go. She'd known this evening would be their first time before she'd left home. She wanted him and wasn't opposed to a spot of visual seduction, even if it meant stepping out of her comfort zone.

"I am never, ever going to look at that T-shirt the same way again."

Her arms wrapped around his neck and her legs precariously close to his growing erection, Luka carried CeCe from the water and across the grass to the Kombi. He set her on her feet, untied the knot of his T-shirt, and lifted it over her head.

CeCe crossed her arms over her chest but let them fall as he wrapped her in a towel. Shivering but seemingly unperturbed by his naked and dripping body as he stood shielded by the open passenger door, she watched him dry off.

With his towel secured low on his hips, Luka pulled her closer and buffed her skin with the velvet cotton of her beach towel. They kissed, long strokes of his tongue against hers, their surroundings forgotten as they reconnected.

He guided her to sit inside the van, the willow above embracing them in its light green lace. "You still okay with this?"

She nodded. "This is our moment."

They lay back, side by side. She nipped in her lower lip, but when Luka opened the towel and kissed her from neck to navel, CeCe reached for him without restraint, her fingers feather-like on his skin until she closed around him. He pumped into her fist, his heart beating faster with every stroke.

Cool to the touch and scattered with goose bumps, her skin glowed in the sunlight streaming through the van's back window. Luka cupped her breast and lightly pinched the tight bud, perfect in color and size, the swell of her under his hands feeling like heaven. He longed to smother her nipples in caramel and lick the rich sweetness off her skin until she came, then do it all over again.

He felt suddenly nervous and unprepared. Because, despite wanting to have sex with her every time they met, he hadn't expected it to happen today. Not really. And first times could be nerve-racking, especially when the seduction had played out over several days.

CeCe cupped his face, her expression soft. "I'm a little nervous," she murmured.

Yeah, me too. "Don't be. We don't have to do anything you're uncomfortable with."

She nodded. "I'm comfortable."

Luka reached for his jeans and the condoms he'd slipped into the front pocket. He sat back and watched as she gave consent through each touch and breath and those intriguing hazel eyes. And when he ripped open the packet with his teeth and rolled it on, she studied his every move, her eyes wide.

Snuggling in beside her, one hand cupping a breast again, he felt the beat of her heart beneath his palm. His lips found the curve of her neck, and as he caressed her skin, nuzzling and sucking gently so as not to leave his mark, she let out a low moan, her breath heavy in the air.

Along the roadway, a throaty car changed from third, to fourth, to fifth—drowning out the ripple of water over rocks. Luka looked up. Sex in a public place had never been his thing, but as the daylight flattened, the willow's green canopy was all he could see through the van's back window. He closed his eyes in a moment of hesitation, half expecting her to hesitate too, but instead, she traced her thumb around the outline of his lips.

"Hey, it's okay." She pulled him closer. "No one will find us."

He chuckled. "Somehow, I don't think you'd be too concerned if they did."

Luka shifted his weight until he lay half on top of her. He'd planned to take things slow, to enter her with care and savor the moment, but as she raked her nails down his back, he throbbed harder, the innocence he'd imagined no longer a reality.

"I would so," CeCe whispered, her legs opening to him, "but I want you to see me. And I want to see you. Your body is all kinds of beautiful, and I can't tell you how much that turns me on."

Shadows of willow leaflets danced across her skin, forming intricate patterns of lace. No woman had ever told him he was beautiful before, not in such a way, and Luka recalled the times he'd watched her, thinking the exact same thing. Her body was all kinds of beautiful as, he suspected, were her heart and soul.

With one hand behind her head and the other on her breast, he kissed her long and deep, and she groaned again. And as they joined, CeCe holding his expression in the depths of her hazel eyes, he struggled to maintain control.

Sweat soaked their skin, and when he let her go with reluctance, CeCe shivered with the chill of the darkened sky. He reached for the quilt they'd tossed aside and covered them both. She stayed on her back, her hand to her chest as if to calm her beating heart. Next time, they'd spice it up with different positions, but as he'd moved into her rhythm, she'd told him she liked missionary. Liked the weight of him...the size of him... how he kissed.

She turned to meet his gaze, her smile lightening the mood. "Thank you. That was amazing."

"I thought so too."

CeCe played with the edge of the quilt. "How long does it take before you're...?"

"What?" Luka chuckled. "Ready to go again?"

"Yeah."

"Depends. Come home with me, and we'll find out."

9

NAKED SURFING

As it turned out, Luka's recovery had been quick and strong. And by the time they'd made it back to his studio, CeCe could think of nothing but the intensity of what might happen once they walked through the door.

He'd pressed her back against the wall as soon as they were inside. Not in a display of dominance, but gently, his hands cupping her face as he kissed her. She was naked under her voile skirt, and the feeling of his erection and his murmured words of assurance added a layer to the sex that she'd never experienced before.

Afterward, they lay on his bed, feeding each other slices of sweet, white-fleshed nectarines from the tree in his backyard, and when she finally headed for home, it was after two in the morning.

Before she left for work a short six hours later, CeCe packed a few things into an overnight bag, just in case he invited her to stay again. She ate breakfast, the sensation of him a distant tingle between her legs, and waited for her father to leave the house before confiding in her mother.

CeCe rose from the table and put her plate in the dish-washer. She turned and rested her elbows on the breakfast bar. "I thought I might stay in town tonight."

Her mother looked up from her coffee. "What, again? Don't you need a decent night's sleep after your early morning sneak in?" She sipped.

"No, I'm good."

"So, what's he like?"

CeCe hesitated. She often stayed at Molly's so she didn't have to drive home if they'd been out. But her mother seemed to have a sixth sense when it came to CeCe and her love life, or lack thereof. She smiled at the thought of him. "Gentle."

"Okay. But you know if you ever need us, just to call, don't you?"

"Of course." She walked over and kissed her mother on the cheek. "You're the best."

"Thanks, but you realize I don't keep secrets from your father."

CeCe chuckled. "Course you do. We all keep secrets, Mum. Life would be so dull if we didn't."

As she went to leave the kitchen, her mother called her back. "I know you've been through a lot lately, sweetheart, but it's nice to see you smile again. Anna would have wanted that. She was such a bubbly girl before she met that Dillon."

"Yeah, I guess."

***

The following day at dawn, with CeCe at the wheel, they traveled south along the coastal highway toward Sandwater Bay. While there had been many moments over the past few days when she'd thought the happiness would burst from her chest, this morning had to be one of the best she'd had lately.

The previous night had been hot and humid, making sleep difficult, but despite this and their seemingly insatiable desire for one another, CeCe didn't feel tired.

She parked in her usual spot behind the dunes at the far end of the beach. The surf was slower here and quiet for a change, suiting her level of skill. It normally roared its arrival onto the shore, but that morning, the entire world still seemed to be drowsing.

They sat in the sand and watched the sun rise over the Bay of Plenty, CeCe resting between Luka's jean-clad legs as his arms held her—loose enough to flee, tight enough for her not to want to. The beach was deserted, and as she briefly closed her eyes, the soft sough of the surf and the warmth of his scent had her wishing he'd never let her go.

The sun now above the horizon, a shirtless Luka stood and stretched his arms over his head. CeCe marveled at the sight of him: every muscle defined to perfection, his skin glowing and blemish free.

"Have you ever surfed naked?" he asked with a grin.

She looked up, the taste of salt settling on her lips. "No. Have you?"

"Sure. Want to give it a try? It's awesome."

"But what if someone comes?"

"You can leave your towel on the beach, and I'll grab it for you while you hide under the water."

"But then they'll see *you* naked."

He shrugged. "Doesn't bother me. Being naked is a great leveler, don't you think?"

"Maybe." She laughed. "But you're just saying that because

you have an amazing body with a most impressive piece of equipment and a six-pack."

Luka bent down, picked her up, and tossed her over his shoulder as she giggled her protest. "You have an amazing body too. But if you don't strip soon, we'll miss our chance." He slapped her playfully on the butt and ran up the beach to the van.

They undressed side by side on the sand, and as he stepped back to study her, he smiled. "Have I ever told you how freakin' beautiful you are?"

CeCe gazed up at him through her lashes. "Maybe once or twice last night."

He opened his arms. "Come here."

She remained in his embrace for a moment, his warm skin against hers comforting as always. She'd never had a boyfriend like Luka before; well, not that he was really her boyfriend. When Easter rolled around, he'd leave, and she didn't know how this fling of theirs would fit into his plans. But Anna's death had taught her to live in the now, and this was that now. This beach, these waves, this contentment.

She'd worry about 'later' when it turned up, uninvited.

Naked and free, they surfed and kissed and lazed on their boards, holding hands as they recited their favorite song lyrics to one another, CeCe almost falling off her board in fits of laughter when he sang her an Australian folk song about plum trees and gum trees.

They returned to the Kombi where they dined on a breakfast of apricots, granola, and yogurt, then lay in the back, a sprinkling of sand and salt on the cotton throw beneath them.

"That was awesome. I'll want to go naked surfing all the time now."

He raised a brow. "Not without me, you won't. You need a watchdog when you're surfing naked."

She beckoned with her finger, a flirty smile on her lips. "Here, boy. Come here."

Luka tackled her until they were both giggling. Nuzzling her neck, he growled softly, then pulled back and held her gaze.

They kissed; Luka tender in his approach as always—soft lips and considerate hands. But just as she went to reach for him, he stopped her. "No, you don't. I need a shower first. Last time I suited up after a surf, my dick chafed like crazy." He jumped into the driver's seat, still wrapped in his towel. "And as there are no showers out here, you either point me in the direction of the nearest river, or we head home."

"I vote for the river. There's a turnoff a couple of miles up the road." CeCe slipped her dress over her shoulders and followed him into the front seat. The want was building in her core, but a slight hesitation surfaced as she wondered who he'd previously slept with at the beach. However, she pushed that thought from her mind. Luka hadn't been a virgin when they met, and neither had she, so there seemed little point in paying it any heed.

Luka started the engine and nudged the Kombi into gear. With his tanned skin, easy smile, and sun-kissed locks tousled by her fingers, he looked so handsome behind the wheel. When she leaned over to kiss him, he took her hand, and as they drove along the highway, she realized this was what she'd been waiting for to fulfill her New Year's resolution.

A guy, the beach, and a perfect summer fling.

1 0

RIVER RUN

As the highway faded from sight in the rearview mirror, Luka parked beside a cabbage tree and cut the engine. Although the trip from the beach to this stretch of river had taken less than ten minutes, he'd been uncomfortably hard the whole way. He shifted in his seat, willing himself to establish some control.

As Luka walked along the riverbank, checking the water's depth and testing the temperature with his foot, CeCe stripped the covers from the mattress in the back and fluttered them in the open air, sending sand cascading onto the grass in front of her.

"Is it cold?" she asked from above him, her hair wild with salt and wind.

"Not too bad." He turned. "Anyway, cold water's good for you. Coming in?"

"Yep. I'll just get undressed."

Naked, they slipped into the water and gravitated toward one another. CeCe's breasts tightened, and she lay back, her hair now forming a sleek veil around her as she floated beside him.

He pulled her upright, her face flushed and covered in

droplets dripping from her hair and lashes. They kissed, eager and urgent and ready for each other despite the lack of foreplay. When he pulled back, she lifted his hand and sucked his fingers into her mouth one by one as he watched her. And when she wrapped her legs around his waist, it took all his strength to slow things down. To wade with her to the bank and lay her on the rug beside the van.

Her towel lay draped across her navel, covering nothing it should as Luka rummaged through his jeans pocket, desperately searching for what he needed. She watched him, her eyelids heavy with desire and her hands to her breasts.

They'd kissed a lot in their short time together. He loved the tenderness of it, the taste of her intensifying arousal—her words of encouragement as he moved from her mouth to her neck and down to her navel.

As he caressed her thighs, she opened for him, the faint scent of river water rich in his nostrils and the sounds of the highway barely registering as the blood pumped faster through his veins.

CeCe's hands went to his hair, fingers playing with the strands as he nuzzled into her. And as she arched off the rug, her grip tightened to a notch short of painful as she lost herself in the moment.

Seconds later, when she rolled over and offered herself to him, Luka's desire robbed him of any remaining semblance of control. He took her with urgency until they both collapsed, their skin glazed with sweat.

"You're an amazing lover," CeCe murmured as they lay together, shielded by the Kombi on one side and the river on the other.

Luka rolled over and propped himself up on one elbow to admire her postcoital beauty—breathtaking in its simplicity—

her hair drying into curls and the slight sun blush across the bridge of her nose. He smiled. "I love being with a sexually confident woman. It makes me horny."

CeCe raised her brows. "So I've noticed."

Luka flopped onto his back and closed his eyes against the sun filtering through the cabbage tree fronds above. He recalled her face as she came, one side pressed to the rug, the other flushed with passion. Her falling apart fascinated him. She did so without restraint, moaning his name as she squeezed her core tight, her hands gripping whatever she could reach.

"Luka?"

"Yeah." He kept his eyes closed, one bent knee touching hers and the sun warm on his face.

"Am I too young for you?"

Opening his eyes, he took her hand, her skin cool and smooth to the touch. "We wouldn't be here if that's what I thought. Why do you ask?"

"It's just…you've obviously experienced much more of life than I have, and I kind of feel like a newbie around you."

Luka returned to his side and stroked wisps of hair from her face. Apart from that first day, when she told him she was eighteen, he rarely thought about their age difference. "Do you think I'm too old for you?"

She shook her head. "No. You're just right."

"Good." He leaned forward and kissed her. "You had me worried there for a moment."

11

PERFECT DISTRACTION

CeCe smiled when Luka opened his door. Shirtless as usual, he wore another brightly colored length of cotton tied off-center just below his navel. She'd understand if it was a warm night, but after two days of rain, the air was unseasonably cool. She motioned to his lavalava. "Do you have one of those skirts for me?"

"Why? Are you planning on getting half naked?"

"Perhaps I could be persuaded."

A grin on his face, Luka stepped back in invitation. CeCe wanted to go to him, to wrap her arms around his neck, but she always found that first contact the hardest, so she waited for him to make a move. Although they'd been seeing each other since the beginning of January, it still felt a little foreign. With Easter less than three months away, their use-by date was looming, and she didn't want to be left with a bruised heart. She wanted to enjoy their time together for what it was and move on without regret when it ended.

He looked exhausted, as if he didn't have the energy for her. CeCe knew she should have called first, but she still hadn't used the number he'd scribbled on the bookmark. She didn't know why. She'd always been so available to Travis, so much so that she'd sometimes lost any sense of herself. Most days, he'd scarcely allowed her time to breathe.

"You look shattered. Should I go?"

"Yeah, I've been studying—I'm finding it pretty tough." He stepped forward and took her hand. "But please don't leave. You're just the distraction I need."

Luka kissed like he meant it. Always. There was no hesitation, and as she relaxed in his arms, the tension of the day eased.

He released her and stepped away. "I've something for you." CeCe watched as he opened his chest of drawers and pulled out a sarong in various shades of aqua. He shook out the fabric and dangled it from his index finger in an invitation for her to come closer. When she reached out to take it, he grabbed her around the waist and gently pushed her onto the bed.

Luka positioned himself between her legs, his hands efficient on the zipper of her jeans. She raised her butt in assistance, and as he continued to undress her, the excitement at just the look of him flushed her cheeks until they warmed.

Her jeans and panties on the floor, Luka started on the buttons of her top, and as he worked his way down and peeled it off her shoulders, he never once broke eye contact. He picked up the sarong and draped it across one side of her body and down between her legs. She wasn't wearing a bra, so the touch of the cool cotton as he teased it over her right breast heightened her senses to the point where she felt compelled to close her eyes.

He lifted the fabric before letting it flutter over her. Once. Twice. After the third time, his lips found her breast through the thin cotton, and his attention had her arching off the mattress in desperate want.

Standing at the side of the bed, Luka let his lavalava fall to the floor. He was already erect, so very erect. With hard planes of muscle on his torso and strong, lean legs, he had the body of a surfer—all sun-kissed skin and tousled hair. CeCe loved everything about him. Not only his body and the way he commanded her release without compromise, but also, his keen mind as well.

He chuckled.

"What?"

"You sure know how to make me feel good about myself without saying a word."

CeCe shrugged. "I love seeing you naked."

Luka leaned forward and kissed from her breastbone to her bare pubis and back again. "And I you."

"Do that thing."

"What thing?"

"You know." Her hands in his hair, CeCe hesitated as he moved closer to her need then whispered, "With your tongue, and your lips, and your breath."

He gazed up at her, his eyes bright. "My pleasure."

Afterward, they slept, the thrum of the rain on the iron roof soothing in its steadiness. CeCe awoke to the rhythm of his breath on her neck, and his erection pressed against her. As she eased back the covers, Luka stirred and wrapped one arm around her waist.

"Don't go. Not yet." He pulled her closer, his arms holding her tightly as usual. "I hate it when you leave. I miss the warmth and the spell of you."

She looked back over her shoulder and smiled. "The *spell* of me?"

"That's what you've done, isn't it? Cast a spell? Worked your magic?"

She laughed and wriggled free. Standing next to his bed, she picked up the sarong and tied it above her breasts. "Go back to sleep. You're hallucinating."

His hands clasped behind his head, Luka studied her in the half-light of dawn. "If I am, this is the horniest hallucination I've ever had." He reached over and snatched the sarong free, leaving her standing naked before him. "This stays here for next time."

"I thought it was a gift."

"One that will hopefully keep on giving." He grinned. "Anyway, I have to get up soon. I'm going home for a few days after work."

"When will you be back?"

"Tuesday night. Text me while I'm away. Just once."

She gathered up her clothes from the floor beside the bed and slowly dressed as they watched one another. "I just might."

Luka began reciting his number, but she leaned over and silenced him with a kiss. "I have it saved in my phone, and don't worry, Chopper Guy, I'll still be around on Wednesday."

"Maybe we should go out for dinner and a movie next weekend. On a date."

CeCe hesitated. Blew him a kiss. "You think?"

12

A FAVOR

"We've got a problem."

Luka looked up from his desk as Brad walked through the door carrying a white box. They didn't have a uniform in the Tulloch Point Search and Rescue office, the service was too small and underfunded for that, but Brad wore the same outfit every day. Khaki shirt and brown pants, black leather shoes with heavy soles, and a name badge identifying him as Bradley Jones, Coordinator.

"What kind of problem?"

Brad's smile broadened as he sat the box on his desk. He obviously needed a favor. "Our chemistry teacher's pregnant and confined to bed rest, and the school year begins first week of February. We've found a replacement, but she can't start until after Easter."

Luka shut the lid of his laptop, grabbed his phone and water bottle off the desk, and stuffed them all into his backpack. His shift had finished twenty minutes ago, and he wanted to hit the road before dark. "That's a shame. And what do you mean by 'we'?"

"You know I'm married to the principal, right?"

Brad had mentioned that fact at least half a dozen times, but he was the kind of guy who'd repeat a story without even thinking about it. "Yes, so you've said."

"Carole thought maybe—"

"No."

"You can't just refuse without knowing the details."

"Watch me. No."

"Look, we're in a tight spot here. There are at least twenty kids in year thirteen chemistry and almost double that number in year twelve. Four days a week until Easter. That's all we ask."

"I'm taking a break from teaching." Luka grabbed his jacket off the hook beside the door and shrugged it on. "In fact, I plan to make that break permanent."

"But you only taught for two years."

"Yep. It's not really my thing, and right now, all I want to do is pass my chopper license."

"But you're an excellent teacher."

His brows drew together. "What? Who told you that?"

"Carole called the principal at your last school." Brad sat at his desk and opened the box of donuts. He offered it to Luka, who declined. "Will you at least consider it?"

Luka watched Brad bite into a donut and sighed. He'd taught for a couple of years after completing his science degree but soon realized dealing with a bunch of hormonal teenagers wasn't how he wanted to spend his days. Apart from that, the routine of it didn't suit him. He was a night owl who loved the outdoors. In hindsight, Luka had no idea why he'd chosen the teaching route in the first place.

"Do us this one favor, and we might be able to get you some extra hours in the chopper," Brad continued.

"Come on. Play fair. You can't dangle that juicy carrot in front of my nose and expect me not to sniff at it."

"Course I can. We're desperate—you're available. And it's only one term."

"Yeah, but it's four days a week. I'm busy enough as it is." He sighed. "Anyway, I'm heading home for a few days, so I'll pretend to think about it, but I'm not making any promises."

"Good man."

"See you Wednesday." Luka grabbed a donut and took a huge bite. "Thanks. Good donut."

Outside, Luka swore under his breath as he pushed the button on his key fob. More hours in the chopper meant he'd gain his license sooner. But the teaching trade-off?

No. Just no.

"What are you going to do about the board, Dad?" CeCe asked as she and her parents finished their evening meal. Her father had been on the Tulloch Point High Board of Trustees for several years, but he'd planned to retire at the end of last year when CeCe graduated and his term ended.

Then Anna died.

"They want to co-op me for another year. What do you think?"

CeCe shrugged. "Go for it. But you're asking for my opinion, Dad." She shot an amused smile at her mother, who offered one in return. "Are you sure you're feeling all right?"

"Very funny. I just thought, with you going back to school, it wouldn't hurt to do another year."

"I don't mind, honestly."

"Oh, and Carole Jones texted this morning. They might have found a new chemistry teacher for the first term," Frank said.

"Great." CeCe sipped her water. "Anyone we know?"

"Well, you know him," he replied. "It's that guy who helped you when you sprained your ankle."

The saliva immediately dried in her mouth as his words tumbled across her mind. She set down her knife and fork. "Who do you mean? The doctor?"

"No, the guy who gave you a ride into town. That Search and Rescue guy."

CeCe fought the panic rising in her throat. She picked up her water glass but put it back down. *No way!* "Luka? But... he's a paramedic."

"Yes, as a volunteer. Anyway, he's got all the bells and whistles as far as qualifications go, so let's hope he's keen. Otherwise, I might have to come and teach you guys myself. Right"—he drained his coffee—"I need to make a few calls."

CeCe stood and smoothed down her jeans as her father left the room, her heartbeat racing in her chest. She cleared the table, stacked the dishwasher, and chatted away to her mother— meaningless words tumbling from her mouth as her stomach tightened in knots.

Later, as she readied herself for bed, CeCe stared into the bathroom mirror, her hands grasping the side of the basin for support. She told herself that Luka being her new teacher wouldn't be a problem. She was eighteen, old enough to vote, drive, and drink alcohol in a bar, so she could see who she liked.

Then she remembered another male teacher who'd had an affair with a senior student the year before last. Their circum-stances had been different—the twenty-year age gap for a start —but when people found out about them, the entire town shunned him. The girl ended up dropping out of school not long after he resigned. Rumor had it, they'd run away together, leaving behind his stunned fiancée and the student's distraught parents.

But this was different. With Luka only in Tulloch Point until Easter, what would the harm be? CeCe splashed cold water on her face and patted it dry. She had this. They were responsible adults, free to do whatever they wanted.

And she wanted Luka.

However, as she lay in bed later, CeCe couldn't stop thinking about Mr. O'Leary the teacher. She imagined him standing in front of the class, writing on the whiteboard, or sitting on the auditorium stage with the other teachers, inflexible in their formality as they tolerated stuffy assemblies.

Why had Luka failed to mention it last night? Had it just slipped his mind? After all, he probably had no idea she'd be in his class. Why would he?

During breakfast on Monday morning, CeCe's father received a text from Carole Jones confirming Luka's appointment, and as he relayed the news, she held her breath. Within the space of forty-eight hours, Luka had gone from being her lover to her teacher.

Doubt settled over her. What had she been thinking with her blasé attitude and I'm-a-mature-adult mantra? She wasn't mature, not by any stretch of the imagination. Now Luka would be on the staff at her school, a person of authority to look up to, and to make matters worse, CeCe knew nothing about chemistry. She was only taking it because it was a requirement for her degree. He'd be scrutinizing her work and marking her assignments.

Her worst nightmare.

She'd texted Molly several times during the weekend to arrange a catch-up for early in the week. But Luka? She couldn't even bring herself to open his name in her Contacts, let alone send a debut message.

That Wednesday, CeCe worked a full shift, finishing at five thirty. During the day, she'd half expected to see Luka browsing through the crime section, flashing her flirty smiles as he so often did, but today, he was conspicuous by his absence.

After freshening up in the staff restroom, CeCe walked the few short blocks to the Japanese eatery on Coronation Drive for her six o'clock dinner date with Molly. The place was half empty when she got there, which wasn't unusual for early evening. While CeCe stood waiting to be seated, her cousin dashed in.

"Hi." Molly stopped to catch her breath. "I almost didn't make it. Some idiot just about ran me down with his souped-up Camaro."

"Are you okay?"

"Shaken but not stirred." She paused as they were shown to their table. Having no need to study the menu to know what they wanted, Molly looked up at their waiter, his pencil hovering over a tiny notepad. "Two vegetarian bento boxes and a couple of Asahis, please."

As the waiter walked away, Molly leaned over the table. "What the hell is going on with this school shit?"

"Well, according to Dad, Hot Chopper Guy's my new chemistry teacher."

Molly frowned. "I thought he was with Search and Rescue."

"Yeah, he is, as a volunteer. But he taught for two years after finishing his degree."

"You've discussed it with him?"

85

"Not the job at school, but he told me he'd been a teacher and that it wasn't his thing. He said he was here to finish his helicopter license. Other than that, I don't know much about him."

"But you Googled him?"

CeCe pulled her phone out of her bag. She swiped and tapped the screen, then offered it to Molly. "Yep. Take a look."

Her cousin frowned as she scrolled. "The Rata River Equestrian Center? What's the connection?"

"I think it must be his family's business. There's a photo of him in the gallery."

"But he doesn't talk about it? What *do* you two talk about? The five best positions for screwing each other's brains out?" Molly returned the phone.

CeCe grinned. "Stop it. We agreed not to get too deep in the domestics of each other's lives."

"Makes sense. Keeps the mystery alive, at least for a while, anyway. Because, while I'll never buy into that 'all men are the same' BS, they do all fart in their sleep and scratch their balls every chance they get."

Suppressing a laugh, CeCe shook her head. It was hard to stay troubled when Molly was on form.

"What? It's true."

Their meals arrived, and they both ate several mouthfuls before resuming their conversation.

"Are you really okay?" CeCe asked. "You seem kinda down."

Molly shrugged. Her long hair hung in a loose plait over one shoulder, and as she pulled at the bottom strands, her expressive eyes saddened. "You know that guy I met from the band? Jesse?"

"The drummer?" CeCe picked up a piece of sushi with her chopsticks and took a bite.

"Yeah. Anyway, he threw me the L-word, and I caught it with both hands."

"Well, that's good, isn't it? A bit soon, but..."

"Yep. Except he woke up around five on Sunday morning, got out of bed, gathered my clothes, and told me to leave. It was weird—no explanation, no goodbye kiss, no nothing. I did my walk of shame with birds squawking obscenities at me, and now he won't return my calls or texts."

"Really? How did he seem, you know, after you got dressed?"

"I've never felt a cold shoulder like it. And as I walked to the door, he switched off the light and said nothing more."

"Wow. I'm so sorry."

"Yeah, me too." Molly picked at her food. "Anyway, we're supposed to be discussing you and Hot Chopper Guy, not my shitty love life. So, what are you going to do?"

"No clue. I'm loving the sex, but...what do you think?"

Molly sipped her beer. A deep thinker, her advice was usually spot-on. Pity she never took it herself. "He's only here until Easter, correct?"

"Yes. And the permanent teacher starts after Easter, so that's what"—CeCe counted the weeks in her head—"nine weeks away."

"That's a long time for a fling. Better to end it now than play teacher's sexy pet. You know what this town's like. He won't get a fair deal if anyone finds out. You might, but you're a local. He'll end up looking like a grooming asshole while you're the innocent student, swept off her feet by a predatory older man."

CeCe glanced around the restaurant, which had filled up

without her even noticing. Molly made a good point. Luka was leaving at Easter, so maybe it would be easier to deal with the separation now rather than waiting another nine weeks.

And yet…

"He's only twenty-six. Hardly a predatory older man."

"It's happened before, that's all I'm saying. Get out before you're in too deep."

CeCe thought for a moment. "You think?"

"This is not about protecting yourself—it's about protecting Luka. His reputation."

MOTHER'S INTUITION

As CeCe turned left into the orchard's driveway, thunder rumbled in the distance, drowning out the song on the radio. Despite the forecast for fine weather, the start of the week had been cold and wet, and as she pulled up outside the implement shed, large droplets of rain splattered onto the windshield.

Inside, the house was dark and still, a lone lamp awaiting her return. Her father often went to bed early, but she was surprised to find her mother had also retired for the night. CeCe longed to talk to her, to toss the words in her head around until they slotted into order and made sense.

Clifton Falls seemed the only solution. If she went to school there, she and Luka could be together again when he returned home after Easter, and no one would be any the wiser. But the odds of her father agreeing to boarding school were zero to none. Her only chance was to convince her mother.

She boiled the kettle and made herself a chamomile tea with a dash of honey, just enough to enhance the flavor.

When she'd called in to see Luka on the way home, his studio was dark, and his SUV absent from the driveway. Now, sitting alone at the breakfast bar in the low light, CeCe thought it was probably just as well. She needed a clear head for the conversation they were about to have.

CeCe looked up as her mother shuffled into the kitchen. Andrea pulled the cord of her robe tight and knotted it off-center, her curls falling in tousles about her face. "Hi. How was your night?"

"Good. The kettle's hot if you want some tea."

Her mother reached for a mug and a tea bag then flicked the kettle's switch to bring it back to the boil. "Do you want to talk about it?"

"What do you mean?"

"The dilemma you've been dragging behind you for the last few days." Cup in hand, Andrea pulled a stool around to the kitchen side of the island and sat opposite her daughter. "Is this about the new chemistry teacher? Is he the guy you've been seeing?"

She nodded. When the swallow didn't help shift the lump from her throat, CeCe pressed her lips together and lowered her head. Her mother reached across the island and squeezed her hand. "Hey, it's okay."

"Luka won't want to keep seeing me when he finds out I'm a student."

Her mother frowned her concern. "You haven't told him?"

CeCe shook her head, tears threatening to spill. "I planned to tonight, but he's been away." She sniffed. "And it's not the sort of thing to explain in a text, is it?"

"No, I guess not."

"Anyway, how do you know?"

"Your mood changed as soon as your father mentioned him. I knew you'd been seeing someone, but I hadn't imagined it was the guy who picked you up that night. I thought maybe you were back with Travis and needed some time before telling us."

CeCe let out a sigh. "What a mess."

"It's only a mess if you make the wrong decision. You can't continue this, not while he's your teacher. And you've only been seeing him, what, two, three weeks? Time to step back and let him do his job, don't you think?"

Silence stretched between them. That's not what she thought. Not at all. All she could think of was ways to get around the fact that Luka would be her teacher until Easter.

"I've been thinking." CeCe sipped her tea, letting its warmth soothe her. "What if I boarded at Immaculate Heart?"

"What? In Clifton Falls?"

"It's only for a year. Then we could see each other when Luka goes home after Easter, and no one would have to know. Besides, Mitch is there. It's not like I'd be going somewhere where I knew no one."

"But you haven't discussed this with him, have you? How do you know what he wants? The guy's only here for a few months. Have you talked about a future together?"

"No, it's not like that. It's just a fling, but..."

Her mother shook her head. "CeCe. Even if Immaculate Heart had a place in their boarding hostel, your plans and his plans might not be on the same page."

"So you're advising me to bow out gracefully?"

"I'm advising you to think very carefully. Because if you carry on seeing Luka while he's in a position of authority at your school, there might well be consequences. Not only for you but also for him. He could lose his job."

"But he doesn't even enjoy teaching. He told me that."

"Okay, so talk to him and see where he stands. You might find he's unwilling to compromise on this."

CeCe leaned back on the stool, her hands on the counter in front of her. She drummed a finger impatiently, keeping time with the beat of her heart. *Tap-tap, tap-tap, tap-tap.*

Her mother stood and placed her mug in the sink. "Come on. You'd better get to bed. Things will look clearer in the morning."

CeCe knew that wasn't true. She'd expected clearer mornings since finding out about Luka, but each had been just as misty as the last. "Please don't tell Dad. Not yet."

Her mother held her arms wide, and CeCe stepped into the hug. "I won't."

14

ROCK NOTES FOR ANNA

After finishing work around two on Thursday, CeCe drove out to Sandwater Bay and sat in the van, staring out at the rain-clouded sky. She picked up the flat rock she'd found at the river one day. Smooth and gray with a white seam running through the middle, it looked like the shape of a heart if you used your imagination.

They'd done this when they were younger—she and Anna —written notes on small, flat stones and passed them to each other during class. They'd started off as a way of communicating about cute boys at school but had soon morphed into something more meaningful.

But when Anna met Dillon, she'd stopped sending notes. Eventually, their communication had dwindled to a few generic texts and small talk over the occasional after-school milkshake. Even then, as soon as Dillon pulled up outside, Anna would race out to meet him.

CeCe grabbed a fine tip Sharpie from her bag, letting the words flow into her head as she forced back those pesky tears.

Holding the rock steady in her left hand, she wrote with her right, and when finished, read it under her breath.

A,

Some days, when forced to
make a decision I don't want to,
I miss your voice, your insight, your smile in my eyes.
Where are you now? Floating above the cloud,
watching me struggle?
Or are you sitting on a rainbow,
wishing we were still together too?
C xoxo

The ocean was flat and surprisingly warm when CeCe waded into the surf, the rock note for Anna clasped in her hand. They'd spent a lot of time at this beach. It was where her brother had taught them both to surf and where Anna had fallen in love with Mitch when she was only thirteen. Not that he'd ever noticed.

CeCe swam toward the horizon until her feet could no longer touch the bottom. Despite the overcast day, surfers bobbed on their boards farther down the beach, waiting their turn in the lineup, and several people strolled along the shoreline—some with dogs fetching sticks, others alone.

Goggles in place, she slipped under the water to bury the rock in the sand, then surfaced and swam back to shore.

As CeCe walked up the beach, a bright ray of sunlight peeked through the clouds, bringing with it a spark of warmth. She lay face down on her towel to dry off, the fingers of her right hand tracing a pattern in the sand—L&C encased in an arrowed heart—then quickly scattering it into oblivion as she wondered why Luka hadn't called into the library to see her.

Sensing someone watching her, she looked up to see Travis and a couple of his friends sitting on top of a nearby dune. He stood and brushed the sand from his shorts before walking her way. When he reached her, he sat without invitation, his knees bent and sight fixed on the horizon.

He fiddled with his sunglasses. "How have you been?"

CeCe sat up and faced the same way, a sudden cool breeze making her shudder. *Restless...troubled.* "Good."

"Some of us guys are heading up to Koru Bay tomorrow afternoon. We thought we'd stay the night. You should come. I was going to text you, but then I saw your Kombi."

She gathered the words that had floated around in her head since he'd dumped her. Words she'd shuffled and reshuffled many times but never had the guts to say. She inhaled and let them drift out: "You hurt me, Travis. Maybe I hurt you too, but when I needed you, you accused me of being morbid and boring. So I'm sorry, but boring girls don't go away for the night with a group of guys. They stay home and work in the library and keep their hearts locked tight. And you might think boring girls have to settle for second best but screw you. This boring girl knows that second best is not good enough."

CeCe stood and grabbed her towel. She didn't want to cry in front of him, but as she strode toward the Kombi, the sand hard and cool beneath her feet, the tears wouldn't be denied.

Travis chased after her. "CeCe? Wait!"

By the time he reached her, she'd already started the van. He leaned on the open window. "I'm sorry. We're good together, babe. Please, I want a second chance."

She depressed the clutch and shifted the van into reverse. "I already gave you a second chance. You just never realized."

15

MAKING A DIFFERENCE

Back home, CeCe parked the Kombi in front of the implement shed and rested her head against the steering wheel. Although she and Travis had split up almost four months ago, he still had an effect. Their infatuation started with a schoolgirl crush—she'd watched him strut around school as if he owned the show, and even though he was a year behind her, she'd still found him cute. One day, he'd kissed her in the gymnasium equipment room, and they'd started hanging out soon after.

The hourly news on the radio caught her attention. An American couple had gone missing in the ranges to the west of the national park. She wondered if Luka was out looking for them, and for a moment, she wanted to be out there too, adding her weight to the search effort. Making a difference.

CeCe jumped when her father opened the door. "Are you coming in for dinner?"

"Yes. I was just listening to the news." She reached over and turned it off before following her father toward the house. "There's a couple missing up by the Hikuwhai Hut."

"Yeah? I'm sure that teacher friend of yours will find them. Brad reckons he has an uncanny knack for sniffing out leads."

"He is not 'my teacher friend.' He just happened to pull me out of a rabbit hole."

Frank entered the mudroom and began washing his hands. "Where have you been, anyway?"

"At Sandwater Bay. I saw Travis there."

"Oh, yeah? How was that?"

CeCe shrugged. "Awkward. He wants me to go surfing with him tomorrow."

Frank dried his hands as CeCe washed hers. "Would that be wise?"

"Don't worry, I said no." She turned to him with a smile. "But you're asking my opinion again. Normally you'd speak your mind and *tell* me what to do."

He shrugged. "Maybe, but as you keep reminding me, you're almost nineteen. You know how I feel about Travis, but in the end, it's your decision whether you see him or not."

CeCe followed him into the kitchen and kissed her mother on the cheek. "Quick, grab the thermometer, Mum. Something's seriously wrong with Dad. He just told me I was old enough to make my own decisions."

Her mother laughed. "Don't worry. It's merely a phase—he'll grow out of it."

As her dad took a seat at the table, CeCe helped her mother serve the meal. With him in a good mood, maybe now was the time to bring up the subject of schools.

"Actually, I've been thinking about school."

Frank accepted his plate from Andrea and turned to stare at his daughter. She tensed under his gaze as his easy mood from moments before vanished. "Don't tell me you've changed your mind again."

"I still want to go to university, but I'm not sure if I'm doing the right thing. I mean—"

"Whatever you decide," he countered, "surely repeating your final year should be the next step. You need chemistry. Without it, you'll struggle once you get to uni."

"Yes, I know. I've not changed my mind, but I'm not keen on going back to Tulloch Point High with the younger kids." CeCe sat across from her father. "I thought maybe I could go to Clifton Falls and board at Immaculate Heart."

Her mother placed a bowl of salad on the table and took her seat while giving CeCe a knowing glance.

"Why on earth would you want to board at Immaculate Heart?" he spluttered. "You wouldn't last a week at a boarding school. You're hardly an Immaculate Heart girl, and I mean that in the nicest possible way."

CeCe dished salad and potatoes onto her plate but passed on the pork schnitzel in favor of crumbed eggplant. "So, what do you suggest? I go back to Tulloch Point High and slum it with the younger kids? Settle for some mediocre school in a mediocre town?"

Her father took a deep breath. "Look, we've been over this until my jaw hurts even thinking about it," he said sternly. "They're giving you another chance. That 'mediocre school,' as you put it, is prepared to give you another chance."

CeCe stared at the plate of food before her, her appetite lost in her father's words. She couldn't tell him about Luka. Not now. But the thought of sitting in his class, watching him at the whiteboard, having him mark her assignments, and the other students finding out about them made her sick to her stomach.

"Maybe I could give Immaculate Heart a call tomorrow," her mother said. "See if they might have a place."

CeCe had expected her mum to tell her dad about Luka, even though she'd asked her not to, but obviously, she hadn't.

"No, Andrea. School starts in a few days, and I'm not paying thousands of dollars for some snobby boarding school when we have a perfectly good high school in our own backyard."

"It still wouldn't hurt to inquire," Andrea replied.

"Is it Travis?" her father asked. He looked at her mum. "She saw him today. I've never liked that boy. The kid's a smart-ass. And now he's unsettled her."

"It's not Travis. I need to get away, Dad. I know you don't understand, but please. I can't go back to Tulloch Point High. I just can't." CeCe stood and carried her plate to the counter. Having eaten less than a quarter of her meal, she covered it with plastic wrap and placed it in the fridge. "I'm sorry, Mum, but I'm not hungry right now. I need to go out for a bit."

Frank placed his knife and fork down and sighed. "Will someone please tell me what's going on?"

"What do you mean?" CeCe asked.

"You've been sneaking around for days. In and out of town in that rust bucket of a van, down at the beach on your own. I'm exhausted just from watching you. And before you spout off about how you're almost nineteen and can live your own life, don't expect us to stop caring just because you've clocked another year around the sun."

CeCe rounded the table and pressed a kiss to her father's cheek. She'd rarely taken her parents for granted, even when she was younger. She knew too many kids from dysfunctional families not to realize that her own family was one to cherish. "I know, Dad. But I'll be okay, so please don't worry about me." She looked up. "Can I borrow the Corolla, Mum? I'll be back in an hour or two."

"Course you can. I filled it with gas today so you can use it for school. The Kombi's not really suitable if you're giving other kids a ride."

"Thanks."

Luka's place was dark and silent when CeCe pulled up outside. Thinking he might arrive home at any minute, she sat for a while, her phone in her hand as she thought of what she should say.

She stepped from the car and walked down the driveway in the dark, the light on her phone illuminating her steps to ensure she didn't trip over any tree roots. Her stomach tied in knots, she knocked on his door. Nothing.

A swing hung from a large oak tree in the backyard, its seat weathered with age and rope rough to the touch. She sat in it for a while, swaying back and forth, her thoughts shifting from *why* *to why not?*

There seemed no reason for them to break up. They were two adults who could keep a secret. She didn't have to go to Clifton Falls this term. By the time Easter arrived, her father might have changed his mind about Immaculate Heart, and she and Luka could still be together.

She checked her phone: after eight. Where was he? Chilled, CeCe walked back to her car, doubts and convictions still battling it out in her mind until she could scarcely think straight.

When CeCe drove past the small Search and Rescue building on her way home, it was a bustling hive of activity. Along the street, cars lined the curb, and as she pulled into the only available parking space and cut the engine, a chopper whirred to a stop on the nearby helipad.

She sat for a while, observing the comings and goings. Then, just as she was about to pull away, Luka walked around the side of the building, dressed for business in a navy blue flight suit. His aviator sunglasses rested on top of his head, redundant as he talked with other crew members. She'd never really thought about his day-to-day life, but seeing him now, standing tall with the other men, she felt a sense of pride for the man who meant so much to her.

She wanted to leap from the car and run to him, but he appeared preoccupied. It was all very well him visiting her at the library, but his work wasn't exactly conducive to dropping in for a chat.

So instead, she picked up her phone and flicked him a text.

Hey, it's CeCe. We need to talk. xx

16

WITHOUT CALLOUS INTENT

As the working hours dragged, CeCe longed to escape the noisy world inside her head and return to the night of that Christmas party, when she'd left in a huff to get away from Travis. If only she could retrace her steps to achieve an alternative outcome, she'd call Mitch or even Molly's mum to ask one of them to come and collect her.

No rabbit hole, no meet-cute, and no sex with Luka O'Leary in the back of the Kombi.

Instead, she'd have met *Mr. O'Leary* on the first day of school, sat through his chemistry class, and gone home with a teeny crush. But that crush would have gone no further than her imagination, as his position would not allow it.

"Hey."

Her hand flew to her chest. "Don't do that. You gave me a fright!"

Luka looked her up and down, but it wasn't his usual lazy gaze. "Are you okay?"

"Yes, fine, but kind of busy at the moment." She slotted a book into place and picked up another from the cart.

He hesitated. "Sorry I haven't been in touch, but it's been full on since I came back with that couple missing. I have tonight off though. I thought we could grab dinner if you're free."

"Um…maybe not dinner, but I could call past after work. Actually, there's something I want to talk to you about."

Luka took hold of her arm and turned her slightly to face him. "Yeah, so you said in your text," he whispered. "The first text you send me, and it's 'we need to talk.' Are you sure everything's okay?"

CeCe glanced over to see Miss Libby watching them from the reception desk and swallowed hard. "I really should get back to work. We'll talk later."

His jaw tight, he stepped back, the hurt evident on his face. As they stood in awkward silence, she longed to blurt out, "You're my teacher." But now was neither the time nor the place.

"Okay." Luka handed her the book he'd been holding, then turned and walked across the floor and out through the main door without once looking back. She wanted to follow him. To explain. But instead, she stood with the book in her hand and the words stored on the tip of her tongue, awaiting a more convenient time.

As CeCe pushed the cart toward the back storeroom, Miss Libby waved her over with an enthusiastic hand. She knew CeCe and Luka were seeing each other and had appointed herself as a surrogate agony aunt. "Trouble in paradise?"

Hoping to see him still outside, CeCe glanced toward the door, but he'd gone. "I think we've struck our first hiccup."

"Don't worry. Hiccups pass. Just don't let them choke you."

CeCe couldn't help but smile. "I won't."

"He's special, that one. But how old is he?"

"Twenty-six."

Miss Libby raised a brow. "So, eight years between you. That can be a stretch at your age, child. Just take things slowly, won't you?"

"He's leaving at Easter, so…"

"I see. Does that worry you?"

With Luka now her chemistry teacher, CeCe had more to worry about than Easter. Her hand went to her neck to scratch an itch in the very place he liked to caress her. "A bit, but it's just a fling."

"So that's what you're telling yourself?" The older woman chuckled. "People say if you're meant to be together, you'll find a way. But sometimes, life's not that kind, and we let the good ones slip away while holding on tight to the dregs." She shrugged. "But you know what?"

"What?"

Miss Libby stood, lifted the cardigan off the back of her chair, and draped it over her shoulders. "The older I get, the more I realize I know sweet Fanny Adams about life, especially when it comes to men."

"Yeah, me too."

The older woman picked up her handbag. "And with that little pearl of wisdom, I shall bid you farewell."

As he drove home along Coronation Drive, Luka replayed their conversation in his head. CeCe had never given him the cold shoulder before, but that's what their exchange had felt like. A swift brush-off.

Standing in the shower later, he thought of the American couple who'd gone for a 'stroll' in the national park and failed to return. He'd been at work since five that morning, and he'd still be there now if Brad hadn't insisted he take the evening off. But he was confident they'd find them.

After his shower, he lay on his bed, still wrapped in a towel. The next thing he knew, CeCe stood at his bedside, urging him to wake up.

Confused and unsure of his surroundings for a moment, Luka lifted his head from the pillow and smiled. "Hey. What time is it?"

"Almost six. Sorry, I should have let you sleep."

He rubbed his eyes with the heels of his hands, and as he sat up, the towel slipped from his waist. "Shit. I was miles away." He stood and pulled on his boxers, then a pair of clean jeans from the pile of laundry in the basket. "Sorry about the mess."

CeCe studied the room. "No problem."

Ignoring the resistance in her body language, Luka stepped forward, cupped her face, and bent down for a kiss. "Hi."

Her response less than enthusiastic, she frowned and stepped back.

He took her hands, let them drop again. Something was definitely up. "What's going on?"

"May I have a drink? Water's fine."

Luka opened the fridge and grabbed a bottle of sparkling water. He poured two glasses and added a slice of lime to each. "Shall we go outside?"

She took the offered drink and sat at the kitchen table.

Guess not.

"I know…about your new job."

He took the chair opposite and sipped his drink. "At the high school? Who told you?"

"Dad. He's on the board of trustees." No eye contact on her

part. Her father being on the school's board was news to Luka. But why would that upset her?

"I've been meaning to tell you, but it's been crazy busy this week. I said no initially but reconsidered over the weekend. And I didn't have your number until yesterday, so—"

"Luka. Stop!" CeCe's hands flew up to emphasize her point. In the short time they'd spent together, he'd never once heard her raise her voice, never seen her angry.

He leaned back in his chair and watched her grapple with her thoughts. She picked up her glass, took a sip, put it back down.

"I dropped out of school last year—partway through August —I'm not sure exactly when, and I've been working at the library since September." She traced a finger around the lip of her glass. "But as I've said before, it's not my dream. I planned to study business management once I left school, but I've thought a lot about it lately and now, I want to go to Otago to study science."

At first, he thought she was asking him to tutor her, but when she lifted her gaze, a large knot formed in his gut.

"I'm going back to school next week to repeat my senior year so I can graduate. When Dad told me you were the new chemistry teacher, I pleaded with him to let me go to boarding school instead. But he wouldn't hear of it. So, unless he changes his mind over the next few days, I'm stuck at Tulloch Point High."

Luka raked his fingers through his hair as the meaning of her words sank in. CeCe was now not only his lover but his pupil as well. He released a sigh. "So that's what you wanted to talk to me about?"

"Yes. But I've had time to think it over, and I don't see why anything needs to change between—"

"Shit, CeCe, there's nothing to *think* about. We can't see each other if I'm your teacher. That's a line I am not prepared to cross, and besides, what about the people who already know? Your co-workers at the library, your friend Anna?"

"Why not?"

"I've told you why." Luka stood and paced the room. "You can't just stroll into my classroom and expect me to teach you damn chemistry by day and then have sex with you at night like it's the most natural thing in the world." He paused for a breath. "Why didn't you tell me you were returning to school?"

She looked down. Picked at her nails. "It didn't seem important."

"Yeah, well, it is now. We have one chance here to do the right thing, do you understand? If I could go back and turn down the job offer, I would, but I've given my word."

CeCe stared up at him, her eyes wide. "And your word means more to you than us?"

"It's not that simple, is it? And if you don't understand that, you're not as mature as I thought."

She held his gaze, but the words Luka expected never came. He needed her out of his space before he weakened and ended up consoling her the best way he knew how: naked on his bed. "Look, I know we agreed this was just a fling, but let's take a break until Easter, then we'll work something out."

Frown lines tracked across her forehead and for a moment, he thought she'd agree. It wouldn't be easy, but they could make it work.

"No." Her voice remained even. "What's the point?"

"The point is," he countered, "nothing's black and white here."

"Maybe, but you're going home after Easter, back to your city life. And next year, I'll be at uni, hundreds of miles away.

Long-distance flings don't tend to work, do they?" CeCe stood and picked up her handbag from the kitchen counter. "Thanks though. It was nice while it lasted." A sad smile accompanied her goodbye. "Guess I'll see you at school unless Dad changes his mind by Monday."

She stepped back and opened the door, leaving it ajar as she moved outside, beyond reach.

The wind slammed the door shut, and Luka stood in stunned disbelief, her words 'nice while it lasted' ringing in his ears. Panic surged in his chest. If anyone had asked him a few days ago about his relationship with CeCe Dobson, he'd have called it a summer fling without callous intent. But now?

Luka flopped back on his bed and watched the ceiling fan spin. He'd been starving when he arrived home from work. Now he couldn't even rouse himself to check out the fridge.

"Shit!"

Her father looked up from the newspaper when CeCe walked in the door. "You're home early. Decide not to stay in town tonight?"

"Nah, I need an early night."

"Are you ready for school on Monday?"

CeCe sat at the table. "About that… I'm not sure I'll make it back to school."

"Not this again." Frank leafed over the last page of the newspaper. The seconds ticked by. He stood, folded the paper, and placed it on the sideboard. "Your mother and I are going into town to see a movie. We can talk about this tomorrow. I won't have my evening out ruined by your lack of insight.

You're a bright girl, Sydney. Don't throw it all away because you can't be bothered to make a difference in your own life."

Sydney?

"But—"

He held up both hands for her to stop, then turned on his heel and stalked out the back door without another word.

Her mother appeared from their bedroom with a necklace in her hands. "Put this on for me, will you, sweetheart?" She held it out to CeCe. "How was work?"

CeCe fastened the clasp. "Okay."

Craning her neck, Andrea peered into the adjoining media room. "Where's that father of yours? We're going to be late."

"In the car. I told him I didn't want to go back to school, and he called me Sydney."

"Oh dear."

"Yep. I guess I'd better wash and press my uniform."

"It's done. I did it this morning." Her mother smiled softly and opened her arms wide. CeCe stepped into her knowing embrace. Some of her friends never hugged their parents, but the Dobson clan had always been big on physical affection. "Thanks, Mum. Have a good night. I'm sorry I've been such hard work lately."

Her mother patted her on the back and chuckled. "It's just a stage. You'll grow out of it."

The heat of the evening cloying in its closeness, CeCe lay on her bed, the French doors open to the veranda. Across the lawn, hundreds of avocado trees spread their green-leaved branches in all directions, and outside her bedroom door, petunias sulked in their pots, desperate for a drink of water. She'd do that soon, but for now, she just wanted to mope.

In the back of her mind, CeCe had known her fling with

Luka would be short-lived. Such was the nature of the beast. And, as Miss Libby had pointed out, sometimes life was unkind.

Her phone pinged. She picked it up and glanced at the screen.

Luka: We should talk before school starts. Text me a time and I'll make sure I'm here.

CeCe threw it down on the bed and went outside to water her plants. She wanted to text back a simple *Why?* But what was the point? He'd made his decision, and his reasons were sound, no matter how much she might wish they weren't.

She dreaded the thought of seeing Luka at school every day. He'd dress in smart casual, carry a messenger bag, and probably coach rugby or soccer or some other sport. He'd be popular with the guys, but even more so with the girls. Because Luka had a charm about him that couldn't be denied, and the few times they'd been together in public—at the burger bar and the library—she'd noticed how women watched him.

She grabbed her phone again and ran her fingers over the keypad.

CeCe: Let's not draw this out. Sometimes talking is overrated.
Luka: So is doing the right thing.
CeCe: Roll on Easter.

Worried that he might misinterpret her meaning, CeCe reread her last text and cringed. She went to send an additional message of explanation but stopped herself. Back and forth communication on a tiny screen annoyed her.

And, besides, what more could she say?

MR. O'LEARY

That first humid day of school on the third of February, CeCe had chemistry last period. She walked to class alone, and when she got there, took a seat at the back, one over from Travis. He glanced her way, but she didn't return his look. When her phone pinged with a text, she checked it to find two words on the screen.

'Teacher's slut.'

What?

Luka, or Mr. O'Leary as she must now call him, arrived five minutes late but offered no apology. CeCe watched him remove his laptop and stow his bag under the desk. He looked up, and as their eyes met, the hairs on the back of her neck lifted. Wearing black dress pants and a crisp blue shirt, he seemed out of place. This wasn't her Luka, the man who loved lounging around home half naked. Luka, who commanded her to come, more than once, and held her loosely in his arms as she slept.

He cleared his throat, looked at her again as if seeing things, then turned to the whiteboard and wrote his name across it in a flourish of upright font.

"Afternoon, everyone. My name's Luka O'Leary, and I'll be your chemistry teacher until the end of term. I ask that you leave any BS, bad attitude, and gang patches at the door and that all phones are off during class. Respect my rules, and we'll get along just fine. Flaunt them, and we won't. Simple as that. Now, any questions?"

A girl called Angela, who sat in the front row, raised her hand. "Some of us want to know your political persuasion, stance on racism, and sexual orientation. We refuse to be taught by a homophobic, white supremacist, right-winged member of the jerk-off party."

CeCe suppressed a smile. Luka was part Māori on his father's side, but as for his political beliefs and the rest, she had no idea. However, he was often vocal about the advantages of living in a democratic society.

He moved to the front of his desk and held Angela's gaze for just a moment too long. "What's your name?"

Angela straightened in her seat. "Angela Hohepa."

CeCe held her breath, waiting for his curt response.

He smiled. "*Kia ora*, Angela." Luka continued his reply in fluent *te reo* Māori. Several of the students laughed at something he said, including Angela, but as CeCe knew only basic *te reo,* she couldn't pick up on his humor.

She understood one thing, though: their new teacher was a charming man with a glint in his eye and a grin to match. By the time he'd finished his spiel, every straight girl in the class was probably in lust with him, and at least one of the two gay guys as well.

"Oh, and if you're wondering," Luka continued in English, looking around the room, "my star sign is Taurus, and I love apple cake, just in case any of you guys are good bakers."

As Luka moved back behind his desk, the class laughed

again. "Right. Let's get to work." He ran his sight down his laptop screen then looked up, straight into CeCe's eyes. He set the first challenge. "Where's Sydney Dobson?"

Prick!

She wanted to stand, march straight over to the door, and slam it on the way out. Instead, she raised her hand a fraction.

He hardly looked at her. "Sydney, please recite the first twenty elements by atomic number."

CeCe hesitated and felt herself pale as the other students turned to stare at her. Having never studied chemistry before, she was unfamiliar with the periodic table. She barely knew what a Bunsen burner was. "Hydrogen, helium, lithium…boron—"

"Incorrect. Please learn that part of the table by Friday." He scanned the room. "Anyone else?" Angela raised her hand and recited the list with ease.

The tone had been set.

For the rest of the period, Luka ignored CeCe, as if she were any other student in any other class. But as she headed out the door at the end of the period, he called her back. "Sydney, would you mind waiting behind for a few minutes."

"Yes. I would." She kept on walking.

As CeCe left the classroom, she found Travis waiting for her. Again, she kept walking, her backpack heavy on her shoulders, her mood in no way conducive to idle chit-chat with her ex.

"CeCe? Wait up." Travis reached out and grabbed hold of her elbow.

She stopped. Yanked herself free. "What do you want?"

"I didn't send that text. I swear."

Travis trailing behind her, CeCe strode down the corridor, past the lockers, and out the front door. "Whatever."

"Brandon was mucking around with my phone, and he sent it. It was a joke. He said he saw you and some guy that looked like O'Leary at the beach one day. Are you guys together?"

She ignored his question. "Yeah, well, that says it all, doesn't it? You and your friends think it's okay to slut-shame girls, that it's funny? Get a life of your own before trying to destroy someone else's. I've been through enough BS lately."

Hightailing it across the quad to the school gates, CeCe kept her head down as the straps of her backpack dug into her shoulders.

"Time you moved on, babe," Travis yelled after her. "You can't cart that morbid shit around with you forever."

CeCe stopped and turned to face him. Gathered courage. Stepped forward. "You don't move on from grief, Travis. You carry it with you...every single day." She slapped her chest. "It's in here. It floats on the waves at Sandwater Bay and sits in the passenger seat of my Kombi. And that stupid comment is why we're over. You just don't get it, and you never will."

As she crossed the road to her mother's Corolla, she could feel Travis watching her.

Leaning against a lamppost, Levi, one of her passengers, frowned over at her ex. "Are you okay?"

Levi was a cocky kid. Sixteen years old and already a good head and shoulders taller than her. She greeted him with a smile. "I'm fine."

"The brats aren't here, so guess I call shotgun."

"Yeah, they have swimming lessons this afternoon." CeCe still didn't like anyone sitting in the front passenger seat. That seat was Anna's. But what could she say? That the seat was reserved for a dead girl? She opened the driver's door then glanced over at Travis, who hadn't moved an inch. "How was your day?"

Levi grinned at her over the roof. "I received a detention first period."

"What for?"

"Told Ms. Butler to piss off."

"Levi! No wonder you got a detention. Get in the car."

They climbed in and fastened their belts. CeCe turned to look at him. "Okay. Life lesson for this week. Never tell a teacher to piss off. Ever. Or to F off."

"She deserved it. Called me a moron."

"Yeah, well, two wrongs just make both of you look stupid. Remember, a little bit of diplomacy can go a long way."

He grinned. "Is this how it's going to be? All this touchy-feely stuff every time I hitch a ride?"

CeCe matched his grin as she flicked on her indicator. "Not every time. Just when you're being a dick." She pulled out of the parking space and onto the road.

"Did you meet the new chemistry teacher?" Levi asked as they traveled east along Parkvale Drive. "Some of the senior girls were talking about how hot he is."

Checking her rearview mirror, CeCe winced. "Yep, I met him."

She ignored Levi's stare.

"And?" he finally asked.

"And nothing. He's my teacher."

18

THE STANDOFF

As part of his paramedic training, Luka had learned how to keep calm and maintain a neutral expression in most situations. But when he'd looked up earlier to see CeCe sitting at the back of his class, surrounded by a half dozen male students, he'd struggled to hold his reaction in check. Especially after her *Easter* text message.

He slumped back in his chair and picked up his phone, thinking he should text and ask to meet up so they could discuss what happened like adults.

His day had been difficult, leaving him angry and sad in equal measure. Now his lack of sleep the night before reflected in his mood. And that afternoon, as she'd walked past him in her summer school uniform—white shirt, navy blue pleated skirt, and sandals—she'd looked so young.

Much too young.

A knock at his front door startled him. As he stepped into the short hallway, Luka could see CeCe through the blind slats, and when he opened the door, she entered without invitation.

He followed her into the living space. "What are you doing here?"

"You wanted to see me."

"Yes, at school, not here."

"Sorry, but I was in no mood to stay after the way you treated me. What happened when you stepped into that class-room? Did you decide to be a bully because my last text bruised your ego a tad? Is this what it's going to be like from now on?"

Luka shook his head. Lowered his voice. "Until a week ago, I thought we had an understanding. So excuse me, but this new normal is going to take some getting used to. And if you want to get ahead in my class, do the work and learn the basics."

"Fine, but I don't understand bond energies and systems in equilibrium and stupid periodic trends in behavior. It's way over my head, and I've no idea what to do about it."

"Yes, well, that's your first hurdle. If you think it's all stupid, how will you ever respect the learning process?" He sighed heavily. "Have you considered dropping chemistry and taking something else?"

Anger flared in CeCe's expression. "Why? So you can forget I ever existed?"

"Let's get one thing straight—I will never forget that you exist, understand? But you can't just rock up at my home unin-vited like I still owe you my time. I've no doubt you can do well if you apply yourself, but you won't get far with that attitude. And another thing, why are you taking level three chemistry when you haven't even done level two?"

"Because Mrs. Jones thought I could handle it. And you know what? We're always told we can be whatever we want, but that's just another lie loaded with pressure. We can only be what our brains allow us to be. I couldn't be a neurosurgeon no matter how hard I tried. I don't have what it takes. But I want to do chemistry."

"But why? What's driving you to take up a subject you've never studied before? Because let's face it, chemistry's no walk in the park. It's hard work."

He noticed her hesitation. Most likely, she had no idea what her goal or motivation was. Maybe she hadn't even thought about it.

"I want to have my own cosmetics business one day. My skin's sensitive, and I can never find skincare that suits me. Other people are doing it, but I think I can do it just as well if not better."

Surprised by her reply, Luka held her gaze. He would never have pinned her for the ambitious, entrepreneurial type. But then, the carefree woman she'd presented to him when they were lovers differed vastly from the girl standing before him now. "Well then, maybe you'll have to try a little harder."

She didn't miss a beat. "Maybe you need to teach *a little* better. I can only learn what you teach me."

"That's bullshit, and you know it." Luka pulled out a stool from the island and she surprised him by taking it. He leaned his butt on the counter, arms folded. "I'm guessing your father refused to move you?"

"He did. So unless you resign, you're stuck with me."

"And you didn't think to give me a heads-up? I asked you to text me."

"I figured you'd see my name on the roll, so—"

"Well, I saw a Sydney Dobson and assumed it was you. I never knew CeCe was a nickname. Something else you didn't think to tell me. And you're repeating the year, but you can't recite the first few elements of the periodic table?"

He watched her inhale, exhale, trying to keep her reaction in check perhaps. "I told you that I haven't studied chemistry before."

CeCe was right. He'd been a bully by singling her out in class, and he was still being one now. "Does your father know about us?"

"No, and since there *is* no us anymore, it's a moot point."

They stayed on opposite sides of the island, CeCe seated, Luka standing. "Look, I'm sorry. But that 'roll on Easter' text really pissed me off. It's like suddenly you can't wait to see the back of me."

"That's why I hate texting. Messages can be misconstrued."

He rubbed the back of his neck. As far as he was concerned, there had been no misconstruction. She'd made herself perfectly clear. "I'm running Thursday morning tutorials for a few students from my other class, starting next week. Be there by seven thirty, and you can join us."

"I can't come to school early."

He frowned. "Why not?"

"Because I give some younger kids from our road a ride most days. The school bus is full."

He paused. "Okay, well, I'll email you some online resources. Let me know if you need anything more, but please don't come here again. I don't want anyone else finding out about us."

CeCe stood and picked up her bag from the floor without hesitation. He followed her down the hallway and opened the door. "Yes, sir."

He sighed at her attempt to bait him. How had their fling so rapidly turned into a shit-show? "And please don't call me sir."

She glanced back. "And don't call me Sydney."

As she walked down his driveway, Luka stood in the doorway and watched her, the knots in his stomach tightening.

If he had any sense, he'd tender his resignation at the end of tomorrow's staff meeting. But that would mean going back on his word, and going back on his word wasn't in Luka's makeup.

Luka didn't see CeCe the following day, and as he lay alone in the dark until well after midnight, thinking of her, vivid details of their time together played on his mind. He'd never met any of her friends, and when they'd first started seeing one another, he'd wondered if she came from a broken home. He had no idea why. Maybe it was the troubled vibe he sometimes caught when she thought he wasn't watching.

He missed her. The way they'd talked into the early hours on those nights when it was too muggy to sleep. But she'd never shared her story or given any real indication of what made her tick.

Thinking about it, he'd never been so infatuated with a woman before. But when he saw her in his class, that infatuation soon turned to trepidation. Luka had never understood how a teacher could fall for a student; he saw it as a professional line one just didn't cross.

But life sometimes swept a color wash over the black and white we painted for ourselves, and now, he didn't know how to handle his growing passion for CeCe Dobson.

Sitting at his computer before class the next morning, Luka brought up her results for the previous year. Until the end of the second term, her achievements had been impressive, with high marks in all subjects. After that, she hadn't passed a single standard and had eventually dropped out.

As students filed into the classroom, Luka clicked out of the screen. CeCe arrived a few minutes late, but he ignored her as she took the same seat as before. From his position at the front of the class, he watched her, then watched Travis watching her.

Ignoring Travis, she took copious notes, her head down over her notebook, concentration furrowing her brow. When class was almost over, she raised her hand. Luka glanced back from cleaning the whiteboard. He turned. "Yes, CeCe."

She cleared her throat. "You asked me to learn part of the periodic table." Her eyebrows knitted together. "Are we being tested on it?"

"Not today."

After the bell rang, Luka stood to dismiss the class. He shut his laptop and slotted it into his messenger bag as CeCe waited until the rest of the students had left the room.

"So, I spent all that time for nothing?"

His thoughts in turmoil, Luka had tossed and turned all night, and he flinched at her tone. The maturity he'd once found endearing had vanished. He looked down at her and gathered his response. "Learning the basics is never for nothing. It's often the difference between a pass or a fail. Don't expect me to give you validation for something you should have known in the first place." He grabbed his phone and keys from his desk drawer and stuffed them into his pocket. "You're a senior student in this school—perhaps it's time you started acting like one."

"Fine. And you know what?" Without giving him time to respond, she continued, "I'm really looking forward to Easter."

He didn't miss a beat. "Yes, so you've already said."

CeCe stormed out the door, and he watched her leave, feeling like an utter bastard. But more than that, he wanted to pin her up against the wall and take her like he meant it—without contrition or restraint.

Luka rubbed the back of his neck, the many reasons he'd

decided to leave the profession flooding his thoughts. Was he a good teacher? How could one evaluate one's own academic qualities in the classroom? He wanted her to succeed, but he wondered if their past association would hold her back.

Granted, being in his class after what happened between them couldn't be easy for her, and unfortunately, she appeared to lack the emotional maturity to deal with it. Some days, he did as well.

Later that afternoon, Luka watched from the side window of the classroom as a group of half a dozen younger kids congregated on the tennis courts. Just as he was about to turn away, CeCe strode toward them, dressed in her PE gear and with a sports bag slung over her shoulder. The students gathered around her, and they conversed back and forth, her face full of smiles.

As he watched them interact, he realized she must be their coach. They volleyed for a time, CeCe helping the younger ones with their backhand. Luka enjoyed watching tennis, especially if it was live, but no matter how hard he tried, he had zero racquet skills. It appeared CeCe Dobson had more to her than he'd first thought. It was a shame she'd never get to give him a lesson.

If the janitor hadn't arrived to clean the room, Luka would have stared out that window for the rest of the afternoon. Then he remembered. He shouldn't be watching her at all.

19

RUMORS

The wind picked up as CeCe turned into Old Cemetery Road. Tears welled in her eyes as she neared the main gate, but she wanted them to fall, knowing she'd feel better later if she set them free and got on with it. Mr. O'Leary, with his holier-than-thou attitude and unrelenting stare, was pissing her off. He was mad, and she understood why, but he didn't have to be such a jerk about it. She'd known too many jerks in her time and didn't care to meet any more.

CeCe hung a right onto the main cemetery drive and parked in the shade of a pin oak. She'd raided her mother's garden that morning, wrapping the blooms in wet newspaper before placing them in a small cooler on the back seat of the car.

The posies were always dainty—budding roses and delicate annuals cupped in bright green foliage. Being dainty herself, Anna had loved both the word and the design. CeCe's mum called these compact floral creations tussie-mussies, and when she'd Googled it, to her surprise, the term was an actual thing.

Hoe in hand, Bob the gardener greeted her as she passed. He worked most days spring through autumn, tending the graves with no expectation of monetary recognition. Bob had started with his wife's grave, then one day, he'd stayed a little longer to tidy up the row, and the next a little longer still. By the time he'd turned eighty, he'd found a new life purpose—tending flower beds and the graves of forgotten or unforgiven souls who'd been laid to rest in the company of his wife of fifty-one years.

She sat next to Anna's headstone. The grass felt slightly damp underneath her school skirt, but CeCe didn't care. She'd told her best friend about Luka the week after the rabbit-hole incident. How he'd lifted her over the fence and dropped her off at the hospital. About the touch and smell of him—the cadence of his voice. Anna would have loved that story. Some nights, she'd read romance novels until the early hours. Now she wanted Anna to know that the 'happy ever after' was, in this case, a crock of shit. Love may conquer all, but lust certainly did not.

"I have a story," she began as she arranged the flowers in a vase at the base of the headstone. "You remember I told you about Luka, the meet-cute guy who flies a chopper? The first official fling of my life? Well, it's all turned to crap."

CeCe stayed for a while, talking in whispers about school and Luka and how emotionally close to the edge she felt at times. In the days leading up to Anna's death, they hadn't been in contact, and that was always her first apology.

Her last regret.

When she returned to the car and glanced through the back window as she reversed, the sight of Bob, all alone next to his wife's grave, tore at her heart.

Levi lounged against the wall, waiting for CeCe as she left her classroom the following afternoon. "Can I bum a ride home?" He fell into step beside her, loping along in his usual ungainly fashion.

"Course you can." She stopped at her locker and opened it. "But I thought you had cricket practice."

Levi leaned on everything, as if he struggled to hold himself up without support, and the lockers were no exception. "Coach stood me down this week."

After stuffing her bag with what she needed, CeCe shut the door and locked it. "How come?"

He shrugged. "I might have mouthed off without thinking. Guess Coach didn't see the funny side."

As they walked across the quad in silence, CeCe suppressed a smile. It wasn't until they were in the car and she'd pulled away from the curb that he spoke again. "The word's out, you know that, don't you?"

CeCe had no idea what he was talking about. She turned to look at him. "What word?"

Levi hesitated. "You and O'Leary. Everyone's gossiping about you guys."

Her stomach tightened. "Are they? What are they saying?"

"That you're bumping uglies. Is it true?"

As she waited to turn right at an intersection, CeCe kept her eye on the traffic while processing his words. She'd wondered how long it would take for Travis and his friend Brandon to shoot their mouths off. "Don't believe everything you hear on campus, especially from guys like Travis Bostock."

"I don't. But I just thought you should know what people are saying. Travis reckons you've been sleeping with O'Leary since before Christmas. But then, he's a stupid prick. Thinks every girl in school's in love with him."

"Yeah, well, I'm not sleeping with Mr. O'Leary. And I don't want to talk about it anymore. But thanks for the heads-up."

They traveled in silence for a while, listening to Point Rock FM until CeCe veered left into Levi's driveway and pulled to a stop beside their mailbox.

"Do you want me to put everyone straight, you know, just subtly?" he asked, one hand on the door lever.

CeCe turned to him and smiled. The kid didn't have a subtle bone in his body. "Nah, let them think what they like. I don't care."

"Okay. If you say so." He raised an eyebrow to make his point. "Thanks for the ride."

But as Levi shut the door and shuffled toward his house, CeCe knew that wasn't true. She cared. No girl wanted to be singled out at school for sleeping with a teacher. She'd heard it said more than once that a lie travels faster than the truth. But the gossip about her and Luka wasn't a lie. It *was* the truth. She had slept with Luka, and as much as she told herself she didn't want to repeat the experience, that was also a lie.

CeCe showered and changed, and just on five, she left to drive back into town for a movie night at Molly's place. As she parked at the supermarket to pick up some ice cream, the streets hummed with people on their way home from work and skateboarders weaving in and out of cars.

When she returned to the Kombi, CeCe sat in the driver's seat and glanced in the rearview mirror. "Shit!"

She bounded out the door to inspect the damage. Some idiot had written 'teacher's slut' in shaving cream all over the back of the van. She grabbed a towel from her beach bag and a bottle of water and wiped the window clean, telling herself it was just sticks-and-stones crap.

But as she drove to Molly's, she failed to restrain the tears.

20

CHEMICAL REACTION

As one week slipped into the next, the distance between them increased. Apart from when he singled CeCe out to answer a question in class, they seldom talked at school. There was a coolness to her Luka found hard to ignore. And true to that old adage about wanting what you can't have, he wanted precisely that—CeCe.

Alone in the darkness of his studio at night, Luka struggled to sleep, and when she walked past his desk after class, he wanted to reach for her hand, have her hesitate before relaxing at the touch of his fingertips feathering across her palm. To see those dimpled cheeks as she smiled.

The first few times Luka spotted her van at Sandwater Bay, he kept on driving. It had become one of his favorite surfing spots along the coastal highway, but Piper Bay, five miles on, was almost as good, and CeCe never surfed there.

However, when he noticed the Kombi on this particular day, Luka didn't want to travel farther. He wanted to watch CeCe in the lineup, to chuckle as she struggled to keep her balance and cheer her on when she did.

The sun sulking in the haze, he pulled into a parking space just shy of the sand dunes and searched for her in the water, wondering why she'd come here alone when the surf was so rough. Sure, the beach was seldom empty at this time of the day, but she wasn't a particularly strong swimmer, which worried him.

But maybe she wasn't alone. Why he'd made that assumption, he didn't know.

Luka peered through the Kombi's windows and tried the driver's door, but it was locked. Worried, he searched the waves again, and as he turned to the south, he saw her jogging up the beach toward him. As she drew closer, CeCe slowed her stride to a walk, and when she reached him, bent over to catch her breath.

"Hi. I thought you must be in the water."

Shielding her face from the sun with her hand, CeCe glanced at the surf. "Not today. Too much chop for me. Are you going in?"

"Maybe."

"Actually, could you give me a ride home later? It's on the way."

Trying to gauge her mood, he frowned. Hesitated. "Is there a problem with the Kombi?"

"Yes. It won't start. It's not the battery—we just put a new one in last week. I've called one of my dad's friends, who has a tow truck. But he'll have his kids with him, so he won't be able to give me a lift, and Mum and Dad are away. I was going to hitch a ride with someone, but since you're here…"

"Sure. No problem."

"Thanks. Joe said he'd take a while, so I'll wait with the van."

"Okay. I might go in for a bit. See you soon."

The sand cool under his feet, Luka walked toward the waves, his board tucked under his arm and his heart rate elevating. It was the most she'd said to him in weeks. In some ways, it was as if CeCe the librarian was back, minus her dimpled smile and school uniform.

It had rained overnight, so the water was chilly, and as he waited in the lineup after several uneventful runs, he realized his heart was no longer in it. When the tow truck arrived not long after, Luka sat on his board and watched her interact with the driver—a stocky guy with a beer belly and a ponytail and dressed in a black tank, shorts, and flip-flops.

CeCe stepped forward, and they embraced in a bear hug. They chatted and laughed before the guy backed his truck into position and winched the VW onto its flatbed while she talked to the youngsters in the cab.

By the time Luka left the water, the truck and van were gone, and she sat next to his SUV, waiting for her ride.

"All good?" he asked.

"Yeah. Joe thinks it's the starter motor. He's going to look at it next week."

While he opened the back door and grabbed a towel, CeCe climbed into the front seat, her sight fixed on the waves. Even when he sat beside her, she didn't so much as steal a glance in his direction. Luka loathed this awkwardness, but he had no words either. They'd once lain naked in each other's arms, talked well into the night. Now, it seemed, she couldn't even stand to look at him.

Before starting the engine, he gazed out across the water one last time. Did she remember the days they'd spent here together? That hesitant touch as he'd brushed the sand from her face and tied her bikini straps in a bow?

He turned the key. Reversed. Headed toward the highway

and took a left at the T-intersection. CeCe worried the butterfly around her neck, something he'd noticed she did when nervous.

"I meant to say thanks for passing my last assignment."

Luka shot her a sideways glance. "No thanks needed. You did the work—I just marked it accordingly."

"Even so, I appreciate what you've done for me, with the online stuff, I mean." She kept her focus forward. "Take a right at the next intersection."

As they traveled away from Sandwater Bay, CeCe remained silent, as did he. They'd never been at a loss for words with each other in the past, but now, he struggled to know what to say.

"Boundary Road's coming up. Turn left at the signpost, then first left into Station Road."

The sky had darkened by the time they reached the orchard belt, an area known for its avocados and kiwifruit. And as Luka drove down the straight stretch of road, he wondered if she still wanted him. Thought of him in that way.

"This is me, just up here on the right."

Luka pulled alongside the mailbox and stopped. To the left, a sign proclaiming 'Dobsons' Orchard' dominated the side of a small roadside fruit stall, and on a knoll above them, a villa peeked through the trees.

Finally, CeCe glanced his way. "You can drive up. No one's home."

When he reached a sweeping circular driveway, Luka shifted into first. As the house came into view, it reminded him of his grandfather's place in the Rata River Valley—an old villa, well-loved and lived in—where his parents had first met when his mother was only ten years old. After years of little mainte-nance, the house now sat idle, and Luka couldn't bring himself to visit it.

In contrast, from what he could see—with rambling roses, immaculate garden beds and a velvet green lawn—CeCe's family home had been faithfully maintained. He pulled to a stop in front of the main door and looked about. Along the veranda, a wisteria coiled upward around the posts, covering the spouting in leaves of green, and pots of summer flowers spilled down the steps.

CeCe shifted in her seat to face him. Her hand lifted to the butterfly necklace again, busy fingers running along the length of its chain. "Thanks for the ride."

"No problem. I'll see you at school on Monday."

CeCe stepped from the SUV and shut the door with a light hand, then she bounded up the veranda steps and through the front door.

Luka sat for a deciding moment. He rubbed the stubble on his jaw, knowing he shouldn't follow her. And yet...

He found her crouched beside the breakfast bar, petting the Burmese cat at her feet.

She straightened. "Looks like we have company, Pixie." CeCe opened the fridge and pulled out a casserole dish, placed it in the microwave, and set the timer. As if unaware of his presence, she gathered plates and silverware and glasses, then returned to the fridge for a bottle of wine and a bag of salad greens.

"Are you doing okay?" Luka eventually asked.

She stopped to look at him, her expression troubled. "Do you know what some of the guys at school are calling me?"

He waited, watching as she tore open the bag and emptied half into a bowl.

"Teacher's little slut."

Luka winced at her words. "That's harassment. Why didn't you tell me?"

She shrugged. "According to Levi, the whole school knows about us. This time last year, I was house captain, a peer mentor to a group of juniors, and ready to take on the world. So, yeah, my fall from grace has been spectacular, but I'm slowly dusting myself off."

"Doesn't it hurt you, what they're saying?"

CeCe reached into the fridge for a cucumber, bell pepper, and dressing and continued to build the salad. "Sure. But it's just sticks-and-stones stuff, isn't it?" Her tone softened, and she flirted with a smile. "Maybe one day, when those guys fall in love, they'll understand the hypothesis of chemical reaction in relation to the human species, where pheromones can't be ignored or denied."

In love? Luka narrowed his eyes and stared. Realizing she was making a joke, he chuckled. "You do know there's significant scientific debate about whether human pheromones even exist?"

CeCe removed the casserole from the microwave and placed it on a wooden board on the counter. "Is that so?" Spatula in hand, she indicated to the dish. "Cannelloni?"

It had been a long time since lunch, and Luka resisted the urge to inhale. What was he doing here, sitting in her kitchen, flirting and enjoying her company while she offered to feed him? "I should go."

"You don't have to worry," she murmured. "No one will know you're here."

"Maybe, but we shouldn't make this any harder than it already is."

Ignoring his objections, CeCe dished a large serving of cannelloni onto each plate and pushed one across the island. "Help yourself to salad. Would you like a wine?"

Luka eyed the spinach and ricotta pasta, rich with tomato

sauce and bubbling cheese, and made the split-second decision he'd told himself he would never make. "Thanks. Only if you're having one."

She smiled. "I am."

Instead of moving to the dining table in the bay window across the family room, they remained at the island, CeCe to his left, and his hesitation stowed away for later. On a nearby sofa, her cat slept with a paw over its eyes.

See no evil.

And as they sipped their wine and spoke little, Luka feared this night was about to turn reckless.

21

A LITTLE RECKLESS

Aided and abetted by the wine, CeCe's filter clogged to the point where it failed to function as it should. Here she was, having dinner with Luka in her family home while her parents were out of town.

But did she care? Not at all.

She couldn't help thinking of the last time they'd been together at his place—that final, perfect moment before he'd left for Clifton Falls. Luka had given her the sarong the night before, cotton-soft and swirling with shades of aqua, and as the rain washed summer's dust from the roof in the dawn light, she'd never imagined for a second that their bubble would burst so quickly.

As the alcohol seeped through her veins, they talked without reluctance. There was no need to pretend anymore, to withhold details. Her suitcase of baggage had already been pried open, and its contents strewn across the school campus for all the world to see. CeCe Dobson: the girl who fell out with her best friend, who'd then died before she'd had the chance to stitch up the weeping wound.

CeCe Dobson: the dropout—the teacher's little slut.

With their plates stacked in the dishwasher and words of praise for the meal on his lips, they moved to the veranda and sat in the oversized wicker chairs to finish their drinks.

However, as Luka leaned forward to kiss her gently on the forehead, his breath fresh from the dryness of the wine, she experienced no victorious buzz. There were no second chances on the table, that much she knew. And yet, she also knew that when he walked away, this would be a moment she'd later cling to as she moved through her life.

His gaze regretful, he pulled back. "I should go."

"Are you okay to drive?"

"Yeah. I've only had a couple of glasses and plenty of food." He stood and rested his elbows on the veranda railing, his sight on the lawn and surrounding gardens. "This is a beautiful place. Reminds me of home."

CeCe loved the sound of his voice, that fusion of accents wrapped in a soft classical cadence. She wanted him to stay, to hold him while he slept, and when he turned in her arms, have him do the same in return. "Do you ever get homesick?"

"Sure, sometimes." He glanced her way. "My folks run an equestrian center, so I miss the horses. Not that I live in the Rata River Valley these days. I'm in the city most of the time for work."

"Do you ride?"

"Yes." He turned to look at her. "You?"

"I dreamed of learning when I was younger, but horses and I don't really gel. They scare me, and they know it."

"Yeah, they get nervous when they sense someone's uncomfortable around them. Much like us, I guess."

She moved to his side and stood with her back to the lawn

so she could look at him. "I sometimes feel uncomfortable around you, especially when we're in class."

"Yes, me too."

"Do you ever let yourself remember?"

Luka nodded, then drained the last of his wine. "Of course. Despite what you may think of me, I'm not immune to what we had. I just don't want to make our lives any more complicated."

Sensing his growing detachment, CeCe led the way inside. "Thanks for the ride home. Guess I'll have to take the Corolla to the beach for a while."

His smile was tinged with regret. "It won't have the same appeal."

"No, I suppose not." CeCe slipped her hands into the back pockets of her jeans to keep them still. She couldn't reach out. Not now.

Luka placed his empty wine glass on the kitchen island and turned, one step closer to the door. "Anyway, thanks for the delicious meal. Sure beats takeout any day."

"No problem."

Outside, they stayed several feet apart, CeCe scuffing her toe across the stones of the driveway as she mentally commanded herself to get a grip. Luka opened the driver's door of his SUV and stood holding the inside handle. "I'll see you next week."

CeCe nodded. Smiled the polite smile of departure. She saw no need to speak, and even if she did, she'd struggle to form the words. And as she watched him drive away, it struck her that life in the vastness of this world—with its series of heartaches and lessons interspersed with moments of joy—sometimes made little sense.

Without Luka, the house creaked with emptiness, and despite the mild March evening, CeCe shivered as she crossed the family room to close the French doors. Just as she was about to click the top deadbolt into place, she heard a car traveling up the driveway. She ran into the living room and, with one knee on the sofa, peered out the window. Luka stared out the windshield, appearing lost in silent contemplation, and as she stepped into the hallway, CeCe failed to calm her racing heart.

By the time she opened the front door, Luka already stood at the bottom of the veranda steps. In his hand, a white paper bag, the type with a woven handle like they sold in packs of five at Kmart for a couple of dollars.

"Did you forget something?"

"Yes." He offered her the bag. "Your book. I've been meaning to give it to you at school, but it keeps slipping my mind."

"Oh, okay. Thanks. What did you think?"

He glanced over his shoulder at his SUV, its door ajar, then back again. A slow smile lit up his face. "Are all the books you read that steamy?"

She shrugged. "I prefer intimacy to violence. I've never understood how violence is so acceptable in literature, but sex often isn't."

His smile slipped slightly. "Fair point."

CeCe refused to release his gaze. Luka stepped backward toward his SUV, and as he shut the door, her physical reaction to his decision was immediate. "What are you doing?"

He took three of the five veranda steps, his hand resting on the rail as if he needed a steadying anchor. "Being reckless."

She made her way to the French doors off her bedroom and stepped inside. Luka followed, the tread of his shoes on the veranda boards no more than a whisper. And as muted light spilled in from the hallway, he slipped his hands around her from behind, his lips soft against the side of her neck.

"Turn around and look at me," he whispered.

She did as he asked, her heart racing and mouth dry. "I didn't think you were the reckless type."

His sigh deep and conflicted, Luka rested his forehead against hers. "Tell me to go then." He reached for her hands, his thumbs smoothing over the knuckles, and kissed her.

CeCe shook her head. "So the decision's mine?" Her hands went to the buttons of his shirt. One by one by one. "If you don't want to be here—"

"Oh, I want to be here, so, so much, but..."

"But?"

"You know the 'but' as well as I do." He lifted his chin and closed his eyes as CeCe slipped her hand into the waistband of his jeans.

"But surely you won't deny me after that kiss? Deny us this one last secret?" She unzipped his fly and coaxed his jeans to the floor, then gently pushed him backward. "Lie on the bed."

"So you're in charge?" Luka pulled her down with him. They kissed, tender lips on tender lips, graceful but so very erotic as he slipped one hand under her T-shirt and cupped her breast. "I don't think so."

With her legs trembling and breasts impossibly tight, CeCe closed her mind to Luka's 'but.' He'd thrown out the chance, and she'd happily caught it. Later on, if he wanted to pretend she'd seduced him, so be it. "I'm not the one who came back uninvited."

"Only to return your book."

They kissed again. "Liar. You made a conscious decision to be here. If you can't live with that, we should stop right now."

Luka groaned as her hand slipped into his boxers. He was rock hard under her touch, and as she moved to stroke him, he smiled. "I can live with it."

Her T-shirt off and discarded on the bedroom floor, CeCe straddled him and watched as he removed her sports bra. She wondered if he could smell the sweat on her skin from her run. She wished she'd showered, but now, that would have to wait.

Their kisses built in tempo—hot and demanding and so full of passion that CeCe struggled to ground herself. Until that moment, sex between them had been gentle, albeit intense. But this groping and sucking and frenzy of hands and tongues stole the breath from her lungs.

"I love the scent of you." Luka twisted her G-string around his fingers, and the tiny seam gave way.

"You've ripped my panties," CeCe gasped as he settled between her legs and coaxed them open.

He looked up at her, a soft grin changing his expression to playful. "Now I'm going to make the rest of you come apart."

They'd fallen asleep just shy of midnight, covered only by a crisp cotton sheet and their spent desire. There had been no conversation afterward. Luka's expression spoke for him— tender and loving, mixed with a touch of sadness and regret as he held her close and planted feather-light kisses in her hair.

CeCe woke around three to Luka's lips caressing her nap. Their second time lacked the intensity of the first. It was the kind of sex she'd come to expect of him—where he whispered his commands as his hands gently guided her into different positions, and he'd pull back, time and time again, wanting the moment to last.

Afterward, Luka rolled onto his side to face her. His gaze held on tight, and as the emotion rose in her throat, tears she hoped he couldn't see welled in her eyes.

"When are you leaving?"

He sighed as a calloused palm cradled her face. "Easter Monday."

CeCe closed her eyes against the tears and snuggled closer, knowing this would be their last time. He was right: they'd both been reckless. It was time to let go.

Nursing a groggy head from the wine and lack of sleep, and with his morning erection begging for attention again, Luka slipped out of bed and gathered his clothes from the floor. CeCe lay with her hair fanned out over the pillow and her breasts peaking underneath the cotton sheet. He studied her, knowing this would be the last time he'd kiss her. Touch her. And as he dressed in the shadows of her room, despondency engulfed him.

Shoes in hand, Luka leaned over, brushed a lock of hair from her face, and kissed her on the cheek. "Take care, beautiful," he whispered before stepping through the French doors and leaving their stolen moment behind.

Outside, dawn cast a misty light over the tree rows, and as he drove along the coastal highway and onto Coronation Drive, he replayed that moment when he'd followed CeCe into her bedroom.

He smacked his hand down on the steering wheel. "Damn it, Luka. What the hell have you done?"

2 2

BOILING POINT

Most of the other students were already seated when CeCe entered Luka's chemistry class on Monday. She took her usual seat without even a casual glance in his direction. Luka called the class to order, and when he looked her way, she still didn't meet his gaze. When the period was over, she left the room as soon as the bell rang, eye contact avoided at all costs.

He'd texted her after finishing work on Sunday, but apart from a brief thanks for the lift back to the orchard, it was as if Saturday night had never happened. Driving home from school on Monday afternoon, the windshield wipers struggling against the heavy rain, Luka found it difficult to concentrate. He texted her again that evening, but she never replied.

All week he thought of her, relived the moment he drove back up the driveway and followed her inside, but every time he picked up his phone to call her, a hesitation kicked in. CeCe wasn't the wallflower type. If she wanted to contact him, she would.

But she didn't.

Until Thursday.

CeCe walked into his classroom just as he was about to leave for the day. Stood by his desk. Dropped her bag at her feet. At first, he couldn't read her mood, but as he searched her face, the look of regret was plainly evident.

"About Saturday," she started. "Someone saw us together at the beach. I don't know who, but the rumor mill is churning. I don't want you to look at me or even text me. It only stirs things up."

Luka watched her expression falter. Noticed her chin tremble. She inhaled deeply and blinked back tears.

"I know the other night shouldn't have happened," she continued, "so let's pretend it didn't and move on. No texts, no stolen glances."

He brushed his fingers against hers. She halted her intended backward step but didn't look at him. Luka moved closer and skimmed the back of his hand across her cheek.

CeCe closed her eyes at his touch and let out an unsteady breath. "Please don't do this."

"Hey, it's going to be okay." He hesitated, trying to find the right words for a wrong situation. He was about to reassure her when Carole Jones pushed through the door. The principal considered the two of them, her expression a mixture of disbelief and disappointment. Seconds passed in silence.

"CeCe, please leave." Carole's instruction left no room for retort.

After a moment's hesitation, CeCe flung her bag over her shoulder and marched from the room.

The principal turned to Luka. "You, in my office. Now!"

His stomach tied in knots, Luka grabbed his jacket and followed her down the corridor, across the rain-soaked quad, and into the admin block. Carole didn't slow her stride or glance back once, and when she opened the door to her office, Frank Dobson, his face like thunder, already lay in wait.

As she closed the door and settled behind her desk, Luka tried to gather his wits.

"I assume you two have been introduced?" She gestured toward the empty chair in front of her. "Sit down, Luka."

He'd met CeCe's father when they'd both attended a school meeting on cyberbullying. He'd found him pleasant enough, if a little curt. But now, as he caught the older man's stare, his gut flipped. "Mr. Dobson."

Frank took a deep breath then sighed, but there was no response to the acknowledgment, no extension of his hand.

"The board has received a formal complaint about your association with my daughter," Frank eventually said. "The second such complaint since we employed you."

What? Luka struggled to keep his reaction in check as he looked at Carole for an explanation.

She regarded both men in turn. "There was an informal question mark over Luka and CeCe's *friendship* when Luka joined the staff. As they're both of age, and it was an unsubstantiated rumor, I left it where it belonged. Off campus."

"So what have you got to say for yourself?" Frank asked Luka.

Luka couldn't believe how calm the man was. According to his colleagues, Frank Dobson could be a real hothead, but the man before him appeared in total control. Scarily so. "What am I being accused of?"

Luka watched Frank slowly come to a simmer. "So, we have a smart-ass, do we? You know darn well what you're being accused of."

"Look, if you want to ask me a direct question, I'll give you a direct answer, but all this innuendo is just wasting both my time and yours."

A few degrees off boiling point, Frank narrowed his eyes. "Fine. Did you drive my daughter home from the beach last Saturday evening after the Kombi broke down?"

"Yes."

"Did you go inside my home while I wasn't there and spend the night with my daughter?"

Some of the fight left him. Out of respect for CeCe, Luka wouldn't lie to her father. "I did."

"So, while the wife and I were away for a relaxing weekend, you were making yourself at home in my house and sleeping with my daughter in a bed that I paid for, is that correct?"

"It was a one-off. I can assure you it won't happen again."

"So what? She's only good for a one-night stand now?"

The hairs lifted on the back of Luka's neck, and a trickle of sweat tracked from his forehead down his hairline. Frank Dobson by reputation was showing his snarling face. "That's not what I said. I care for CeCe, very much, and I won't sit here and minimize what we had simply to save face. But I agree, what we did was inappropriate and, ultimately, lacked judgment on my part."

Frank leaned back in his chair and studied Luka with suspicion. "You're her teacher, for shit's sake. You can't brush this under the carpet with some lame 'lack of judgment' excuse."

"I'm not trying to excuse what I did. I've given you my account. It's not like I can undo what happened that night, and in truth, I don't want to."

"Well, I must say, I'm extremely disappointed that it's come to this, Luka." Carole crossed her arms over her chest. "Sleeping with a student is gross misconduct."

"You think I don't realize that?"

"Then why did you do it?" Frank asked.

Luka rested his elbows on his knees and scrubbed his hands up his face. "Because some days, doing the right thing is too damn hard."

The three of them sat in awkward silence.

"You do realize she's being bullied, don't you?" Frank eventually continued.

Luka looked up at Frank. "She mentioned some name-calling."

"Unfortunately, it goes much further than that," Carole offered, her voice soft with concern. "We caught two students defacing CeCe's van with shaving cream the other day, and according to my sources, her locker's been egged more than once. Not only that, one of our prefects heard a senior boy call her 'teacher's slut' as she walked past. We slapped him with a week's detention, but we can't protect her twenty-four-seven, particularly on social media."

The bile rose in Luka's throat. He'd done this. Dropped CeCe in a heap of crap just because he couldn't leave well enough alone. "This is bullshit. Why wasn't I informed?"

"We're informing you now," Carole said. "And frankly, Luka, I'm not sure I trust you to keep your reaction in check."

Luka held his tongue. She had a point. He wondered if the 'teacher's slut' comment came courtesy of that idiot Travis Bostock. "Fair enough."

"And might I suggest you think on this," Frank said, "when it comes to the student-teacher relationship, doing the right thing is the *only* thing to do."

Frank paused to catch his breath, then puffed out his chest— boiling point finally reached. "And let me make myself clear, stay away from CeCe, understand? She's got enough to deal with without you grooming her."

"That's not how it is."

"I wonder if the Teachers' Association would see it that way." Frank stood to leave. "Oh, and by the way, CeCe is no longer in your class, and if you see her around campus or anywhere else for that matter, you'd better look the other way. Get it?" Frank stormed out and slammed the door behind him before Luka could respond.

"Well," Carole said, "what an unfortunate mess."

Luka huffed out a sigh. "Yep. Seems I broke a cardinal rule before I even knew I'd broken it. I honestly had no idea CeCe was returning to school when we started seeing one another."

Carole leaned back in her chair. "Look, CeCe Dobson's a sweet kid, well-liked both on campus and around the town. You were never going to come out of this with a halo flashing over your head."

"She's over eighteen. I did nothing wrong, and now I'm being slapped with the bad-guy label." He shook his head and muttered. "And all because of a freaking rabbit hole."

"It's not about her age, Luka. It's about the ethical dilemma of a teacher sleeping with a student."

The phone rang on Carole's desk, interrupting his response. She held up her hand and took the call.

While he waited, Luka looked around her office. Files and papers filled the shelves to bursting point, and on her desk, a cup, half full of tea, sat in a chipped saucer. The place was a mess. Offices like this reminded him of why he found teaching untenable. The paperwork and red tape drove him nuts, and for schools like Tulloch Point High, funding was always an issue.

He wanted to walk out. Go surfing. Get drunk. But as he waited for Carole to end the call, he knew he needed to tone down the attitude.

She returned the receiver to its base and sighed. "You do

realize that you could lose your teaching certificate? And you don't want that hanging over your head, even when you're set on pursuing other career paths."

Luka knew Carole was right. While teaching would never be a lifelong vocation, he needed to keep his options open, especially if he wanted to travel.

"I accept that you did the right thing when you found out CeCe was returning to school, but your downfall was going back for more."

Luka scrubbed his hands up and down his face. "Who laid the first complaint?"

"It was more a comment spoken out of turn in the locker room. My son was there when it happened, and he brought it to my attention."

"And Travis Bostock was the instigator?"

"Look, Travis and CeCe were sweethearts for over a year. The boy has an ego the size of Australia, and unfortunately, his insight is sadly lacking, but that doesn't mean their breakup didn't affect him."

Luka leaned back in his chair and pinched the bridge of his nose. *Sweethearts.* He hated that word. There was nothing sweet about Travis Bostock. He doubted the kid even had a heart.

"Anyway, while I'd like to keep this in-house, the board might well have other ideas. CeCe's a complex kid who's had a challenging time lately. So I'm asking you, please don't add to those complexities."

Puzzled, Luka mulled over Carole's words. "Okay, you're going to have to fill me in here. What do you mean by 'challenging time'?"

"Her best friend, Anna, died in her sleep, July last year. The girls had been inseparable until some jerk Anna took up with came between them. Didn't she tell you?"

Anna? "No, she didn't."

"CeCe took Anna's death hard and ended up dropping out. We tried to work with her online, but she struggled to commit. Such a shame. She was one of the most promising tennis players we've ever had at the school, but she gave that up too. Her parents are good people, but as you saw, Frank tends to overreact at the first sign of trouble, and in this case, rightly so. Although she seems more stable now, we still need to keep an eye on her."

Luka fought to keep his external reaction professional while his heart hammered in his chest. "I understand."

Carole stood. Her disappointed expression needed no further verbal attachment, but she added one anyway: "I expected more from you, young man."

He picked up his jacket and shrugged it on. "I expected more from myself."

As Luka left the office, the knowledge that CeCe's friend Anna was dead hit him head-on. CeCe hadn't wanted to share stories with him about her friends and family. She'd wanted to separate her time with Luka from reality. To live in their bubble between the beach and his bed.

23

BLUE BUTTERFLY

CeCe was in bed when her father knocked on her open door. Her heart lurched when she caught his expression, and she lowered the book she'd been reading. "Hey."

"Have you got a minute?"

Pulling the duvet up under her chin, CeCe wished she could hide beneath it until her world made sense again. "I was just about to turn out the light."

"It won't take long."

He sat on the chair beside the bed, taking a moment to gather his thoughts. It was something her mother had taught him, so he didn't overreact. He inhaled and exhaled with purpose. If she hadn't been so unnerved, she'd have smiled at the dramatics of it.

"Were you going to tell me...about you and O'Leary? Because if you're waiting for me to find out from someone else, that day has come."

CeCe sat up and rested back against the headboard. Head down, she worried the butterfly around her neck, but that feeling of strength didn't eventuate. She looked up at him. Sighed.

"What do you want me to say? You've obviously heard the gossip."

"Maybe, but I want to hear it from you. Is he the guy you've been seeing? Is that why we've never met him? Because he's your teacher?"

She nodded. There seemed little point in denying it. Both her parents could sniff out an untruth from a mile away. "I never knew about the teacher thing until you told me."

Her father frowned at her. "And he never mentioned it? Don't you find that strange?"

"He didn't know about the job when we started—"

"Started what? How serious was it? Is it?"

CeCe closed her eyes for a moment. "It was over before it began. Lost in the details."

"But sexual?"

"*Dad!* We don't need to have this conversation. It's over. What more can I say?" CeCe flung back the covers and dashed into the bathroom for a box of tissues.

When she returned, he watched her cross the room. "I want you to say that you understand why this has to stop immediately."

"It's already stopped. I told you."

"But that's not strictly true, is it? He gave you a ride home from the beach last weekend, and now there's been a complaint to the school board about you both."

Box of tissues in hand, she sat back on the bed, mumbling a *shit* under her breath as her stomach churned.

"What were you thinking? You could have called Molly or any number of people, but..." Frank held her gaze. "Did he come inside?"

She looked away. Her dad obviously knew Luka had been in

the house, so what could she say? That he'd stayed the night? That they'd clung on tight to their final stolen moment?

"CeCe. You're better than that."

"Am I?" Tears welled, and she swiped them away. "Because right now, I don't care if he is my teacher. I don't care if he doesn't want me or what people think, and I'm sorry if that offends you, but my thought processes are a little skewed these days."

"So that's why you didn't want to return to school? Because you were sleeping with him? You should have told me. Maybe I could have helped."

"Retrospect is overrated, don't you think? And I know you, Dad. You can't let things lie. You jump in boots and all with the solutions and the attitude. We weren't doing anything wrong when we started seeing each other, and now it's over. But sometimes I want to talk to him, and I can't do that at school."

"Yeah, well, I'm asking you not to meet him out of school again either. Not while he's still teaching there."

She frowned. "But I'm old enough—"

"This isn't about your age. It's about safeguarding his reputation as much as your own. Understand?" He leaned forward and kissed her on the forehead. "Don't make Luka pay that price."

CeCe plucked another tissue from the box and dabbed her eyes. As usual, her father made a sound argument, but she had no interest in learning that lesson at present. The lessons had come thick and fast the year before, and she was determined this year would be one of discovering what made her heart sing, not lessons that constrained it.

She wanted to sit in the back of the Kombi with Luka, eating sweet nectarines until the juice dripped down their chins, to surf naked at sunrise, have sex at midnight and again as dawn's light crept through the curtains of his studio home. She wanted him...

"Also, you won't be going back into his classroom. Mrs. Jones has arranged for you to join a correspondence class via video link until after Easter."

"But that's not fair. Luka's a great teacher, and I finally feel like I'm getting somewhere."

"Actions have consequences, Sydney. You know that. You invited him into our home and slept with him without our knowledge or consent."

She dropped her head into her hands and sighed. "What do you think might happen...? To Luka, I mean."

"Who knows. But I'll be voting to dismiss the complaint as unjustified. I'm not saying I agree with what you did, but according to Brad, Luka's a good guy." He stood. "Anyway, get some sleep."

"Thanks, Dad."

As her father closed the door, CeCe flopped onto her front and buried her head under the pillow. Lately, her life had started to make some sense—to slip into order. But that was before she'd met Luka at the beach. Now, despite her father's advice, she failed to understand why she had to compromise.

The bathroom tiles cold beneath her bare feet, she switched on the light above the mirror and studied her reflection. Puffy eyes stared back at her, and as she cleaned her teeth and washed her face, she knew her time with Luka was over. It wasn't a decision she'd made, but one fate had made for her.

And, for some reason, fate had a habit of getting it wrong as far as CeCe was concerned.

Back in her bedroom, CeCe reached into her nightstand drawer for a flat rock she'd recently found. Next, she picked a fine tip Sharpie from the mug of pens on her desk, jumped into bed, and let the words flow.

Dearest A,

Did you ever get the feeling that something you'd searched for,
once found, would lose its significance?
It's like passing a point and knowing your life will never be the
same. Some people call it fate. Others, a fork in the road they
never thought they'd take.
I'm sorry you had to take the road you never wanted to travel. I
hope you weren't afraid...

Love
C xoxo

When Luka arrived at the SAR office the following morning, a large brown envelope sat waiting for him at the front desk. He looked up as Brad strolled in from the break room, coffee in one hand and a Danish in the other.

His boss gestured toward the envelope. "Looks like your results are in. Duncan hand-delivered it just over an hour ago."

The 'Duncan' he referred to was the flight examiner: Duncan McAlister. They'd met several times before his practical exam, and Luka never felt they'd hit it off. Even so, the guy was known for being tough but fair, and Luka respected that. "I'm almost too nervous to look."

Luka pried open the flap and scanned the text, his mind working to process the words on the page. He stared in disbelief and frowned, a clench forming in the pit of his stomach. "It's a fail. My last two modules and I failed them both."

Brad's expression softened. "I thought that might be the case."

Turning the letter over to check if there was anything on the back, Luka shook his head. "Unbelievable."

"Look, it's not the end of the world," Brad said. "You can sit them again."

"Yeah, but it's still a kick in the guts." Deep down, Luka had known he would fail. He'd let his nerves and lack of sleep get the better of him that morning and had tried to put it from his mind ever since, hoping Duncan hadn't noticed.

Luka gathered up the papers and slotted them back into the envelope, taking a deep breath to calm himself. "I thought I was a good pilot."

As he sipped his coffee, Brad said nothing, his expression answering for him.

Luka stared. "What?"

"You failed those modules because you let your indecisiveness get the better of you." Although softly spoken, his boss's words were pointed. "You know it, and I know it. And in this game, you need to leave that shit on the ground, where it belongs. You can't take it up in the air, man. Not if you want to get ahead."

Luka sat in the chair opposite Brad's desk and dropped his head into his hands. "Yeah, you're right. Shit!"

"Look, I get that you're hurting, mate. All that stuff going on at school with CeCe Dobson, you've let your standards slip. Most of us have been there at some point, so cut yourself some slack. At least you get to have another crack at it." Brad's reference to CeCe returned her to the front of Luka's mind. A place she'd sat for over two months now, most of that time invited, some of it not.

"This isn't about CeCe."

"No? Well get out there and prove me wrong. And you'd better work your ass off over the next three weeks. Fail once, and Duncan will overlook it—fail twice, and he won't be happy. I'm not saying you shouldn't have a social life, but don't lose that focus. You came here to do a job, not chase after CeCe Dobson, and if you think her distraction isn't an issue, I suggest you think again."

Luka slouched back in the chair and massaged the bridge of his nose, thinking back to the weekend before his practical exam. The weekend he'd slept with CeCe in her parents' house. "Yeah, point taken."

"Good. And if you ever want a job back here, call me. If a vacancy comes up, it's yours."

"Thanks." Luka glanced around the office. "I'm going to miss this place."

"Yeah, we're going to miss you too. But you have bigger fish to fry, and we both know it." Brad held out his hand for the envelope. "Right, let's have a look at those papers to see where you're going wrong."

24

CHASING CARS

On Easter Monday, a blue-sky day, fresh with the turn of autumn, CeCe stepped from her mother's car and walked down Luka's driveway for the last time. The nectarines on the tree in the backyard were long gone, as was the usual clutter by the hot tub. No surfboard, no wetsuit, no board shorts drying over the rail. If it hadn't been for his SUV parked in its usual place, she would have thought he'd already left.

CeCe stood on the deck and knocked on the door. She should have texted first, but that wasn't their thing.

Dressed in a faded AC/DC T-shirt and slashed-at-the-knee jeans, Luka opened the door. In the narrow entranceway, a large rolling duffel and smaller weekender sat ready for the trip. She held his gaze for a second, then looked away. It had only been three weeks since that night at the orchard, when they'd stolen their last tender moment. Now he studied her as if they were strangers.

Luka stepped outside, leaving the door ajar. "I was just about to head off. You shouldn't be here, you know that."

She fiddled with the chain around her neck, drawing

strength from her butterfly as usual. "I know but I came to say goodbye. We haven't seen each other in three weeks."

"Yeah, I've been busy. And I thought that was the way you wanted it. No contact."

"I needed it, not wanted it. There's a difference." CeCe tried to swallow away the dryness in her throat with little success "Anyway, I want to apologize. I shouldn't have let you stay that night. It was wrong, and lately, my wrong decisions seem to outweigh my right ones."

Luka nodded and ran his fingers across his stubbled jaw "We were both at fault. I wanted to be there, so—"

"Maybe, but I can't help feeling a little bitter right now. And sad." *Honesty.* "But it will pass. I just need time."

He opened his mouth as if to speak, then closed it again. She'd rarely seen Luka at a loss for words. He was a teacher, used to explaining complexities over and over, but today, his explanations seemed thin on the ground.

"Look," he finally managed, "if we were both a little older, this whole shitty situation probably wouldn't mean a thing. But you need the freedom to do whatever you choose without me hovering in your background—waiting for you to text, wondering when we'll see each other again." His attitude softened. "I wish you every success, CeCe, every happiness, but we both know I'm not the guy for you."

They stood in limbo, the fray of their broken affair hanging between them. CeCe looked down, scuffing the toe of her boot along a gap in the concrete path before glancing up again. She wanted to say *I love you.* Ask him to wait for her. But she knew the impossibility of that request. Next year, she'd be at university, with hundreds of miles and the Cook Strait separating them. It wasn't fair to disregard that.

"It's just…"

Luka sighed heavily. "It's just?"

The sound of a car speeding through the nearby intersection startled her, and CeCe glanced toward the road. When she turned back to him, his dulled expression swallowed her words. "Never mind." She swiped away a tear with the back of her hand and cleared her throat. "I didn't want to cry, but I hate this." Sobs rose to the occasion as she struggled to speak. "I hate that we have no choice. No future. That you didn't fight for me."

He rubbed his nape. Huffed a sigh. "Please don't do this."

"I lost my friend last year. Did I tell you that? Anna. She died in her sleep. We'd had an argument about her boyfriend only days before. She never spoke to me again."

His expression softened. "Why didn't you tell me?"

"Because it's such a personal thing, grief," CeCe said. "You want to hide it, but also, it's hard to understand how other people can go about their days as if they've already forgotten the person you're grieving for. And when you don't even get to say goodbye, it's all the more devastating.

"The funny thing is, if Anna were still alive, I wouldn't be standing here right now. I wasn't one for flings or no-strings sex. But a new purpose often follows grief. I wanted to seize the day—be a whole lot reckless and a little bit happy. Now I feel like I have to step back into the unknown."

Luka held her gaze but remained silent.

"People call me privileged, say that I'm a nice girl with a bit of a wild streak. Every Sunday, growing up, we'd sit on the veranda and eat lunch as a family. I have an older brother and two sisters. I'm the baby, the brat. My parents are happy together and do okay for themselves. I've always felt loved and wanted, we all have…so that's privilege right there."

CeCe knew she was raving but couldn't stop. She wanted to tell him about her life, to fill in the details before it was too late.

"But I see myself as a train wreck of a girl who just wants to get this year over and done with so she can move on. Last year, life gave me lemons, so I tried to make damn lemonade. But it was sour and left a bitter taste in my mouth."

She burst into tears. "Now you're leaving," she sobbed, "going back to Clifton Falls where you'll forget all about me, pretend we never met."

Luka moved into her space and engulfed her in his arms, the scent of him filling her senses, making her want—not physically but emotionally. "Hey, come on. Don't cry. It's going to be okay."

She looked down, pressing her lips together as she choked back a sob. "Is it?"

He dipped to catch CeCe's gaze as he wiped away her tears with the pad of his thumb. "Just be true to who you are, and you'll be fine. You've got this."

He let go. Stepped back.

You've got this. Did Luka honestly believe that those three words would spur her on to bigger and better things? All she had to do was take a deep breath, puff out her chest, and she'd be fine?

As if!

"Is that really what you think, Luka? That I've got this? Because right now, I feel like I don't have a clue."

"Come inside for a moment. I'll get you a drink of water." When CeCe hesitated, he offered his hand. "Come on."

Inside, apart from the lack of clothes on the floor, dishes in the sink, and novels on the nightstand, the place looked the same. She'd expected it to be stripped bare but then realized it would have been furnished when he moved in. Luka filled a glass of water from the tap and offered it to her. She took a sip, then another.

"Is that better?"

Of course it wasn't, but with her tears contained, she nodded anyway. What else could she do? There were no choices offered —no solutions—and as she watched him close a window and pull down the blind, CeCe realized the reunion she'd planned in her head would never become a reality. They'd had a fling, one that was now over.

She placed the glass in the sink and turned to face him. "Take care, Chopper Guy, and drive safe." CeCe inched backward. One step, two, then turned and walked away, sensing his stare—the final chemical reaction between them.

Out on the street, she opened the car door and sat in the driver's seat, warm from the sun. And as CeCe looked sideways down the driveway to the studio, Luka stood by the swing under the oak tree, his hands in his pockets, watching her.

CeCe started the engine and drove two blocks down the road to where a greenbelt separated the center of town from the suburbs. She pulled over, leaned back against the headrest and closed her eyes, letting the tears flow until they turned into an ugly sob where she could hardly breathe.

And a little later, as she made a left onto the coastal highway, she watched the world blur into insignificance.

What would Luka be in her future? A speck in the rearview mirror or an obstacle caught in her headlights?

Luka packed his bags into the back of his SUV, thoughts of CeCe refusing to shut up. She'd looked so delicate and sad standing before him, a goodbye falling from her lips. He'd never seen her cry like that before—those uncontrollable sobs—and it saddened him that today was the only time she'd spoken from the heart.

And as CeCe walked onto the street and out of his life, he'd watched her go, hands in pockets and his heart slipping off his sleeve before landing in the muddy puddle at his feet.

There had been an undeniable chemistry between them, a natural connection that neither of them had to force. And now, with CeCe driving away and his bags stowed in his SUV, ready for the trip to Clifton Falls, Luka couldn't silence his doubts.

His head throbbed. If he hadn't gone out with friends last night and ended up hammered on too many vodkas, he might have already been on the road and would have missed her. But he'd stayed later than planned, mostly to help the cleaners with last-minute details while the alcohol left his bloodstream. Had he hoped she'd turn up? Maybe. She'd all but called him a coward for not fighting for her, but she didn't realize that in his heart and convictions, he'd fought for her constantly.

Just not the way she'd needed him to fight.

Wanting to get another look at the orchard in the daylight, Luka took the back road out of town. Now, whenever she stepped into his imagination, he'd have a concrete base on which to place her. Although, to be fair, whenever his thoughts turned to CeCe, it was an image of her naked surfing or lying under her sarong on his borrowed bed that usually came to mind.

The orchard was larger than he'd realized, and from the road, he could just make out the villa through the trees. In the distance, by an implement shed, the Kombi sat next to a vintage truck with wooden sides like an enormous apple crate.

Initially, he'd wondered if CeCe's family life might be less than ideal. He now knew differently and smiled at the knowledge that she had people who loved and supported her to help her through. Even if Frank Dobson was her father.

Idling at the mailbox, Luka leaned through the driver's window and pushed a flat package through the slot.

His parting gift.

Luka cranked up the stereo, and as he drove onto the coastal highway and headed south toward home, he hummed along to a Snow Patrol song, his mind on the last time he'd run his hands over her curves and kissed the hollow at the base of her throat.

The last time, in that moment of want and need and alcohol, they'd forgotten who they were.

CLIFTON FALLS

PART II

Five Years Later

25

LIME TREE HILL

Six60 playing in the background and dinner in the oven, CeCe opened the loft door wide as soon as she heard footsteps in the stairwell. "You made it." Molly hurried up the stairs, and CeCe pulled her into a tight hug. "It's so good to see you."

"You too," her cousin said before stepping inside and dropping her bags on the floor beside the sideboard. CeCe hadn't seen Molly in months. Sure, they talked on the phone most weeks, but it wasn't the same as sharing a meal over a bottle of wine. "And it's great to get out of the city."

"Hey, Clifton Falls is a city too."

"Yes, but tiny compared to Auckland. The traffic's diabolical up there." Molly scanned the room as she removed her coat and draped it across the back of the sofa. "Wow, this place is amazing. When you said you'd be living in the loft above the packing shed, I imagined some dusty dive with no windows and a pinewood floor."

"So this is the first time you've seen it?"

"It is." Molly crossed the room and peeked into the office. She'd always been the inquisitive type. Thought nothing of rummaging through people's pantries and checking out the insides of their fridges. "The last time I came to Lime Tree Hill was with Mum and Aunt Andrea when I was about ten. We drove down for the weekend so Mitch could visit that weird Norman guy."

"So where was I?"

"I don't remember. And when I came to Clifton Falls in February, Mitch and Tayla shouted me dinner at that Italian place on Seaview Road, so we met in town."

"You mean Gino's? They do the best vegetarian pizzas in town." She picked up Molly's overnight bag and motioned toward the hallway. "Bedrooms are this way. You can settle in while I make the salad."

Molly followed her into the guest bedroom and sat on the bed. "How's the job going?" She bounced up and down as if testing out the firmness of the mattress.

"Good. Three days a week leaves me plenty of time to spend in the lab, and they're a great team. We do a lot of soil testing and regenerative stuff."

"Sounds fascinating." Her cousin pulled a face and tucked her hair behind her ears. As usual, she'd flat ironed it to within an inch of its life, and CeCe, whose curls were always on the go, couldn't help being a little envious.

"Stop it. It's a job, and I need the money."

"Don't we all?"

Back in the kitchen, the aroma of basil and tomato did its best to compete with Molly's lingering perfume. CeCe's stomach rumbled. Apart from a granola bar around midday, she hadn't eaten since breakfast but had been too busy to notice until now. She poured a couple of glasses of wine and set them on the counter, then opened the oven to check on dinner.

"So, what should we toast to?" she asked when Molly returned to the room and picked up a glass.

"Country life. It looks good on you."

CeCe took a sip before slicing the tomatoes. "Thanks. Yesterday, Mitch told me I looked tired and drawn, but hey, guess it's par for the course when you're birthing a start-up."

"Nice guy, that brother of yours. Speaking of start-ups, how's Botanical Ce going?"

"Well, I wake up excited for the day, so that's in the pro column. I'll show you my lab later. It's off the implement shed." CeCe pulled plates and bowls from the cabinets and placed them on the island. "I'm just thankful Mum and Dad made it back from London when they did. I couldn't have handled looking after the orchard for much longer." The strain of running the orchard wasn't something she'd normally admit to, but Molly was her go-to person—always willing to lend an ear. "Did I mention Liz came on board?"

"What, as a shareholder?"

"Just ten percent. She's taking care of marketing and building the website. What about you? How's the world of media consulting?"

"My new boss is a chauvinistic pig. I sneak lunch at my desk between e-mails and phone calls, and work sixty hours on a good week. And those are the positives."

"That's tough." CeCe opened a bag of radish sprouts and sprinkled them over the salad. "You should move down here and go freelance. I miss you."

"You think? I do love this area. Anyway, what's that delicious smell? I'm starving."

"Cannelloni. It's still the only thing I'm good at."

Tayla swept through the door at that moment carrying a large Tupperware container, which she offered to CeCe. "Sorry,

sorry. Mum called just as I was leaving. She talked for ages, so I ran out of time to frost my mud cake. And it sank in the middle. But I brought the stuff for the ganache with me."

Molly rose to greet Tayla, and they hugged warmly. "Relax. I bet it will taste fabulous. Where's Mitch?"

"At the movies with a friend."

CeCe grinned at her sister-in-law. "You *can* say his name. I won't disintegrate into a crying heap on the floor." She turned to Molly. "Mitch is out with his best bud, Luka."

"Oh, okay. So it's still awkward?" Molly asked.

"She pretends it's not, but—"

"Excuse me, I haven't even seen the guy since I've been here." That wasn't strictly true. When heading down the stairs one day, CeCe had noticed Luka's SUV parked outside the packing shed, so she'd hightailed it back into the loft and sat in her office until he'd left. "What are you drinking?"

"Lime and soda. Thanks." Tayla joined Molly at the island. "And you've only been here two weeks, so you're bound to run into him eventually."

"Great. I look forward to it. Not!"

"Don't you want to see him?" Molly asked.

"Not especially."

"But you and Luka are kinda friends, right?" Molly continued. "Didn't he visit you the last time you were staying in Clifton Falls?"

"Yes, but I don't know why. It certainly wasn't to reminisce about old times." CeCe scrunched up her face as she recalled his visit—Luka perched on the edge of the chair, ready to make a quick getaway while asking her how she'd been. His hurried goodbye not long after. The untouched coffee sitting on the kitchen counter beside the uneaten apple cake, still round and perfect. "Anyway, that was ages ago, and it was…"

"Complicated?" Tayla reminded her.

"Yes. Very." CeCe and Tayla had briefly discussed Luka before she'd left Clifton Falls that morning, almost eighteen months ago now. On the drive back to Tulloch Point, she'd forced herself to listen to a podcast on business management just to get the guy out of her headspace. By the end of that week, she'd listened to more podcasts than she had in her entire life.

"So what happened?" Molly asked.

In the weeks following that visit, CeCe had asked herself that question more than once. "He emailed to ask if we could meet up. He said some things, I said some things, then he left. Maybe he wanted to lay some ghosts to rest and let me do the same—who knows."

"And it's kinda raw, even now?" Molly reached for the wine bottle and topped up their glasses.

The question stuck in CeCe's mind, refusing to settle. A distinct chill gripped the air drifting in through the open kitchen window, and with all the talk of Luka, she felt a little chilled inside too. She shrugged as she pulled it shut. "It's been almost five years."

"No second chances?" Molly asked.

"Nope. Anyway, now that I'm settled in, I plan to get out more." CeCe opened the oven door, removed the cannelloni, and placed it on a mat at the table. "Meet some new people. Two of the women at work run an adventure group, and they've asked me to join."

"Sounds like fun," Tayla said. "Maybe you might even start dating again."

CeCe chuckled. "Or not. I'm a bit stretched for time and guys just don't seem to get that."

Molly turned to Tayla. "Do you believe fate brings people together?"

"I never used to," Tayla said, "but after meeting Mitch the way I did, I'm not so sure."

"Meaning?" CeCe asked.

"Well, it was...cosmic isn't quite the right word, but maybe fate did play a part."

Both Mitch and Tayla were guarded whenever the topic of their meeting came up, insisting it was a classic 'girl meets boy next door' tale, but CeCe had always suspected there was more to it than that. However, she decided not to push it, especially in front of Molly. "Yeah. Who'd have thought Luka would rescue me from a rabbit hole?"

"What?" Tayla asked.

"That was their meet-not-so-cute," Molly explained. "Walking home from a party one night, CeCe tripped in a rabbit hole and sprained her ankle. Luka found her."

"Really? How did I not know this?"

"Yep. He lifted me over the fence and into the back seat of his SUV, then dropped me off at Tulloch Point General. Turned out I'd left my boot in his car. Boom. Alice and Cinderella right there."

Tayla laughed. "Oh, I love that story! You guys so need to be together. Pity he's seeing someone."

"He is?" Molly asked as they took a seat at the table. "Who?"

"A lawyer at one of the local firms," Tayla said. "Annabelle Sutton."

"Are they serious?" Molly asked.

"Well, she is. Very serious."

"What's she like?" Molly continued as CeCe served the

pasta, pretending she wasn't interested in Luka's girlfriend or how serious they were.

"One of the most outwardly charming people you'll ever meet." As Tayla stopped to eat a mouthful, CeCe fought the image of Luka with someone else. "Petite, power suits and stilettos, never a hair out of place."

"She sounds perfect," Molly said as she dished salad onto her plate.

"Yes, but... I don't know. Luka seems troubled. Like he's floating along on her wave, but isn't sure if he wants to be there. They've broken up twice now, but always seem to get back together."

"Sounds like every relationship I've ever had." Molly laughed and picked up her glass. "Is he still with Search and Rescue?"

"He is," Tayla said. "Does ridiculously long hours. Not that he needs to work, not for the money anyway."

"What do you mean?" CeCe frowned. She hadn't expected this night to be about Luka *or* his perfect girlfriend, but the conversation was getting interesting.

"His father used to be a stockbroker or merchant banker, something like that anyway. He's had good investment advice, and according to Mitch, it's paid off big time. *And* he's building a house. Not that Luka talks about himself much. He's such a private person."

CeCe finished her mouthful while contemplating Tayla's words. To her, Luka seemed a free spirit, not someone who'd own an investment portfolio or build a home.

"Is he your 'one that got away' guy?" Tayla asked CeCe.

"What? No... Well—"

"I was there, remember," Molly interrupted. "You were a mess when Luka left."

"I was eighteen. Stupid in life, stupid in love. Nothing was ever going to come of it. And I'm a firm believer in leaving the past where it belongs."

"If you say so." Molly grinned at Tayla.

"But he does have a certain something, doesn't he?" Tayla continued the tease. "It's those moody eyes and that knowing expression."

CeCe smiled at the memory of Luka's moody eyes watching her undress in the back of the Kombi. The same moody eyes that searched for her as he'd entered the library and, later, watched her from the front of the classroom. The moody eyes she'd told herself she never wanted to see again.

"Okay. Question time," Molly said. "Who's your 'one that got away'?"

"Don't look at me," Tayla replied with a grin. "I'm a married woman, and besides, I don't have one. How about you?"

"Ah, that would have to be Jesse, my drummer boy. He was amazing in bed—well, until he went all weird on me. I haven't seen or heard from him since the night he told me to leave his place after professing his love for me only hours before. It's like he dropped off the face of the earth."

"Yeah, I remember that. It *was* weird," CeCe said.

"So, if Luka wasn't your *one*, who was?" Molly asked.

CeCe looked up in thought and grinned. "I haven't met him yet." She turned to Tayla. "But getting back to Luka, I still can't get my head around him and Mitch being friends, so please warn me if he's going to turn up at any family gatherings."

"He'll be at Mitch's birthday party next month."

"Of course he will." CeCe rose from the table and puffed out a sigh as she collected their plates. "Right, let's get this cake frosted. And please, no more talk about Hot Chopper Guy. I don't want to spoil my dessert." She noticed the smirk on Molly's face. "What?"

"You still have the hots for him, don't you?"

Did she? "Yeah, my knees go weak and my heart skips a beat just thinking about him. Not!"

"Liar."

THE GRUDGE

CeCe studied her recent 'pride and joy' acquisition—the viscometer her parents bought her when they sold the orchard and moved to Clifton Falls back in March, two weeks before lockdown.

With the music cranked up, she was eager to get to work. But as she bent over a carton of supplies, someone knocked on the open door.

"CeCe?" he uttered her name with surprise. But that voice; she'd know it anywhere. Soft. Cultured. *Turn around and look at me.*

A swarm of butterflies invading her stomach, she glanced up into eyes that had once been so familiar. "Luka." She reached for the remote and turned down the music. "Are you looking for Mitch?"

"Yes." He checked over his shoulder as if expecting to see one of the orchard workers. But the staff had all left for the day. "I heard a noise and thought it was him. I didn't realize he'd finished lining the lab. It looks great."

"Thanks." CeCe placed a jar of coconut oil on the counter

and bent down for another, her hand unsteady. "I'm not sure where he is. Have you texted him?"

"Earlier, but I got held up in town." Luka smiled as he studied the space. "I see you must have got the hang of bond energies, systems in equilibrium, and periodic trends in behavior in the end."

She had to stop herself from smiling back. He'd remembered what she'd said to him that day in the classroom. "I did okay. I won't say it was easy, but I managed."

"That's great. I'm pleased for you. So, what are the bases for your formulas?"

CeCe hesitated. At thirty-two, Luka had a relaxed air about him, a confidence that comes with knowing who you are, but he made her nervous, and she didn't want him in her space, acting all interested and friendly. "I'm still at the testing stages. It'll be a while before I sort that out."

He nodded, appearing genuinely curious, but she had no desire to return the favor right now. The memory of him had fascinated her for almost five years; however, that didn't mean she should surrender to that fascination.

"I guess one of the main things is to get the feel of it right."

As CeCe's hackles rose, she shot him a pointed look. "Yes, as with most things in life."

Luka's expression settled into a frown, his smile fading as he held her in suspension with his gaze. "Was that a dig at me?"

She shrugged, just the slight lift of one shoulder, but didn't reply.

"So, you're still holding a grudge after all this time? Shouldn't we be past all that?"

CeCe knew she should keep her mouth shut, and yet... "Maybe, but I won't pretend that you didn't have an effect. So please don't expect me to bow to your apology, or whatever this is."

His frown deepened. "If you think I'm here to apologize, I'm not. I did what I believed was right at the time. Let you go—"

"You didn't let me go, Luka. You pushed me so you wouldn't have to deal with the fallout. Anyway, I'm kind of busy right now. Mitch can't be far away—would you like me to call him?"

Luka huffed. Shook his head. She half expected him to roll his eyes, but they stayed focused on her. "You genuinely believe there was no fallout?" His tone offered an abrupt change. "I went through weeks of investigation by the Teachers' Association and damn near lost my license. So yes, there was definitely fallout."

Now it was her turn to frown. This was news to CeCe. "But I thought they dealt with it at board level?"

"That was the plan, but the other board members outvoted Carole and your father six to two. So even though I'd left the school, the complaint still went through the proper channels, and unfortunately, the details of how we met didn't matter to them. I crossed a line I should never have crossed."

"Why didn't you tell me? You had my number."

"Because I didn't want to put you through any more drama. Besides, what would it have achieved? I asked your father not to say anything, and yes, I'd already decided to leave teaching, but I wanted to keep my options open. My grandfather was so proud of me when I graduated. He'd wanted to go to university when he was younger but had to work the farm, so I felt like I'd let him down."

She paused to steady her breath. "I'm sorry. That must have been difficult for you."

"It wasn't pleasant. So maybe next time I cross your mind, you could try playing the scenario from a different angle. Realize you weren't the only one hurting."

CeCe remained silent, waiting for him to verbalize more of his thoughts from their past. After he'd left Tulloch Point, her younger self had spent months trying to scramble back to the life she knew, and when he hadn't contacted her in the weeks following, she'd been so unsettled that she'd built up a fierce resentment. Over the subsequent years, that resentment still surfaced at times of self-doubt and uncertainty.

"I get that I upset you when I walked away," he continued. "But, like I said, I thought I was doing the right thing. Giving you space to grow up without my interference. Plus, I had a lot going on before I left. I'd failed my final practical exam and had to redo it, so not everything was about you."

CeCe had heard as much through the Tulloch Point grapevine, but not until after Luka had left, when Travis told her in the only way he knew how—in vengeance. "I'm sorry. I know how much it meant to you to pass."

"Yeah, well, in hindsight, my ego got in the way. I guess I had a lot of growing up to do too but didn't realize it back then."

CeCe nodded. He'd been twenty-six when they met. She'd thought he had life all sorted out, but many people suffered from their own version of imposter syndrome, and perhaps Luka wasn't immune.

"Anyway, you're busy, so I'll leave you to it. I wish you every success."

"Thanks."

As he walked away, CeCe sat on a carton and cursed under her breath. After their last brief encounter, she'd often imagined them meeting up again, and in that imagination, the scenario differed from the reality. They'd chat and reminisce, leaving any animosity where it belonged—in the past.

But CeCe had learned how to cling to a grudge from a master. Her father loved the clutch of a good old grudge, and it wasn't until she went to university that she realized how holding on to them can eat you up inside. She'd needed that separation from home and the small-town lifestyle to allow her to see things clearly and ditch her country-girl streak.

Lately, CeCe had congratulated herself on the progress that time and distance had allowed her. She'd moved from Tulloch Point, Botanical Ce was now a reality, and she was back playing tennis. But some days, when tired and alone and struggling with self-doubt, she still blamed Luka for leaving the way he did. Still embraced the hurt.

Maybe she hadn't come that far after all.

Later that evening, as CeCe strolled across the driveway toward the loft, restless and unable to focus on work, a loneliness she kept telling herself she was too busy for stirred. Tayla's comment about dating may have been in jest, but she wondered if it was time to put herself out there.

However, as she sat in front of the TV, a plate of leftovers balanced in one hand and a fork in the other, CeCe couldn't stop thinking about Luka and how self-absorbed she'd been after he left Tulloch Point. His words from that afternoon played again in her head. *You weren't the only one hurting.*

For the past four and a half years, she'd cast Luka in the role of deserter, failing to consider his feelings because she was too engrossed in her own.

She moved through to the kitchen and stacked her plate into the dishwasher then flicked on the kettle. From a side table in the living area, Anna—the blue butterfly resting in the hollow at the base of her throat—smiled out at her from a photograph CeCe took on her sixteenth birthday.

Oh to be a teenager again, with Anna by her side. They'd spend hours taking selfies and flirting with boys at the beach and many more on the tennis court. And as soon as they went to bed, they'd be texting each other about nothing, everything, and everyone.

Tea made, CeCe padded to the sofa, picked up the silver frame, and sighed. "How did I get it so wrong, Anna?"

THE BIRTHDAY PARTY

Walking into Mitch and Tayla's over an hour late, Luka looked around, hoping to catch a glimpse of CeCe. As he'd expected, their house was crowded, with extra tables set up in the large sunroom and along the veranda. CeCe's father greeted him in passing, even offering a handshake, and Andrea leaned in for a hug, saying how nice it was to see him again.

Through his friendship with Mitch, Luka had come into contact with the Dobsons several times over the years. He suspected Frank still saw him as the opportunistic teacher who'd groomed his daughter rather than as Mitch's friend. But then, according to his old boss, Brad, Frank Dobson was known for holding a grudge, and he did it well. Andrea, however, was a different story. Warm and friendly, she always offered a hug and a smile whenever they met.

Luka grabbed a beer from the makeshift bar in the kitchen and went to greet his parents. His mother had never met CeCe, and Luka could tell she was itching to meet the girl from Tulloch Point who'd once filled his summer days with her dimples and laughter.

He hadn't seen her since that unfortunate encounter in her new lab. Despite the awkwardness of their exchange, he'd felt so proud of her that day. As someone who'd taught her, albeit briefly, he'd sometimes doubted she'd ever make it to this point, but according to Mitch, her determination to succeed—already evident at eighteen—was stronger than ever these days. Not that he and Mitch often talked about CeCe. Luka had made it clear from the beginning that their fling was something he didn't care to discuss.

Unless they were drunk. Then they confided in one another like schoolgirls.

He'd considered contacting her after that day in the lab, but whenever he'd contemplated it in the days following, her chilly vibe had made him rethink. Nothing good would come of it, especially now that he and Annabelle had split. He certainly didn't need another affair with CeCe Dobson.

Mitch cleared his throat and tapped a fork on the side of his glass. As the room fell silent, Luka leaned back in his chair.

"Hey, everyone, thanks for coming. I know thirty-four is nothing special as far as birthday digits go, but I think you'll all agree that this year's been a tough one, what with lockdown and everything. So, I thought it was about time we all got together and celebrated what's important. And to me, that's Tayla and our families and friends who support us in everything we do."

Someone voiced a 'here, here!' and a few people clapped.

"Now, before I shut up and let you enjoy the food, Tayla and I have an announcement." He looked at Tayla, who smiled and took his hand. "Mum and Frank, Barry and Jean, you're going to be grandparents again in the new year."

Jean gasped as Andrea jumped from her seat. "What? Are you serious? You're pregnant? When? How?"

Mitch grinned from ear to ear. "Mum, you always taught me

that a gentleman never tells. But we're sixteen weeks, and she's already as cute as a button."

"That's wonderful news," Jean said. "A little girl."

"Okay, guys, buffet's served. Let's eat."

Luka had just filled his plate when that sixth sense of his had him looking toward the entrance.

CeCe.

She stood in the doorway, breathtakingly beautiful in an off-white fitted dress with a high neckline and capped sleeves. She'd straightened her hair. Apart from when it was wet, he'd never seen it straight before, and the whole look of her—the dress, the heels, the makeup—made him take a second glance. In his head, she'd always been that wild teen, floating through life on the swell at Sandwater Bay, but seeing her now had him viewing her in a whole different light.

When he caught CeCe's eye, she looked away as if embarrassed and turned to her escort, laughing at something he'd said. As they joined her parents, Frank studied his daughter's date in his usual disapproving manner, and Luka was thankful it wasn't him on the receiving end of that glare.

Seated next to his mother, Luka struggled to come to terms with her new style. Not that it didn't suit her. It did. But seeing her with this halo of sophistication definitely had an effect.

"That's her?" Vanessa reached for her juice while following his line of sight. "Wow, you let a good one get away there," she whispered.

"Mum, you don't even know her."

"Maybe not, but I will one day." His mother gave him a raised-brow smile. She'd referred to herself as an intuitive for as long as he could remember. When Luka was younger, her uncanny sense of awareness had embarrassed and crept him out in equal measure, but there was no denying her ability to read people, and horses too. "Who's she with?"

"I have no idea, and what's more, it's none of my business."

"Are you sure about that?" his father asked. "It's important to tidy up life's loose ends."

Luka chuckled. He'd always considered his father a man of many wisdoms. One who wielded power and influence without wrapping it up in a package of self-inflated ego. "Speaking from experience, Dad?"

"Course I am." His parents shared a knowing look. "If your relationship with CeCe was considered taboo because she was your student, imagine how it was for us."

Luka didn't know every detail of how his parents got together, but he knew enough. It had definitely been scandalous at the time.

His mother took his hand and gave it a gentle squeeze. "Are you okay—not missing Annabelle too much?"

"I'm fine. It's been a long time coming."

CeCe looked up from her dessert to where Luka had sat just moments before. She'd spent the past half hour trying to ignore him, and now that she'd dared to peek, he'd disappeared. Earlier, he'd offered a brief, almost curt, hello, but soon after, one of his friends had interrupted and dragged him away to meet someone.

Probably just as well. Parties made her nervous enough as it was, and she didn't need his presence messing with her head.

Luka's mother caught her eye and smiled. *Damn.*

Tayla had pointed Vanessa out earlier, so it seemed impolite not to go over and introduce herself. The O'Learys had been good to Mitch over the years, and they obviously knew who she was.

CeCe stood and smoothed down her dress. Nerves fluttered in her stomach as she walked toward them; why, she had no idea. According to Mitch, the O'Learys were perfectly nice people. Luka's father stood as she approached and pulled out a chair. As she sat, she smiled and offered her hand to Vanessa. "Hi, I'm CeCe, Mitch's sister."

Vanessa introduced her to Luka's dad, Liam, who returned her smile and firmly shook her hand. One look at Liam, and she knew where Luka got his bronze skin and chiseled features from.

"Mitch tells me you own an equestrian center in the Rata River Valley," CeCe said. "I've always wanted to learn to ride, but I don't seem to gel with horses."

"It's all in the way you connect with them," Vanessa replied, her smile as warm as the hands that had greeted her. "You're a young soul, plenty of scope to learn."

A young soul? What did that even mean? Vanessa had a kind but piercing stare, like she could see straight through you. CeCe had sometimes seen the same expression on Luka. Despite having only just met her, she could tell his mother was a fascinating character. Warm and friendly, but with a certain edge one couldn't deny.

"Come up with Luka one day," Liam said. "He'll teach you. Has the same gift as his mother."

CeCe imagined that scenario with dread: Luka and her riding side by side in the Rata River Valley. She swallowed hard, suddenly in desperate need of a drink.

They made small talk for a time—Mitch and Tayla's pregnancy news, the food, even the weather. When they struck a brief lull in the conversation, CeCe looked around the room, searching for someone to save her. *Anyone.*

"Luka said you're launching your own skincare range soon." Vanessa smiled. "Impressive. I'd love to try it sometime, not that I've ever been into makeup, but I love a good moisturizer."

Luka?

"I'll send you some samples." CeCe sat forward in her chair. "Anyway, I should probably go mingle. It's been lovely to chat."

Vanessa took her hand. "I look forward to seeing you again soon. And any time you want a riding lesson, just call the center."

"Thank you, but..."

"You don't have to explain." Vanessa stood and took Liam's arm. "Anyway, enjoy your night. We're off to hit the dance floor."

As Luka's parents walked away, CeCe spotted Luka through the French doors, joking with a group of guys out on the veranda. As if sensing her stare, he stared straight at her and offered the faintest of smiles before turning back to his friends.

EX-LOVERS' TRUCE

Maybe it was the atmosphere of the evening or the fact he'd been feeling a little restless after coming out of lockdown, or even the knowledge that Mitch and Tayla were going to be parents. Whatever it was, Luka couldn't stop thinking about CeCe. That girl was in his head and didn't seem to want to leave, and in all honesty, he didn't want her to either.

When he strolled into the kitchen in search of another beer, Mr. Edward, the resident Harrington pug, lay on the window seat, his brown eyes watching Luka's every move. He sat next to the dog and rubbed behind his ears. "Hey, boy. Are you enjoying yourself?"

Luka looked up as Mitch walked in through the back door, carrying a twenty-four-pack of Heineken. The pug gave a feeble woof before shutting his eyes again. Mitch set the carton on the island. "Ready for another?"

"Yeah, go on."

Mitch grabbed a couple of beers and flipped their lids with an opener. He handed one to Luka. "Where's Annabelle tonight?"

"Out of town on business."

Mitch perched on a barstool and took a sip of his beer. "Is everything okay between you two?"

If there was one thing Luka knew, it was he couldn't hide his emotions from Mitch. The guy had an uncanny knack for picking up vibes. "Not exactly." Luka sighed and shook his head. Although their breakup had been a long time coming, the confusion he'd felt for weeks still surfaced occasionally, especially when he'd been drinking. "We've called it quits."

"What? Since when?"

"Three weeks ago."

"Shit, sorry. Why didn't you say something?"

Luka had asked himself the same question just that afternoon. With Annabelle in constant contact, hinting at another chance, it seemed time to make their split official. Tell his family and closest friend and draw a line under it. "I needed time to let it sink in, time to just be me again. Mum and Dad know, but otherwise, I'd like to keep it quiet for a while."

"I understand. Was it amicable?"

He paused with the bottle halfway to his lips. "As much as it could be with Annabelle. It's funny—she texts me more now than she did when we were together." He took a sip. "Maybe she wants what she can't have."

"It's a human condition."

Luka thought about this for a moment. He'd expected to miss Annabelle more than he did, but it was time for them to let one another go. Past time. "I caught up with CeCe earlier."

"Yeah? How was that?"

"Awkward, just like the last time." Luka took a long drink while Mitch studied him.

"Hold on a minute." Mitch narrowed his eyes, and Luka

knew what was coming next. "Do you still have a thing for my sister?"

"Come on," he scoffed. "It's been almost five years. It was a fling. Besides, I'm not drunk enough for this conversation."

"Me neither. Anyway, there's this guy sniffing around her, a rock star, or so he thinks."

Luka frowned. Wasn't it every girl's dream to fall in love with a musician? "You mean he's in a band?"

"No, a geologist. We met him recently when he was doing some field mapping along the river. Nice guy, but not her type, if you ask me. He's a bit of a bore, to be honest." Mitch chuckled. "You should have seen his face when I introduced him to CeCe. He couldn't take his eyes off her."

Luka understood why. With that fresh complexion and soulful stare, CeCe had always been beautiful. That first day at the library, he'd struggled to keep his eyes off her too. "Is she keen?"

"Who knows." Mitch grinned. "According to Tayla, she's still hung up on some guy from her past."

"Piss off. You're just trying to wind me up."

"And it's too easy."

Later, Luka strolled outside and relaxed into a chair on the veranda. The air was fresh but floral, with hints of wintersweet from the stone-walled gardens surrounding the homestead. Across the courtyard, a couple kissed in the shadows, reminding him of how much he missed the intimacy he'd once shared with CeCe. He hadn't had that same connection with Annabelle and knew he never would.

Luka took a swig of his beer as he shuffled his thoughts.

Despite his earlier denial to Mitch, seeing CeCe in the lab had left an impression.

A troubled impression.

He'd told himself that he'd left their summer fling where it belonged—back in Tulloch Point. But the CeCe of today was an intriguing mix of sophistication and drive, and the sight of her fascinated and intimidated him at the same time. If he were honest, he missed those long legs and wild curls, the way she whispered his name. He longed to stare into those soulful eyes and lose himself in her touch. To bury himself deep within her warmth.

Shit.

He knew he shouldn't be thinking that way about CeCe, especially when his breakup with Annabelle was barely cold. But he was a little drunk, and his thoughts refused to toe the line, so he let them drift a little further.

With a science degree under her belt and Botanical Ce's lab up and running, she'd done well for herself since graduating from Tulloch Point High. And as he'd watched her work the room earlier, friendly and gracious, it was as if a sophisticated version of Kombi Girl had returned to the driver's seat. Happy, smiling Kombi Girl—flashing her dimples while conducting conversations with her hands as she used to.

He glanced up as CeCe approached, a glass of rosé in her hand. She sat in the chair next to his without words or invitation, and they both stared up at the sky. With a full moon and the stars winking down at them, the scene reminded him of their nights on his deck back in Tulloch Point.

"Are you enjoying the party?" she eventually asked.

Luka turned to look at her. Small talk had never been their thing, but that was then. "I am. The Harringtons always throw a good party, and it's such a stunning night."

CeCe leaned back and closed her eyes, her legs crossed and her wine glass held in a loose grip. "Yes, it is. I love living here."

"Mitch mentioned you're working part-time in agricultural research. How's that going?"

She glanced his way. "Good. It's busy, though, juggling everything."

Luka shifted in his chair, trying not to stare at the profile once so familiar to him that now held an air of the unknown. "Sometimes, that's not a bad thing. Helps keep us focused."

"It does, and the bills paid." CeCe smoothed her fingers through her hair. Sipped her wine. "What about you? Are you still with Search and Rescue?"

"Yep. Like you, it keeps me busy."

As they sat there in silence, questions flooded his thoughts. Was she already with the rock star? Did he make her happy, set her body ablaze? Did she moan his name during sex and smile when she greeted him good morning?

"Actually, I'm glad I found you alone." CeCe paused and stared out over the lawn. "I wanted to...apologize for how I reacted in the lab. I hadn't realized how bitter I still was, but I'm going to work on that, and..."

Her hand went to her neck but found no butterfly to ground her. Luka wanted to reach for it, hold it in his, so she knew he understood.

"Anyway," she continued, "I'd like us to bury the past and move on. Because with you and Mitch being friends, we're bound to run into each other at times, and I don't want it to be awkward."

"You mean an ex-lovers' truce?"

"If you like." CeCe smiled. "To be honest, I find it rather strange that you and Mitch are friends."

There were times when Luka found it strange himself. They'd met at another game of touch rugby after Luka returned from Tulloch Point. At the post-game drinks, they'd both got hammered; it was one of the few times they'd discussed CeCe in any detail. "Sport does that—brings people together. Still, he took a while to warm to me."

"Mitch tends to be overprotective. Always has been."

Another silence followed, but some of their earlier unease had dissipated. It gave Luka hope that any future contact between them might be more relaxed. Maybe there was something to be said for an ex-lovers' truce, where the past was left where it belonged but not forgotten.

Luka sipped his beer, wishing he had something stronger to settle his nerves. "So, you met my folks?"

"I did. Your mother's a real sweetie."

Luka looked her way. She glowed under the lights of the veranda, her cheeks rosé bright and her smile relaxed. "She is— well most of the time."

"Your dad said you teach riding?"

"Only to friends. Why? Are you keen?"

"Me? No. I love horses, but they never seem to return the sentiment." CeCe giggled like she used to when they first met. "They regard me with suspicion as if they're staring down their noses at an inferior being. A mere mortal, lacking in confidence and ability, and unworthy of their time."

He nodded in agreement and chuckled. "I know exactly what you mean. I didn't learn to ride until I was thirteen, and it took me ages to get the hang of it." He paused. "What else did my mother say? You appeared to be having quite the chat."

"Nothing much." CeCe's wine glass stopped before it reached her lips. "Just small talk." She took a mouthful, finishing her drink.

"So you didn't introduce her to your date, then?" Luka inwardly cringed at his words, surprised his drunken alter ego had loosened his tongue to the extent that he'd mentioned CeCe's date.

"My date?"

"The guy you walked in with."

"You're observant. That's my cousin Patrick. He lives in Auckland, and his flight was delayed, so I slipped away to pick him up from the airport."

"I thought he must be your boyfriend from the way your father looked at him."

"They don't get on, so…"

Luka let that settle for a moment. She didn't mention the rock star, but then, as he'd said to his mother, CeCe's dating status was none of his business. "Would you like another drink?"

"No, thanks. I've said my goodbyes, so I'm going to wander home. I've had all the alcohol I need for one night." As she stood and placed her glass on the table between them, a little wobbly on her feet, Amy Winehouse's voice cut through the air.

"Oh man, I love this song." CeCe kicked off her heels and stepped out onto the lawn. It reminded Luka of a scene from the book she'd given him that day at the library, the one about the chopper pilot and the woman he'd loved and lost. Life imitating art, or maybe the other way around.

The air had chilled, but CeCe didn't seem to notice as she swayed to the music, her arms outstretched. Luka's gaze followed her across the lawn to where the lights from the house dulled into moonlight. When the song stopped, she turned to look at him and smiled, then strolled back to the veranda to collect her shoes.

"Do you remember when we last heard that song together?" he asked.

"Of course. We'd eaten burgers and fries after our first trip to Sandwater Bay. It was playing on the radio when we arrived back at your place."

His eyes found hers. "I've loved this version ever since."

"Me too." She sat back next to him and slipped on her shoes. "I really should go. Thanks for listening to my drunken apology."

"You're not drunk, are you?"

"Oh yeah, I'm definitely drunk. I wouldn't be out here with you if I was sober."

"Why's that?"

CeCe's expression softened. It reminded him of their time together: when she'd turn up at his place unannounced, her concern wrapping around him like a cocoon. "Because life's complicated enough as it is," she murmured.

"Yeah, you're right about that." Luka stood, placed his bottle on the table, and slipped his hands into his pockets. "Come on, I'll walk you."

"I'm perfectly happy to walk alone."

"I know, but I could do with a stroll."

Luka didn't bother going back inside to say goodbye. After all, he was merely walking CeCe home. And when they reached the side door of the packing shed, they'd shuffle their feet and offer a casual goodnight. They'd hesitate for a moment, then she'd climb the stairs alone while he strolled back to Mitch and Tayla's to catch a ride home with his parents.

However, as the moon tracked their progress through lime-laden trees, he couldn't help but wonder if the PG version in his imagination might ever be upgraded to Restricted.

They were silent for the first half of the short walk, but as they approached the packing shed, CeCe chatted off and on, asking him about his work and where he lived. By the time they reached the driveway, Luka could hardly think straight.

That chemistry he'd shared with the girl in the Kombi burned so much hotter for the CeCe she'd become. Perhaps it was the night air, or the booze, or the off-white cocktail dress holding her tight that led his mind to inappropriate thoughts. Whatever it was, if she invited him inside, he'd still refuse. Rebound sex had never been his thing, and it wouldn't be fair to either CeCe *or* Annabelle.

Just as in his imagination, they stopped outside her door. She turned to look at him; a 'thanks for the escort' whispered into the air. Then, without so much as a peck on the cheek, she offered him a smiled 'goodnight,' stepped inside, and shut the door behind her.

Luka stood with his hands in his pockets as the lock clicked into place. Music from the party drifted over the treetops, and when the window above him filled with light, he turned and headed back the way he'd come, smiling at the stupidity of his pleasantly hammered self.

MOOT POINT

CeCe woke to the sound of the sprinklers *tish, tish, tishing* across the lemon grove closest to the packing shed. She snuggled down under the covers and closed her eyes, her head aching and foggy and her mouth like a dried-up millpond.

Luka drifted into her thoughts. She'd enjoyed having him walk her home under the full moon, found it comforting in a way she never would have imagined. But right now, she didn't need a distraction in the form of a sexy six-foot-three Chopper Guy. She needed to put in the hours and save hard to pay for the Kombi restoration and get Botanical Ce off the ground.

Still, what would five years look like in terms of their shared chemistry? Would the desire be the same? Would he hold her afterward as he used to? Bury his hands in her hair as he kissed her? The thought made her shudder. Luka was taken, and CeCe respected that. She would never come between a couple. Ever.

With it being Sunday, her self-appointed lazy day, CeCe tried to drift back to sleep, her conversation with Luka replaying in her head. Eventually admitting defeat, she picked up her phone to check the time—five after eight—then pulled up her Contacts and hit the Call icon.

"Morning, Molly. Did I wake you?"

"Not quite. But it *is* Sunday morning, and I'm still in bed."

"Me too. So, what's been happening?"

"What?" Molly replied. "Since we talked three days ago? Well, I still haven't had a decent haircut since lockdown ended, my last Tinder date stood me up, and it's nice having Patrick away for the weekend. That little brother of mine seriously needs to find his own place. How was Mitch's party?"

"Good. But we missed you."

"Yeah, but you know, work and all that."

"Luka was there."

Molly fell silent on the other end of the phone, as if waiting for CeCe to elaborate.

"I got a little drunk and danced barefoot on the lawn while he watched from the shadows of the veranda," she continued.

"Sounds kind of romantic for a tomboy like you."

"What? I am not a tomboy. I'm a sophisticated grown-ass woman."

"Where was his girlfriend while you put on this little show?"

"I didn't ask. Anyway, nothing happened. He walked me home, and when we reached the packing shed, I said goodnight and went inside. Alone."

"Seriously?"

"Yes, seriously. Even if Luka were single, I wouldn't have slept with him. Inappropriate much."

"Yeah, sorry. But Tayla did say they were on and off. So if he *was* single, would you want to go there again? Hypothetically speaking, of course. Reunion sex is the best."

CeCe didn't know about that. Apart from that final time

with Luka, she'd never had reunion sex. But then, the night they had sex in her bedroom was definitely one to remember. "First, it's a moot point, and second, single or not, I'm far too busy for a complication like Luka right now. He's staying in the past, where he belongs. Besides, imagine what Dad would say if he found out Luka even walked me home."

"CeCe, you're an adult. It's time Uncle Frank kept his opinions to himself. Also, if you're too busy to spend a few hours having sex with a hottie—and I don't necessarily mean Luka O'Leary—your work-life balance is seriously out of whack."

"Well, as soon as I launch the label, I'll take a break. I might even fly up to Auckland, so we can do dinner. What do you think?"

"Sounds good. But don't leave it too long to get back on that horse, hon. It's way overdue."

"Yeah, but my life's a lot less complicated without a man in it."

"Speaking of," Molly whispered, "my latest complication just turned off the shower. Talk soon."

"I thought you said he stood you up."

"That was last week's guy, I've moved on since then. See ya."

Standing at the kitchen sink a few minutes later, a glass of orange juice in one hand, and two pain killers in the other, CeCe contemplated Molly's words. Celibacy had never been a conscious choice; it was more a subtle reaction to meeting one too many bland men at university. Men who kissed with too much tongue, texted way too much, and wouldn't recognize a G-spot even if signposted from the waist down. She downed the pills and sighed. Luka knew a thing or two about G-spots. In fact, Luka knew a lot about sex.

Lucky Annabelle Sutton.

The sound of her phone's text alert lifted her from her thoughts.

Jaz: We're going to HOTY next Saturday. Keen?
CeCe: HOTY? Is that some kind of male review strip show?
Jaz: I wish! Horse of the Year. It's our first adventure since lockdown.
CeCe: And is that what they actually call it? HOTY?
Jaz: Depends who you're talking to…and who's in the saddle. *wink, wink*.

CeCe chewed her lip while considering her co-worker's invitation. She loved watching equestrian events on TV but had never been to a live show. It was about time she tried something different.

CeCe: I'd love to.
Jaz: Cool. Shall we go for broke and book the good seats?
CeCe. Yeah, let's.

HOTY

CeCe, Jaz, and Tracy climbed the steps to the second tier of the packed grandstand in search of shade. Surveying the jumble of jumps before them, CeCe embraced the crowd's excitement, and as they sat in their seats, her childhood dream of learning to ride flashed through her mind.

Before Anna died, they'd talked about taking riding lessons, but it was one of those bucket-list fantasies that they never got around to. Now CeCe doubted she ever would. She reached into her bag for her water bottle and took a swig.

Jaz nudged her in the ribs and offered her a pair of binoculars. "Take a look, six o'clock."

CeCe put them to her eyes and adjusted the focus wheel, her sight on the competitors' entry gate. People milled about, but there was nothing out of the ordinary as far as she could tell. "What am I supposed to be looking at?"

"You'll see soon enough."

As she looked again, a rider came into view. Dressed in white jodhpurs, a fitted black jacket, and a black helmet, he leaned forward to pat his mount's neck, his lips moving in a private whisper.

CeCe frowned as the commentator addressed the crowd over the public address system: "Next, it's number eight, Inca and Luka O'Leary, representing the Rata River Equestrian Center in this, the annual Clifton Falls Horse of the Year. A crowd favorite, he's one to watch, ladies and gentlemen, boys and girls."

"He has to be the hottest equestrian in a jockstrap I've ever seen." Jaz reached for the binoculars. "White jodhpurs and black boots, just shoot me with Cupid's arrow right now, and I'll die a happy girl."

"He's a chopper pilot with Search and Rescue," Tracy said. "I've heard he never sleeps with the same woman twice. But then, I've not met anyone who's slept with him, so..."

CeCe suppressed a smile. She'd never thought of Luka in terms of a man-whore, but maybe he'd changed since his Tulloch Point days. Then again, he might have been a man-whore all along. How would she ever know? It wasn't like they'd spent much time together back then, and they'd never discussed being exclusive. In hindsight, perhaps that had been naiveness on her part.

"Isn't he with that lawyer?" Jaz said. "You know the one I'm talking about, Tracy. They call her the Ice Queen."

"That's right. She's always in the society pages. Annabelle someone."

"Yeah," Jaz countered. "They're probably married by now and have a kid."

"He's not married." CeCe adjusted her sunglasses, giving her sight unhindered access to the lover from her teens as he awaited the starting horn.

"How do you know?" Jaz asked.

"Because he's a friend of my brothers. They're on the same touch rugby team. *And* he taught me chemistry for a while in my last year of high school."

"Shut up," Tracy said as she leaned over Jaz. "He's a teacher? None of my teachers ever looked like that."

"He was. I didn't realize he was into show jumping, though." CeCe tried not to laugh. Luka was an equestrian, a helicopter pilot, and scored a well-deserved ten on the hot or not scale for his skills in the bedroom. And according to Tayla, he cooked a mean curry as well. *Damn!*

As Luka cantered into the ring, CeCe watched in awe. The look of concentration on his face and the way he rose in the saddle had her mesmerized. And as he maneuvered through the course, she couldn't take her eyes off him.

He completed a faultless round point six of a second under the allocated seventy-five seconds, putting him in first place. The commentator's voice boomed over the field: "What a run. A fabulous piece of show jumping there from Inca and Luka O'Leary, provincial champions for two years in a row. Folks, how about another round of applause for the team that hails from the Rata River Valley?"

For the rest of the afternoon, CeCe tried to put Luka out of her mind as she watched the other riders take the field. But when he stood on the podium to accept his first-place medal at the end of the day, she could have sworn his eyes met hers across the filled-to-capacity stand. He glanced away, then back again, but if he was looking at her, the recognition she expected to follow didn't come.

As she lay in bed that night, she thought of him, sitting tall on his magnificent black horse—his muscular legs contained in those white jodhpurs and black riding boots, and determination in his expression. Where would he be now? Out celebrating his win with friends? Flirting with Annabelle Sutton? Telling her how beautiful she was?

And what of those supposed one-night stands? Had he desired them with the same fierce passion they'd once shared, coaxed them with his whispered words? Did he bury his face in their neck as he came?

Had he ever called them in the weeks following?

And then it struck her. Apart from once or twice, when he'd popped into the library to see her, in the short time they spent together at Tulloch Point, Luka had rarely instigated the contact.

31

VISCERAL REACTION

The following Monday, CeCe bounded down the stairs and out through the packing shed door. Her sister Liz had emailed through samples of Botanical Ce's graphics the night before, and CeCe looked forward to spending the day alone, figuring out what she liked and what she didn't. She planned to do a soft launch of most of her product at the farm gate store, plus online through the awesome website Liz had created. There was no point in throwing heaps of money at her new venture if nobody liked the product. Liz had suggested she let it grow organically, which made perfect sense to CeCe. And with the restoration of the 'money tin'—her father's pet name for the Kombi—taking all her spare cash, she had to watch her budget.

Deep in thought as she strode across the driveway, she didn't notice Mitch and the orchard's foreman, Ned, talking to Luka until she almost walked into them.

Luka's gaze settled on her and remained there without an ounce of unease, but Ned spoke first.

"Morning, CeCe." He flashed her a broad smile filled with false teeth. Now in his eighties, Ned had worked at Lime Tree

Hill ever since Mitch's grandfather owned the place, and CeCe loved his infectious grin. "Day off, is it?"

"Not today. I'm working in the lab." She looked at Mitch and Luka. "Morning, guys."

"CeCe," Luka said, his expression so very readable, but his tone one of indifference.

"Hey, Nick was here looking for you earlier," Mitch, the stirrer, said with a straight face. "Wants to catch up for lunch, said he'd call back later."

That was all she needed when she had a full day planned. An aloof Luka staring at her like she was a lost opportunity and Nick with his plans for a cozy lunch. "Oh, okay. Thanks. Have a great day, guys."

The hairs on her nape lifted as she walked away. Did the man still have his eyes on her? Because right at that moment, her entire body was experiencing a visceral reaction she couldn't control.

Damn Luka and their pesky chemistry.

Or perhaps it was merely her vivid imagination playing tricks on her. She carried on across the driveway without looking back, but as she unlocked the door and stepped inside, Luka's expression stayed in her head.

She was just making a coffee when Mitch knocked on the open door, a pail of something in his hands. "How's it going?"

"Yeah, good." CeCe rubbed her temples. She'd been in the lab for less than fifteen minutes and was already tense. "Here." She picked up a jar from the counter. "Try this."

Mitch set down the pail and took the offered spatula. He smeared a dollop of the cream on the back of his hand and massaged it in with his fingertips. "Feels a little greasy."

"Yeah, it does, doesn't it?" She sighed. "Stability's my

biggest concern. I don't want the creams splitting in the jar after a couple of months and the oil floating to the top."

"Ah, the old 'peanut butter' conundrum. Have you considered asking Luka for his opinion?"

"No, I have not, and why would I? Oh…" She flashed him a smile. "You are such a stirrer."

He grinned back in that cheeky way of his. "I just thought, with him having been a chemistry teacher and all, he might have some ideas."

"There's a vast difference between a chemist and a teacher. I hardly know what I'm doing, so I don't think Luka would have a clue. Besides, he's not someone I should spend time with."

"Really? Why not?"

CeCe shrugged.

Mitch laughed. Although her brother had a serious side, CeCe seldom saw it. He'd teased her since she was a little girl, and he loved teasing her even now. "So, you're still pissed at him? After all this time?"

Yes…maybe…kind of. She pointed to the open door. "Don't you have work to do?"

Mitch lifted the obviously heavy pail. "You don't want this then?"

"What is it?"

"A gift. From your annoying ex. Organic Manuka honey from his parents' hives."

CeCe frowned. "Are you serious? They have beehives?"

"That's why he called in this morning—to drop it off."

"But a pail of Manuka honey that size is worth a small fortune, and why didn't Luka deliver it to me himself?"

"He was on call, and his beeper went off." Mitch raised both eyebrows, that cheeky grin still firmly in place. "Have you seen him lately? Apart from today, I mean."

A memory of Luka in his black boots and white jodhpurs surfaced. "Actually, I saw him at Horse of the Year. I didn't realize he was an equestrian."

"Really? I thought everyone knew that. He's been riding for years."

"Yeah, well, I guess it's in his blood. What other talents does he have hidden up his sleeve?"

Her brother chuckled. "You tell me." He went to walk out the door but turned back. "Enjoy your lunch with Nick."

"Gee, thanks."

"Oh, and just a heads-up. Luka will be at the benefit dinner next month if he isn't on call. He's waiting for his roster to come out."

CeCe puffed out a sigh. *Luka in a tux. Shit!* "Why am I not surprised?"

Nick arrived as promised, bearing vegan sandwiches made from some weird yellow 'bread' that stuck to the roof of CeCe's mouth and so full of raw onion that she could hardly eat them. He talked about his job—a lot—a distraction she had neither the time nor the energy for. But she didn't want to hurt his feelings.

By the time Nick left, that tightness in her temples from earlier had turned into a full-on headache, so she headed over to the loft for painkillers and a ten-minute nap.

With a glass of water in one hand and her phone in the other, CeCe sat on the sofa, a soft breeze floating through the open balcony door, providing a welcome freshness to the air. She set the water on the side table and unlocked her phone.

CeCe: Thanks so much for the honey. Please let me know what I owe you.
Luka: It's a start-up gift. Sorry I didn't deliver it myself. I was on call and had to rush off. How's the business going?
CeCe: Slowly.
Luka: You'll get there.

There were days when CeCe wondered if that were true. Sure, to make the dream a reality, she had to focus and put in the effort, but it wasn't hard work she was afraid of; it was what would happen if she failed.

She took a deep breath, her fingers hesitating over the keypad. Maybe Mitch had a point, and she needed a second opinion. But could she do this? Invite Luka into her space? It was one thing to meet at social gatherings, where she was free to leave whenever she chose, but entirely different to work with him. It would be like lab day at school all over again. But then, what did they say about desperate times?

CeCe: Do you know much about stabilizing emulsions?
Luka: Should I brag and say my salad dressings rarely split? Why?
CeCe: I'm not sure I have my mixture of surfactants quite right.
Luka: Assume you don't want to use sodium lauryl sulfate?
CeCe: No. Any ideas?
Luka: Not really. I haven't even been in a lab since leaving Tulloch Point High.

CeCe reread his reply. She stared at the screen, put the phone down, then picked it up again.

CeCe: OK. I'll rethink. Thanks.

The fight left her for a moment, but instead of the nap she'd planned, CeCe picked herself up off the sofa and headed back to the lab as the painkillers kicked in. On the way, she reminded herself that the spark of connection she'd felt with Luka the night of Mitch's party came courtesy of the music, the starlit night, and that last glass of rosé.

It had no place in their everyday lives.

32

RELUCTANT CHEMISTRY

As Luka drove toward Lime Tree Hill Saturday morning, his inner voice kept telling him to carry on to Petrie Bay and lose himself in the waves. It was a flat day with gray cloud sitting long and low on the horizon. His lips quirked in a wry smile. Flat and gray: yep, that pretty much summed him up these days.

He'd thought about CeCe often since that day in the lab several weeks ago. Her fierce handling of their conversation and the way she'd dismissed him without the emotion he'd expected. So different from that last day at Tulloch Point. But that had been the eighteen-year-old version of CeCe Dobson. People changed over the years, particularly when moving from a teenager into adulthood, and the CeCe of today had embraced adulthood in style.

When he approached the packing shed, the place was deserted, unusual for a Saturday. With some hesitation, he walked up the loft stairs and knocked on the open door.

CeCe popped her head around the dividing wall between the kitchen and entry. "Luka. What are you doing here?" She stepped toward him.

Luka fought to keep his gaze from drifting the length of her body. Dressed in leggings and a baby blue hoodie, her hair pulled up into a high ponytail, she looked way too sexy. "I was wondering if we could have a word."

"Sure. I was about to go for a run, but come in." She gestured toward the sofa. "Grab a seat."

As he sat, CeCe crossed to the kitchen and flicked on the kettle, her subtle perfume hanging in the surrounding air. He wanted to close his eyes and inhale but stopped himself. Instead, he studied his surroundings, expecting it to look the same as when Mitch lived there, but she'd given the place a major makeover.

A woven wool rug took up the floor space in the seating area, and around the dining table sat six chairs dressed in various autumn shades of velvet—two rust, two deep-aqua, and two scarlet. Books covered both sofa side tables, stacked high and coordinated by the color of their spines, and on a rustic dresser, a tousled bunch of blush roses dipped their stems into a tall white jug. While the decor surprised him, it suited this new adult CeCe—eclectic but sophisticated. Much like CeCe herself.

Luka picked up a photo from the sofa table and studied it. "Who's this? She's wearing your butterfly."

"That's my friend Anna." She leaned back on the counter, her arms crossed. "I gave her that necklace on her sixteenth birthday. Her parents returned it to me after she died. I used to wear it a lot at first, but I don't so much now."

"She's pretty." Luka studied the picture before putting it down again. "It must have been tough, trying to make sense of her death."

"Yes, very. You hear of people going to bed healthy and not waking up but never think it will happen to someone you know." CeCe smiled sadly. "That first *why?* is the hardest part.

Then comes *why wasn't it me?* before the whole *it was just her time* cliché."

"Had you been friends for a long time?"

CeCe took a jar of tea bags off the shelf above her and unscrewed the lid. "Since we were twelve. We played tennis together. By the time we turned seventeen, we were riding around in cars with boys and down at the beach, having fun." She paused. Took a deep breath.

"Then the year we turned eighteen, Anna met this older guy, Dillon. He was a prize jerk. Used to bum money off her and cheated every chance he got. She wanted me to see him in the same false colors she did, but I was never one to paint guys like him with shimmer and gloss. So we agreed to disagree. In the end, I told her about the cheating, and it ripped us apart, and I mean *ripped*. She never spoke to me again."

"You made the right call."

"I'm not so sure about that. Even after all this time, I still sometimes question my motives. Realistically, I know I couldn't have done anything to save her, but rational thoughts don't protect you from the irrational ones. Her death was hard, but in some ways, the regret's even harder. Do you get what I mean?"

"Yes, of course."

"Anyway, enough morbid talk." CeCe placed two mugs on the counter. "Green tea?"

"Thanks."

"Oh, I meant to congratulate you on your Horse of the Year win."

Luka smiled as he recalled looking into the stands and seeing that mass of curls and striking face. "So, it *was* you I saw, checking me out through those binoculars."

She shrugged, poured water into the mugs and dipped the tea bags up and down. "I've joined this group, and they do something different each month. This month, it was HOTY, no pun intended."

Her giggle had an immediate effect, and Luka shifted in his seat as he relaxed. This was the CeCe she'd channeled when they first met, the one he'd so often longed for over the years. And the more time he spent in her company, the more she reminded him of Kombi Girl.

"Besides, I wasn't checking you out. I was watching Inca."

"Of course, it's always about the horse. Anyway, how did you enjoy it?"

"Loved it. It appears you're quite the accomplished sportsman."

"Yeah, I like to keep fit. You'll never see me in a gym, though. Can't stand them."

"Me neither." CeCe's face lit up with a shy smile, and she stilled. "To be honest, in those white jodhpurs and black boots, you caused quite a stir among my friends."

He chuckled. "And people say men objectify women."

"It's rumored you never sleep with the same woman twice."

WTF? "What? Come on," Luka scoffed as she handed him a mug. "Who said that? You know that's not true."

CeCe shrugged, but her blush was evident. He'd almost forgotten what a flirt she could be when she put her mind to it. "I'm only repeating what I heard."

He took a sip. "So, gossip is alive and well in your Clifton Falls circle?"

"Gossip's alive and well in all walks of life. Sometimes the perception is different, that's all. And besides"—she sat in the chair opposite and placed her tea on the side table—"we humans find handsome men and women intriguing. It's in our nature."

Luka let that comment slide. Women often called him handsome, but he'd never given it much thought. Just like the rest of the world's population, he couldn't help the way he looked.

"Anyway, what can I do for you?" she asked.

"I've been thinking about your text. I know someone who might be able to help you."

She frowned, picked up her mug, and sipped her tea.

"His name's Jay Blakely. He was one of my students when I taught at Clifton Falls High, and he's looking for work until he returns to university next year to finish his masters."

"Thanks, but I can't afford staff."

"He's registered with a government scheme, so they'd pay eighty percent of his wages. It's a reintegration assistance program."

"Reintegration?"

Luka got straight to the point. "Jay's just come out of prison. Served eighteen months of a three-year sentence for manufacturing a Class B drug, so he'd need constant supervision."

"Seriously? He's got a record for cooking up drugs, and you want me to employ him? I wouldn't be able to sleep at night. Is he in a gang?"

"No, he's not in a gang. His mother had stage four breast cancer. When it spread to her other organs, she couldn't tolerate the chemo and had a huge distrust of drug companies. So when Jay came home from uni and saw her in pain, he decided to put his chemistry degree to good use. Word got around, and before long, people attached 'supplier' to his name. He dropped out of uni to nurse her and sold any surplus hash oil to fund an experimental drug and to pay the mortgage."

"That's so sad, but…"

"Look, he's a good guy. Sure, he did something stupid, but don't we all at some point in our lives?"

CeCe picked up her tea again and studied him through the

steam wafting from the mug. She took a sip. "So how did you get involved?"

"Through a friend. Jay's name came up in conversation and I remembered him from school."

"Did his mum pull through?"

"No. She died a month before they sentenced him. Jay was on electronic bail, so he nursed her at home with the help of an aunt."

CeCe nodded. "That's tough."

"Yeah. But he's committed to moving on."

"I don't know." She tucked her feet up and fiddled with the zipper of her hoodie, absently moving it up and down a couple of inches each way while considering his suggestion. "Guess he'd be helpful to bounce ideas off."

"Okay, I'll leave it with you." Luka shifted in his seat. Every time they were together, he felt a little more uncomfortable, and the tease of her pink crop top under the hoodie wasn't helping.

She nodded. "Give me a couple of days."

"So what's next on the agenda for your adventure group?" he asked, changing the subject.

"A chopper ride. The one from Station Winery for the local hospice."

Luka nodded. "That's a great trip."

"You've done it before?"

He finished his tea. CeCe didn't need to know that he owned a chopper and sometimes volunteered for the gig. In fact, he had another stint coming up soon. "Once or twice. When are you going?"

"On the fifteenth. But I'm a nervous flyer."

"Then why put yourself through it?"

"Because you can't be afraid to take chances all your life, or you'll get nowhere."

"I agree." Luka stood and took his mug to the kitchen sink. There was no reason to stay any longer, even if he wanted to. "And don't worry, you'll be fine."

"Hope so." CeCe rose from the chair and followed him to the door.

"Anyway, I'll flick you Jay's contact details…just in case you want to get hold of him."

"Okay, thanks."

He paused on the landing. "Maybe we could go for a surf one day soon."

As CeCe hesitated for longer than necessary, he braced himself for her reply. His invitation had been poorly thought out. He'd misinterpreted the mood of their earlier banter, seeing it as a breakthrough rather than what it was: a good-natured ribbing between two people who'd once shared a bond. Nothing more.

"I don't really have time for surfing these days."

Struggling to quell the disappointment caused by her rebuff, he nodded. "Of course. Enjoy your run."

CeCe closed the door behind him, padded down the hallway, and flopped down on her bed front first. "Argh, men!"

Half an hour—that's all it had taken for him to tip her day upside down. Now, she'd have to drag herself along the river track with thoughts of Luka 'the player' O'Leary annoyingly stuck in her head.

Surfing? Seriously?

She rolled onto her back, wondering why he hadn't text before turning up, then mentally kicked herself for the inappropriate comments about his black boots and one-night stands. *Shit!* What had she been thinking?

More than that, what was *he* thinking? That they could be besties, go off surfing together while Annabelle, *his girlfriend*, met with clients and attended court.

Rude, just rude.

Hearing her text alert, CeCe let that thought go. She jumped off the bed and picked up her phone from the dresser.

Molly: What's up?

CeCe: Not much. Just saw Luka. He invited me surfing.

Molly: How dare he! *insert chuckle* So he's single then?

CeCe: No idea. Surely Mitch would have said if he was.

Molly: Ya think? Mitch doesn't know you still have the hots for Chopper Guy does he?

CeCe: I DO NOT!!!

Molly: Liar. Have you asked Tayla?

CeCe: No, she's visiting her sister. Anyway, my friends from work say he's a player, so…

Molly: You think it's true?

CeCe: Who knows?

Molly: You gonna go? Surfing, I mean?

CeCe: As if. You OK?

Molly: Yep. Great. But I have to go. Looks like my Tinder guy's just turned up for our morning coffee date. SHIT. He has a mullet!!!

CeCe: Hahaha cute. Go you. Talk soon. I'm off for a run.

Molly: Spare me the deets.

There wasn't much to Jay Blakely's resume. In fact, on paper, one would wonder if the man had any life experience at all. Still, what could he say? That he was an expert in the manufacture of hash oil?

And resumes were like that now: two pages, and you're done.

CeCe looked up from her computer when he knocked on the door. Tall and dressed in chinos and a button-down shirt, he looked nothing like she'd imagined. She stood and offered her hand. "You must be Jay. It's nice to meet you. Please take a seat."

He looked older than twenty-four and his handshake was a little weak, but he smiled as he sat in the adjacent chair. "Thanks for seeing me. It can't be easy to put aside judgements based on my past."

Okay. "It's human nature to wonder why someone's spent eighteen months in prison, but I'm not here to discuss your past, except to say that if it wasn't for the reintegration program, I wouldn't be able to afford you at present."

Jay nodded. "I'm under no delusions on that score. At least you've given me an interview. Luka said your business is an organic skincare start-up?"

"Yes. Well, that's the plan."

"You obviously know my recent history, so what else do you want to know about me?"

CeCe stood and took a jar off the shelf behind her. "I have a better idea." She handed him the jar and a spatula. "Try this. I can't seem to get the consistency right."

Jay rubbed the cream between his fingers. "Yeah, I see what you mean. It can be a problem when working with all-natural raw materials. Can you bring up the Turbiscan and zeta poten-

tial results? You may need to up your concentration of surfactants to see which one's the better choice."

Impressed by his formality and no-nonsense approach,
CeCe crossed to the large desktop computer, shuffled her
mouse, and clicked on a file. "Yes, I've looked at that, but the
one I want to use is the least stable of the three I've tested."

"Okay." Jay sat on the stool in front of the screen and pulled
a pair of glasses from his shirt pocket. He put them on. "Let's
see what we're dealing with, shall we?"

33

SHAKY RIDE

As soon as she clicked her seatbelt into place, CeCe knew she'd made a big mistake by agreeing to come. She'd joined the Carpe Diem group with Jaz and Tracy as a way of balancing her increasingly busy life. Living in a lab day in and day out wasn't healthy, but if she had her way, she'd be back at Lime Tree Hill, working on Botanical Ce rather than taking a chopper joyride on her precious day off.

While Jaz and Tracy chatted all the way from Clifton Falls CBD to Station Winery, a twenty-minute drive, CeCe watched the world pass the minivan window. As the road twisted and turned around rolling hillsides of fertile farmlands, her stomach did the same, and by the time they hit a straight stretch of highway, she was fighting an annoying case of motion sickness.

They traveled along an avenue of maples until they reached the winery's entrance. Their driver parked beside a semicircular building constructed of cedar and stone. Manicured gardens of native grasses and flowering shrubs surrounded the exterior, and to the west, a forest of pines stood tall, filtering sunlight through the treetops.

As they walked through the main doors—large and imposing with circular knobs fashioned from burnished metal—and into the tasting room's foyer, a strange energy filled the air.

Jaz moved to her side. "Guess who's here?"

"Who?"

"White jodhpurs, black boots—"

"Luka?"

CeCe looked at the three choppers lined up outside and froze at the sight before her. Luka—navy flight suit, hair hanging over his forehead, and mirrored aviators—stood chatting with two other men. She muttered an F-bomb under her breath. Surely he wasn't one of their pilots.

Of course, it shouldn't have surprised her to see him. The day had already started badly when she'd slept late and nearly missed the pickup. Now Luka, in all his sex-on-legs glory, was almost close enough to touch. Their gazes met. Offering no smile, he didn't look away until he'd had his fill.

When they ushered their group across the tarmac toward the men, he stepped forward to greet her with a kiss on each cheek and a husky, "CeCe, it's good to see you again."

Then, just to add to the confusion of an already stressful day, Luka turned his attention to the others without another word. She studied him from behind, those coveralls molding his butt to perfection, and before she could censor her thoughts, the memory of a naked Luka stretched out on her bed after the last time they'd had sex flashed through her mind.

The man really did have the most perfect bare butt she'd ever seen.

Jaz nudged her with her elbow and whispered, "What was that all about?"

"Nothing," CeCe whispered back while trying to usher her thoughts into line. "I told you—he's a friend of my brother's."

"Well, he didn't share any of his particular brand of nothing with me."

"Or me," Tracy said. "And none of my ex-teachers ever looked at me like that."

"You say that as if it's a bad thing," Jaz said. She turned to CeCe. "Don't tell me you guys have a history."

CeCe grinned. "Stop it."

Twelve women had opted into that day's 'escapade,' as Jaz called it, eight who loved to fly and four who didn't. Being a bona fide member of the latter group, CeCe dreaded the thought of Luka being her pilot. She'd only been in a chopper once before—ten years ago when she and her father took a joyride as part of a school fundraiser. After that, she'd vowed to never again sit her butt in a helicopter seat.

The group had activities such as abseiling, white water rafting, and Japanese cooking classes planned, and CeCe was keen to be involved in every single one. So when they'd mentioned the sightseeing trip, she knew it was time to face her fear.

CeCe dug her fingernails into her palms and glanced toward the main doors, plotting her exit strategy. If she told everyone she had an upset stomach and made a dash for it, no one would question her.

As if sensing her unease, Luka looked her way. Aviators in hand, he strolled back over to talk to her. "You okay?"

CeCe assumed her confident face. "Fine."

He narrowed his eyes. "Don't be nervous. You couldn't have picked a better day. Or a better pilot."

"Very funny." She shook her head at his ego talking. "Anyway, what are you doing here? Surely you have people you need to rescue."

He chuckled. "Returning a favor. It's a charity gig, so what could I say?"

"Am I with you?"

Luka gave her a private smile, one she'd once been so familiar with, and leaned closer. "Yes. Is that a problem?"

CeCe looked away, wishing she could still make a run for it. Until now, their recent meetings had been on her terms. But not today. "No. It's fine."

"Good. And if you ask nicely, I might even let you ride shotgun."

Spellbound and embarrassed in equal measure, CeCe held her breath as Luka walked away, her breasts tight under her T-shirt and her cheeks impossibly hot.

Jaz smiled in amusement. "Okay, now I *know* something's going on. Are you going to tell me what you guys were whispering about, or do I have to drag it out of you?"

"There's nothing to drag out." CeCe followed Jaz across the lawn to the three waiting choppers. "That man is a walking contradiction."

"Most men are, but damn, he does contradiction with a capital C."

While waiting to board, CeCe introduced her new friends to Luka. He shook their hands with his usual charm, making small talk as he flashed that sexy smile. Climbing on board last meant being seated next to him, and as she put on her headset and watched him do the same, she tried to calm her nerves with several deep breaths.

She found the flight exhilarating, no doubt about that, but while she loved being so close to the Pacific as they zipped along the coastline, CeCe couldn't get used to the motion. Every time he dipped to show them a point of interest, her stomach dropped.

Luka, on the other hand, seemed perfectly at ease in the pilot's seat. And as she watched him chat with the other women through his headset, she felt a pang of envy at how relaxed they all appeared. However, she quickly pushed aside the emotion when he addressed her. "How's it going, CeCe? Hanging in there?"

"Only just."

He took her hand and squeezed it, his large and warm on top of hers as his aviators shielded his expression. His touch lingered on her skin long after he'd pulled back. Her hands held each other in her lap, thumbs busy over the knuckles as she glanced out the side window at the fertile plains below.

"Don't worry, I'll get you back in one piece."

Knowing that wasn't true, CeCe looked away. She'd never returned in one piece from any of her encounters with Luka O'Leary. Each time, he took a little more of her heart.

When they landed, she expected him to stay and talk, but he didn't. With his aviators firmly in place and that tight butt on display, he strolled across the tarmac to greet the other pilots, before climbing back into his chopper and flying away.

34

TROUBLE IN A TUXEDO

Smoothing the fabric over her hips, CeCe studied her reflection in the full-length mirror and frowned with a second thought. With wide straps running from the front to the back necklines, another set crisscrossing the shoulder blades, and a choker neck detail, the black velvet dress had a definite BDSM vibe about it. *Damn!*

She was about to attend a benefit dinner showcasing excellence in sustainable horticulture. With Lime Tree Hill as major sponsors, Mitch and Tayla had invited CeCe and her parents to join them. And when their young housekeeper, budding fashionista Valentina, asked CeCe to wear the dress—one she'd designed for a college assignment—CeCe hadn't had the heart to refuse. However, looking at it now, those second thoughts were fast turning to thirds.

As she slipped into a new pair of silver heels, CeCe wondered if Luka would make it tonight. She smiled at the thought. Hopefully, if he did, he and her father wouldn't have to sit anywhere near one another.

She scanned her profile again and then, with her back to the mirror, glanced over her shoulder to check out her butt. The dress fitted perfectly, but to her, it looked at least one size too small. Apart from floaty beach maxis, she rarely wore dresses, and with this one accentuating every curve, she now remembered why.

CeCe grabbed her phone and took a selfie of her reflection, which she messaged to Valentina. As she stood at the window, waiting for Valentina's reply, she raked her fingers through her hair as she thought of the evening ahead.

Valentina: OMG! You look fabulous. And that red lipstick is the star on top of the Christmas tree!!!
CeCe: Love the dress but I feel like I'm being primed for a kinbaku session. It leaves so little to the imagination.
Valentina: A what???
CeCe: You're almost 18. Google it. But maybe go incognito.

When Valentina eventually texted back again, CeCe was in the back of her father's car as he drove down Seaview Road toward the town hall.

Valentina: #blushing. How do you know about these things?
CeCe: Not by experience, that's for sure. I read about it in a Bryce Courtenay novel.
Valentina: Which one? I want to read it now!
CeCe: I'll let you figure that one out.

Chuckling to herself, CeCe slotted her phone back into her clutch. The kid had butted her head against life, but her determination to succeed in spite of a challenging family environment was such that CeCe couldn't help but admire her. Plus, she enjoyed Valentina's wicked sense of humor.

The town hall puffed out its chest with pride as CeCe walked down the red carpet and into the foyer with her parents on either side. Magnificent floral displays fashioned from locally grown flowers and foliage flanked the entrance, and the scent of jasmine and honeysuckle filled the air. And as they ascended the stairs with the other guests, the dress moved against her curves like a second skin. It was the most sensual she'd felt in a long time.

When they entered the grand ballroom, where a server greeted them with a glass of champagne and a smile, CeCe looked around at the sea of tuxedos and designer gowns, each one as exquisite as the next.

She was about to follow her parents to their table when she caught a tall male in her peripheral vision. Luka O'Leary. Hot Chopper Guy—successful entrepreneur (apparently) and the best sex she'd ever had—stood in profile not ten feet away. Hands buried in his pockets, laughter on his lips, and a neat haze of stubble on his jaw, the man certainly knew how to hold the floor.

Following CeCe's line of sight, her mother shook her head and cleared her throat. "Oh, dear me. Trouble in a tuxedo at two o'clock. And I thought your father looked smart."

CeCe tried but failed to suppress a smile. There was nothing special about the tux, or the shiny shoes, or the white shirt and black bow tie, but the sight of Luka made her heart beat a fraction faster. She had to stop herself from fanning her face.

He looked well. More relaxed than the other times she'd seen him recently. The lines on his forehead had smoothed, and he appeared less troubled. No doubt about it, he suited the tux, but his Chopper Guy getup was still her favorite look on him. And as Pilot Luka slipped into her mind, naked from the waist up and with aviators dangling from his hand, her face flushed.

Her father leaned in close. "You wore that dress when you knew Mitch had invited him too? Didn't your mother teach you how to be demure?"

"Guess not. But don't worry, Dad. I'll behave. And besides, he's taken."

"I wouldn't be too sure about that," her father muttered. "I can't see a date, can you?"

It was at that moment Luka looked over and noticed her. His eyes widened, but he quickly corrected his body language. As butterflies swarmed in her stomach, he gave a polite smile and returned his attention to the conversation he'd left only seconds before.

Luka's parents came over to greet them, followed by Mitch and Tayla—her baby bump rounded under her gown. They made pregnancy small talk for a while, and as Tayla led CeCe and her parents to their table a little later, CeCe felt a longing for the man who'd flown her along the South Pacific coastline.

Luka and CeCe might not have been seated together, but he could see her, and she could see him. And he watched. Not in an obvious way, but with brief peeks and the odd glimpse out of the corner of his eye.

Once or twice, he offered a slight smile, but otherwise, his dark eyes seemed to hold her all over with barely a glance. She merely picked at her food, listening to the conversation around her with only mild interest.

As the waitstaff cleared their plates, she found herself glancing Luka's way yet again until Tayla leaned in close and whispered, "You'll never guess what Mitch told me earlier."

"Give me a clue."

"Luka's broken up with Annabelle."

"Really? When was this?"

"I'm not sure, but Mitch said he's known for a while."

"And he never mentioned it?"

"Not until tonight. Luka asked him not to tell anyone."

"My brother always has been good at keeping secrets."

Tayla chuckled. "Yes, but not usually from me." She followed the direction of CeCe's gaze. "Are you doing okay? You hardly touched your meal."

CeCe selected a baby eclair from the dessert platter. "Just being in the same room as Luka makes me nervous. Brings it all back." She popped the treat into her mouth and moaned as the cream and chocolate danced across her palate.

"Yeah, Mitch used to make me nervous too. On our wedding night, we went to Little Brown Barn. He ordered the shoulder of lamb for two, and I just about ate the lot."

CeCe laughed. "Why were you nervous on your wedding night?"

A blush bloomed on Tayla's cheeks. "You know, it's nerve-racking, getting married."

CeCe let that comment slide. She still wondered about Mitch and Tayla and how they got together, but neither of them had ever talked about it. "Yeah, I guess."

Tayla rubbed her baby bump. "Now I've got something else to worry about, and I honestly don't think I'll relax again until this little button is earth-side and screaming her lungs out."

She squeezed Tayla's hand. "I'm so happy for you both, well, the three of you."

"Thanks. But enough about me. What are you going to do about Luka?"

CeCe glanced back at the man in question, still engaged in conversation with the other guests at his table. Before she left home that evening, she hadn't anticipated the pull she'd feel when she saw him again, but he hadn't even come to say hello, so...

"Nothing. We had our time, and over the years, I built up a resentment toward him that he probably didn't deserve. I know now that his lack of contact was simply his way of encouraging me to stretch my wings. But at the time, it didn't feel that way."

"Do you think he still loves you?"

A definite 'no' surged to the tip of her tongue. "We never said those words to each other. It was just a fling. Besides, love stings like a bee sometimes." CeCe picked up a second eclair.

"Yes, but it can also soothe and inspire and make you feel fantastic. You should give it another whirl." Tayla helped herself to a lemon tart, plucked the blueberry off the top, and ate it. "But not with that Nick guy."

CeCe feigned offense. "Why is it that no one in the family approves of Nick?"

Tayla covered her lips with her hand while finishing her mouthful of pastry, then scrunched up her nose and giggled. "He's a perfectly nice guy. But you must admit, he's a bit of an old woman."

"You sound just like my brother. Besides, we're just friends, *platonic* friends. Although, he has asked me to go hiking with him next month."

"Are you keen?"

"Kind of. I do love being out in the bush, and maybe spending some time in nature would do me good."

Tayla looked up as someone approached from behind. CeCe didn't need to turn to know it was Luka; she could tell by the look on her sister-in-law's face. Luka pulled up a chair next to CeCe and sat, his body turned in her direction. "How are you both enjoying the night?"

"Loving it," Tayla said. "But if you'll please excuse me, I need to find the restroom."

CeCe remained silent as Tayla stood and walked away. *Traitor.* With the rest of her table either mingling around the coffee station or up on the dance floor, she and Luka were now alone.

"I still can't get used to seeing her pregnant," Luka said as they watched her leave. "She's glowing."

"It's lovely, isn't it?"

"Mitch is on cloud nine."

"Yes. He's always wanted kids."

As they dragged each other through the ritual of small talk, CeCe wanted to tell him to stop. To ask him what had happened between him and Annabelle. Or perhaps to walk away, just as Tayla had. To take off down the stairs and out the main door so she could stride along the boardwalk until her racing heart calmed.

"Anyway, how have you been?" he asked after a moment.

"Okay. I've been meaning to thank you for putting me onto Jay. He's such a switched-on guy. I'm keen to keep him on once his trial's over."

"That's great."

"And you? How have you been?"

Luka pulled at his bow tie. "Restless."

She frowned at his cryptic response. It wasn't like him to admit such a thing. "Why's that?"

Luka gave her a knowing grin, then leaned in close to her ear and whispered, "Because I can't stop thinking about my sexy as fuck ex-girlfriend, and it's doing my head in."

What?

"Is there any chance of a reconciliation?" CeCe asked, assuming he meant Annabelle.

Moody eyes the color of cognac searched her gaze. "I don't know. Is there?"

His words had an immediate effect. As heat flared between her thighs, she clenched them together. When her father appeared at her side a second later, CeCe barely noticed him.

He offered his hand to Luka, who stood and accepted the greeting with a smile. "You two catching up on old times?"

"Something like that," Luka said as he returned to his seat.

Frank turned to CeCe. "Think we're about ready to call it a night." He frowned. "Are you okay? You look a little peaky."

Her face impossibly hot and Luka's words searing her like a branding iron, CeCe felt more than a little peaky. "I'm fine. It's just so warm in here."

Her father hesitated. "Okay. I'll go find your mother. Be back in a sec."

CeCe watched her father walk away. What did Luka think he was doing, speaking to her like that? She turned to look at him, his knowing expression giving plenty away as the corner of his mouth twitched in the start of a smile.

"I can drop you off later if you want to stay a bit longer," he said.

Sexy as fuck!

"But you've been drinking."

He shrugged as if that didn't matter. "You could always stay with me in town. We'll grab an Uber."

CeCe stood and picked up her clutch from the table, feeling her skin heat under the molded fabric of her dress. No other man had ever had that effect on her in public. "I don't think that's a good idea, do you?"

His lips curled a fraction more, reminding her of the heat they once shared. "I think it's a great idea. But your call."

She shook her head. "Goodnight."

Making her way through the crowd, CeCe felt Luka's stare track her across the ballroom as she searched for Mitch and Tayla to say her goodbyes. When she glanced back, her *sexy as fuck* ex-teacher sat in the same place, still watching her. His eyes held a knowing smile, and in that moment, she ached for him, longed to kiss him with passion and breathtaking urgency as she had years before.

GIRLFRIEND INTERRUPTED

Luka had known she'd be there. Mitch had warned him, so he'd at least be prepared. But would he ever be prepared where CeCe was concerned? Because when she'd entered the ballroom, the cut of her dress holding her tight and lips slicked with red, he couldn't believe his eyes. He'd never been interested in restraining a woman during sex, but there was something about the choker collar and straps of CeCe's gown that had him rethinking it.

In the end, rather than grabbing an Uber, his parents had dropped him off at their townhouse. On the drive there, he'd expected his mother to mention CeCe, but she hadn't, and Luka was thankful for that. He didn't want to talk about her. Not with his wits dulled by too much alcohol. His mother always wanted answers, but when it came to CeCe, he had none.

Although they often stayed with Luka in town after a night out, they'd wanted to get back to the Valley, so he'd walked through the front door to a silent house. After opening the double doors onto the deck, he went to the kitchen for a glass of water and two painkillers, removing his bow tie and unbuttoning his shirt on the way.

Luka settled in one of the leather chairs flanking the fireplace, the glass of water in his hand and CeCe dominating his thoughts. The way she'd smiled when she walked in. That sexy dress with its choker neckline. Those red lips shining like a beacon from the sea of the curls framing her face.

And as he reflected on the evening, other snippets floated into his head. Her shy hello and interrupted goodbye. His inappropriate *sexy as fuck* comment that had her flushing a crimson pink.

He'd stayed on for another half hour after CeCe left, downing shots with Mitch and a couple of guys from their touch rugby team. As a result, alcohol still blurred his senses. He picked up his phone and unlocked it, wrestling with the voice of reason that echoed in the back of his mind. It was after one in the morning, and he knew he shouldn't contact her. Not when he was hammered. Besides, she'd be home at Lime Tree Hill by now, or maybe she'd stay with her parents overnight.

And yet, there seemed so much to say.

When the doorbell rang, Luka thought he must have drifted off, and the sound was a distant part of a dream. Until he heard it again. For a moment, he wondered if kids were playing a prank, but when it rang for the third time, he jumped up to answer it.

Luka couldn't see anyone through the glass panels on either side of the entry from the hallway, so when he reached the door, he checked through the peephole. He closed his eyes briefly and took a deep breath.

She'd stepped away by the time he'd unlocked the deadbolt, her shoulders hunched as she walked toward her car parked on the side of the street.

"CeCe?"

She hesitated, making a snap decision in her head perhaps, then turned slowly. She stepped toward him, her expression apprehensive.

"I thought you said it wasn't a good idea."

"I did." Her gaze flicked back to her car. "Sorry, I should go. I…"

He reached for her hand, cold and small in his. "Don't go, please. Come inside."

CeCe lowered her head. Stepped past him. Turned. "I couldn't sleep," she whispered, her eyes filled with invitation.

Fuck!

"How come?" He closed the door, his hands unsteady on the lock.

"I have too many thoughts jumping to conclusions in my head."

Luka stared without restraint. Just like the night of Mitch's party, this CeCe was all brand new. And while the lips had lost some of their shine, the dress certainly had not. Those straps, the collar, the fabric molding her curves—he struggled to take his eyes off her. "So what was the upshot?" was all he could manage.

She gave a little one-shouldered shrug. "That I should stay home, go to bed, and forget all about you and your 'sexy as fuck' comment. That I'm too busy for this complication and don't want a case of morning regret."

His hands still unsteady, Luka lifted her wrap from where it rested over one shoulder. "And yet, here you are."

CeCe smiled coyly, her fingers raking through her hair as he hung the wrap on the coat hook. "Yes. Is that okay?"

"Only if you promise no regrets."

"Promises were never really our thing though, were they?"

"I guess not."

She hesitated. "Tayla said you're recently single. Is that true?"

He nodded.

"It's just—"

"Hey." Luka brushed a curl away from her face and tucked it behind her ear, surprised at the relief he felt. She was here. Close enough to touch. "I wouldn't have invited you if there was someone else."

Her hand went to the choker around her neck, but she didn't look away. "When did it happen?"

"A few months ago...just before Mitch's birthday party, in fact."

"I'm sorry, I never knew."

"Yeah, but I needed some time to adjust. Even when it's been a long time coming, there's still a process to go through. Things to sort out. Mum, Dad, and Mitch were the only ones who knew."

Now it was her turn to nod. They stood in silence for a moment, the kind of silence that follows awkward questions and honest answers. Silence they didn't need to fill.

"So, we're good?" He leaned one arm on the wall beside her, half caging her in.

"We're good." CeCe glanced back at the door. "Still, it's kind of daunting...being here."

He cupped her face, soft under his palm. "I know. I feel it too." Luka watched her form a brief smile. He leaned in without hesitation, his lips finding that hollow between her neck and collarbone. "I'm so glad you're here."

"Me too." She tilted her head to one side as his touch skimmed across her skin. "But you shouldn't be doing that."

"Shouldn't I? Why not?"

"Because," she whispered, "that's my place, remember?"

"I do remember." He kissed her neck again, his tongue joining in before he blew a breath across its path then pulled back. "Do you want me to stop?"

CeCe held his gaze as she wrapped her arms around his neck. She shook her head. "I'd almost forgotten…"

"Forgotten?"

"What it feels like…that want."

They kissed, urgent and breathless, Luka's hands cupping her butt and her breasts pressing into his naked chest. "I want to fuck you in this dress," he whispered. "I've been thinking about it all night."

She made a noise in the back of her throat, a cross between a pfft, and a giggle and whispered, "Dare you to try."

"What did you say? You dare me?" He watched her chest expand and contract under the straps that restrained her as he dropped his shirt to the floor. "Dare accepted. You really think you're ready for this?"

"I've been ready since I left the town hall."

"And I've been ready since you walked into the ballroom. In fact, I've been ready for weeks." Luka squeezed his eyes shut and sucked in a breath as her hands went to work on his fly.

"You didn't even notice me walk into the ballroom," CeCe murmured as she reached for his erection, the shock of her cold hands making him harder still.

He dipped his head to make eye contact and grinned. "What? Every guy in that room noticed you. That choker is so damn hot."

Their foreplay amounted to not much more than that. CeCe turned to face the wall and braced her arms above her head. Luka pushed his body into hers, his lips needy on her nape as he lifted the hem of her dress to waist height. He peeled her panties down her legs, and she stepped out of them, still wearing her silver stilettos.

"Luka?"

"Yeah?" he panted as he kissed his way up her body.

"Condom."

"Shit!" He opened the drawer of the hall table, pulled out a condom, and ripped it open with his teeth. "Sorted."

They finally made it to Luka's bedroom well after two. By then, CeCe felt a little chilled, and all she'd wanted was for him to hold her while she slept. For a moment, she thought he might ask her to leave. But when they'd climbed into bed, he'd pulled her close, and she'd snuggled into him, resting her head on his shoulder, just like she used to.

"Luka?"

He tightened his hold. "Yeah?" he murmured, keeping his eyes closed.

"Why do you keep a condom in your hall table drawer?"

A slight hesitation before he spoke. "Just in case a beautiful woman turns up after midnight with no regrets on her mind."

CeCe pulled the sheet over her breasts. "Oh. Okay. I guess that makes sense."

He chuckled. "Actually, I was about to put it into my wallet one day when Mum walked in, so I slipped it into the drawer while she took off her coat then forgot all about it. Until last night."

She hesitated. "Do many beautiful women turn up at your door after midnight?"

He pulled back to look at her and smiled. "What, so we're sharing more secrets now?"

"Not secrets, just curiosities."

"I can't say it's happened lately."

Luka's voice was soft, reassuring, making CeCe realize how insecure she'd felt until that moment. Maybe it was the gossip about him being a man-whore, or the thought of his ex. Whatever it was, she was determined not to let morning regret creep into her thoughts. "I still can't believe I'm here…and that we didn't make it past the hallway."

"I'm glad you came, but I have a curiosity too."

"Which is?"

Luka turned onto his side so they were facing one another. "What's going on with you and that geologist guy?"

"Nick? We're friends, nothing more."

"Not lovers?"

She shook her head and took a slow breath. It was surreal, lying in his bed next to him, talking in the dark as if their connection had never been strained or severed. "No, not lovers."

"That's what Mitch said, but I just wanted to be sure."

"Like you, I wouldn't be here if there was someone else."

He brushed his lips against hers, the touch gentle and reassuring. "I hope I didn't offend you with my 'sexy as fuck ex' comment."

"You were talking about me? But I was never your girlfriend."

"You were kind of. My girlfriend interrupted."

Girlfriend interrupted. She liked that term, thought it suited their relationship perfectly. "Yeah, maybe I was."

As hard as he tried, Luka couldn't sleep. His mind as restless as his legs, he slipped out of bed and went into the kitchen for a glass of water. He stood at the sink and stared out over Carter Bay as fishing boats headed into the channel and out to sea. The sky alight with the dawn, he relived the moment when she'd arrived at his door. How they came together like they'd never been apart, how she'd held on tight as he carried her to bed, how incredible it felt to lie beside her again. To hold her again.

Even now, he could hardly believe it had happened.

Standing there, alone with his thoughts, Luka reflected on how privileged and straightforward his life had been since leaving Tulloch Point. He'd passed his helicopter license, had purchased land, and recently, his own chopper. The home he'd dreamed of building for years was well on the way, and he had a close circle of friends. What more could he want?

CeCe.

But would she be prepared to give him a second chance?

His head throbbing, he refilled his glass and gulped it down.

"Hey, there you are. You okay?"

Her voice sending a shiver directly to Luka's groin, he turned to look at her. "Yeah, fine. Can't sleep though."

Wide hazel eyes communicated her concern in dawn's luminescent light. He'd miss those eyes, the compassionate way she looked at him when he was troubled. "How come? Is it work?"

"No." He pulled her close, his arms encircling her waist, that sixth sense of his playing havoc with his usually rational mind. "It's not work."

"What is it then? Do you want to talk about it?"

Luka took a deep breath, released it. Her words reminded him of the younger CeCe. She cared about other's hurt, even then, and it was something he'd never forgotten about her. "It's you."

She brushed a kiss against his lips. "Me? Why would you be troubled over me?"

"Because life's complicated, and I feel like you're out of reach."

CeCe stilled before offering no counter to his comment except, "Would you like me to leave?"

Luka shook his head. He didn't want to be alone, not after the night they'd spent together. He'd been alone for too long and too often since their Tulloch Point days, even when with Annabelle. "Not yet."

AN URGENT KISS

CeCe didn't stay for breakfast, and for Luka, their parting was one of the most awkward morning afters he'd ever experienced. And that was saying a lot. Dressed in one of his T-shirts, tied in a knot at the center, and a pair of leggings she'd found in her swim bag on the back seat of her car, she left around eight. And as he stood and watched her drive down the hill toward Seaview Road, he wanted to pull out his phone and call her. To suggest they go surfing or head up to the falls for a walk.

But no matter how much he longed for her to brighten up his otherwise dulled-off day, as he turned and headed back inside for breakfast, his phone remained in his pocket.

The day failed to improve until he hit the water later that afternoon. After a few mediocre runs, it was close to dusk when Luka looked across Petrie Bay to where the rumble of rain clouds touched the horizon. The wind had dropped around six, and as he took his last wave, thoughts of CeCe finally evaporated.

However, as he drove along the coastal highway toward town, past Lime Tree Hill and her home above the packing shed, he couldn't stop thinking about her in that black dress and silver stilettos. Her nervous smile as she'd stood on his doorstep with only one thing on her mind.

Pulling into his driveway, Luka half expected to see her car parked outside, but the space remained empty. He cut the engine and sat in the garage, running his fingers over the stubble on his chin as she invaded his thoughts once again. He wanted to call her to say hi. To ask if she was okay, and later, to hold her in his arms as she slept and miss her as soon as she left.

As Luka walked down the hallway and into his bedroom, he imagined her lying on the bed, naked under the top sheet, her eyes wide with anticipation.

But CeCe hadn't texted as promised, not that it surprised him. She didn't want commitment or promises or text exchanges where they asked about each other's day. And maybe, just maybe, there was an element of revenge going on.

But one thing he did know. He no longer wanted the fleeting excitement of a fling. After his split with Annabelle, he'd balked at the suggestion of another long-term relationship, but with CeCe now living in Clifton Falls, he'd found himself reevaluating his lifestyle choices more and more.

Not that this was some opportunistic thing. Even though she now lived in the same city and was more geographically available, lately he'd learned to focus more on what he wanted out of life rather than what he didn't.

And he wanted CeCe.

After a quick hot shower, Luka dressed, grabbed his keys off the hall table, and found himself driving back along the highway toward Lime Tree Hill before he'd even considered the consequences.

The loft lay in darkness when he pulled up outside, so he strolled across the driveway and knocked on the open laboratory door. CeCe turned from her desktop screen in fright, one hand to her chest.

"Luka! You scared me half to death."

"Didn't you hear me drive up?"

CeCe removed her safety glasses. "No, I was concentrating."

"Have you eaten?"

"Not yet." Frowning, she checked her watch, then unbuttoned her lab coat. "Time got away on me. Were you at Mitch's?"

He shook his head. "No. I came to see you."

She narrowed her eyes but remained silent.

"You keen for a burger?" he asked. "We could drive into town. I'll drop you back later."

"Actually, I made dinner for Mitch and Tayla this afternoon. She's nesting and thinks she has to feed me all the time, so I thought I'd return the favor. There's plenty left if you'd like to stay."

Luka relaxed. After the way she'd left him that morning, he'd expected her to offer the same aloofness, but she seemed just as happy to see him as he was to see her. "As I recall, last time we ate dinner together, I got myself into a shitload of trouble."

"It's cannelloni, so I can't promise it won't happen again." CeCe smiled as she brushed past, and he realized how much he enjoyed this flirty side of her. "Come on."

They ate at the breakfast bar, the scene reminiscent of the last night they slept together at Tulloch Point. While they made it through the meal—even through the dishes—with easy conversation and warm smiles, the more they talked, the more tension tugged in the background, drawing them deeper into each other's worlds.

He wasn't there to have sex with her again, or perhaps that was just the lie he'd told himself on the drive over. Because every time they were in one another's company, he couldn't wait to be inside of her, and he could tell by the subtle vibes she gave off that she felt the same way.

CeCe moved to the sideboard, and he watched as she placed two old-fashioned glasses on a tray and poured a nip of whiskey into each. He stood next to the sofa but didn't take a seat. She handed him his drink and held her glass against his. "To second thoughts."

Not second chances, not new beginnings, just *second thoughts*.

Luka took a sip, then leaned forward and kissed her, her tongue warm with the taste of whiskey and her eyes bright with a come-to-me smile.

CeCe reached for his glass and placed it on the side table, then did the same with her own. She stepped back, her gaze holding his as she worked the buttons of her blouse while he undid his shirt. Her blouse fell to the floor, and she stood before him in a nude-colored bra with see-through panels along the cleavage and slit-at-the-knee jeans sitting low on her hips.

Maintaining eye contact, she made short work of his belt buckle, and when he tugged his shirt free, she flattened her hands against his chest. His pecs had been sensitive since his late teens, and as she traced a finger over his nipples, they tightened under her touch. He inhaled sharply. "You want to take this to the bedroom?"

She gently pushed him back onto the sofa, shimmied out of her jeans, and straddled him, the rug soft under his feet. "Or we could stay here." Her voice steady, she whispered the words, and his excitement presented itself in the usual way as he struggled for control.

He cupped both hands to her breasts and squeezed with slight pressure. He didn't want gentle—gentle belonged to their Tulloch Point days. And as she returned his kisses with urgency, rocking back and forth in his lap, he realized she didn't want it gentle either.

Luka was still fully dressed, and as he pulled out a condom from his jeans pocket and placed it on the pillow beside him, she watched him wide-eyed. "Undress me," he commanded.

"Yeah? Is that what you want?"

"Fuck, yes! You make me so horny. Just the sight of you."

STOLEN MOMENTS

Slotting a pod into the Nespresso machine, CeCe's thoughts turned to Luka as he showered in her bathroom. She hadn't really wanted him to stay for breakfast. Not because she didn't enjoy his company, but the morning after the benefit dinner had been awkward, and she found it hard to focus on work when he was constantly in her head. With Botanical Ce launching soon, it meant long hours in the lab from now on.

Besides, what did they really have? A few stolen moments along with their shared memories?

Off-the-charts chemistry?

She knew why he'd come. Sometimes, it hurt to be alone, and Luka wasn't immune to loneliness. But she couldn't figure him out. When he awoke, he'd been distant, as if something was troubling him.

They'd talked for a while before getting up. Thinking back, maybe her insistence that she was stretched for time didn't go down well. Then when she suggested they shower together, he'd said he was in a hurry and would only take a few minutes.

Dressed and ready to go, he strolled into the kitchen and kissed her on the cheek. "Thanks for the shower."

"No problem." She watched as the last of his coffee dripped into the cup. "Would you like some breakfast?"

"Just a coffee would be great."

She took four slices of toast from the toaster and placed them in the rack before setting his coffee in front of him. "Help yourself to toast. I made extra."

Luka picked up his cup and took a sip and then another, but he didn't speak.

CeCe couldn't stand the silence. What was he doing? Trying to decide whether he was interested...or not? Shuffling words around on the tip of his tongue? Last night had been amazing, but now they were acting like strangers scrabbling for a second chance.

Holding her coffee in both hands, CeCe rested her butt against the counter. She inhaled its aroma. "How's work?" As soon as the words left her mouth, she wished she could grab them back. Small talk wasn't his thing, but her nervousness often made her babble on about nothing.

"Good. Busy." He sipped. "But I've a week off soon. I thought maybe we could go away somewhere together."

"Actually, I'm kind of committed until I launch."

"What about next month—the weekend of the third?"

CeCe hesitated before deciding honesty was the only way forward. She didn't have to feel guilty for planning to spend time with a friend. "Sorry, I've already got something on that weekend. With Nick. Remember I told you about him?"

He rubbed his index finger over his top lip as he studied her. *Silence.* She wanted to butter him a slice of toast, cut it in half and smother it with honey, but the knife stayed on the plate, and her hands remained wrapped around the mug.

The change in his expression was barely noticeable. A quick look down at his cup and then back to her, the distance between them hovering over shaky ground. "I remember," he finally said.

"Are you okay?"

Luka massaged the back of his neck, indicating he had something important on his mind. "Not really," he murmured. "I don't think I can do this."

She took a seat beside him at the island and braced herself for what was about to come. "Do you mean you don't want to see me again? He's just a friend, Luka."

"Yeah, so you said."

"Are you upset because I have guy friends? That's hardly fair."

He paused and sipped his coffee. "Look, there's just so much baggage from our past that we've never dealt with, but here we are, hooking up like there's no tomorrow."

"Twice, we've hooked up twice."

He let her words hang for a moment, the twitch in his jaw visible under his skin. "You once accused me of not fighting for you, but I did fight for you...fought for you to be free of me. I realize I hurt you, but I hurt too, even before it was over."

Having no desire to fill the ensuring void, she waited for him to continue.

"Some nights, after we'd been together, I'd lie awake with that empty feeling inside and ask myself if that was all we had —stolen nights and two-in-the-morning goodbyes. And I won't pretend what happened between us back then was just some drunken hookup that I don't recall or have chosen to forget. That's not who I am."

CeCe remembered his words from that day in the lab: *maybe next time I cross your mind, you could try playing the scenario from a different angle.* She'd mistaken Luka's resolve for indifference, thought because he was older, he hadn't hurt as deeply as she had. But she was wrong. People all hurt differently, but also, very much the same.

"Didn't you feel empty," he continued, "driving back to your parents' orchard alone after spending half the night in my bed?"

"Of course I did," she said softly. "But I was eighteen, and all kinds of mixed up. I didn't know how to handle a guy like you. I still don't."

"Maybe our first step is to move on?"

"Isn't that what we're doing?"

"Is it?" Luka sighed, shook his head. "Despite what your rumor mill says about me, I've no interest in one-night stands or casual reunion sex."

CeCe swallowed hard, his declaration and her physical reaction different to how she'd imagined their morning after playing out. "So, you're saying it's all or nothing? Is that fair?"

"No, probably not." He brushed a strand of hair from her face. "But the chemistry between us screams for attention. We both know it. And sure, you're busy with your friends and job and new business, but what are you so afraid of? That you might like me more than you want to? That I'll expect commitment?"

While she'd never seen herself as a commitment-phobe, perhaps Luka had a point. She hesitated while contemplating his question.

"Commitment hurts. It means you have to show up, even when you don't want to, and I don't have time for that sort of complication right now."

"Yeah, well, that's what adults do, CeCe. They show up.

And I'm not some Chopper Guy from those novels you read. Relationships take hard work, and I don't want to show up just for sex."

"Is that truly what you think?" she countered, her voice rising a fraction. "That I have a romanticized version of you in my head, based on some hero from a paperback? Because apart from last night, when you *did* show up just for sex, you've hardly made yourself available. That day at Station Winery, you struggled to keep your eyes off me, but you still walked away without so much as a backward glance, just like when you left Tulloch Point. I brushed it aside because I thought you were in a relationship, but now I know different, I don't get it."

"But that's what I'm trying to say." Luka massaged his temples with his fingertips as if the whole conversation was frustrating him. "When I left Tulloch Point, I didn't realize how much you meant to me. I was young and cocky, and the sex was great, but when I found out I was your teacher, I had no choice but to let you go. I'm sorry for the way things turned out. Sorry I drove back up your driveway that day the Kombi broke down. Sorry I got out of the car, followed you into your bedroom, put you in that position."

She took a pause, just like her father did when facing a challenge. His *sorry* wasn't an apology, but rather a way to voice his regret. "We were both at fault that day, but as you say, we need to move on."

"We do. But searching for you through a sea of faces in some crowded ballroom and stealing a few moments of your precious time at a party is not enough for me. Being your 'complication' isn't enough."

CeCe frowned. "So you'd rather step away than enjoy what we have?"

Luka searched her gaze. "I'm giving you the space you need. It's the least I can do right now."

It was now CeCe's turn to rub her temples. She went to speak but had no idea what to say. Did he want her or not? And what was he giving her space from? Him?

He stood and picked up his jacket from the sofa. "Anyway, I have to go, or I'll be late for work. Thanks for the coffee."

Hands flat on the counter, she swiveled in her chair and watched him leave the room. When she turned back to the island, she looked at the toast still in the rack, the untouched butter and honey, and his half-empty coffee cup, and tried to figure out what had just happened.

At work the next day, time dragged as CeCe waited for the clock to strike five. She was tired of thinking about Luka. She just wanted to get on with her life—her business, her job—and had little energy for anything else. But that didn't mean she didn't care for him. Because she did.

Mitch stood at the packing shed door when she pulled into her parking space.

"Is everything okay between you and Luka?" he asked before she'd hardly had time to open the car door.

"Who knows? I thought so until yesterday, but…" She shut the door, leaving it unlocked. "Apparently, he's giving me space."

Mitch nodded as if he understood.

"Have you been talking to him?" CeCe asked as she followed him into his office.

"Briefly." Mitch sat at his desk and shuffled papers into a neat pile. "So, you've obviously hooked up?"

"Did he tell you that?"

"No, but—"

"Mitch, you know I'm not going to share that information, so please don't spread that unfortunate rumor through the family grapevine. Dad would have a coronary."

"As if I would. Anyway, there's nothing wrong with a spot of reunion sex. You're both single."

"Yes, but I don't need the hassle of a moody guy in my life right now."

"And therein lies his problem."

CeCe sat in the chair opposite. "Meaning?"

"Annabelle worked ridiculously long hours, and her job came before everything else."

"Is that why they broke up?" she asked with a frown.

"Among other things. She never had time for his friends or family, and in the end, I guess he couldn't handle that."

CeCe thought back to the night Luka visited her eighteen months before. "When did they start seeing each other?"

"Officially, just before Tayla and I got married. She chased him for weeks before that though, so they were casual for a while."

"And he came to visit me not long after?"

"Yeah. I think he needed to get a few things off his chest." Mitch shut his laptop and slotted it into a messenger bag. "Anyway, maybe space is a good idea. Luka's a great guy, but he's an over thinker, which can be to his detriment at times."

CeCe nodded. "Yes, I get that. What I don't get are his mixed messages." She stood. "I'd better go. I need to spend a few hours in the lab tonight. Jay's coming out to give me a hand."

"Yeah, I'm calling it a day too. We're going to Tayla's

parents' for dinner." Mitch followed her out the door and locked it behind him. "How's the Kombi coming along?"

"Leaching cash from the exhaust pipe every time I turn my back. But I'm sure it will be worth it in the end."

CATCH ME

CeCe stared out through the living room window to the western hill line, a shadow of unease washing over her. Light rain hugged the ranges, the sky overcast with only the occasional patch of blue. She checked the weather app on her phone again. The cold front was moving in from the east faster than earlier forecast.

She thought of Luka, having to fly in conditions just like these. They'd not seen one another since that day at the loft. According to Tayla, he'd gone down to Queenstown to visit his sister, but he hadn't bothered telling CeCe. She reached for the blue butterfly around her neck and held it for a moment, still struggling to get her head around what happened between them after he'd stayed the night. She unclasped the chain and put it on the sideboard.

Pushing wayward thoughts and her fears aside, CeCe watched as Nick pulled up in his SUV. She'd managed to keep him in the friend zone, and for that, she was thankful. In all honesty, she couldn't imagine what a relationship with him would be like. *Bland?*

As for having sex with him, she didn't even want to go there in her mind, let alone in person.

CeCe opened the door and smiled at Nick as he entered the loft. He offered the palm of his hand. Resting in its center was a crystal the size of a large egg. "Good morning. This is for you."

She took the stone and ran her fingers along the ridge. With its white base and dark honey top, it reminded her of a castle sitting high on a hill. "Wow, it's beautiful. What's it called?"

He followed her inside. "Citrine Quartz. It promotes creativity and imagination and purges toxins from the environment."

"Gosh, you sound more like some new-age guru than a scientist." She placed the stone on the sideboard, next to a vase of daphne and her blue butterfly.

"Even scientists have much to learn. Are you ready to go?"

"Yep." She glanced out the window again. "But what's the weather doing? The forecast isn't great."

"Don't worry. We're only going for two nights, and it's an easy three hours to the hut. If anything comes of it, we'll hunker down until it blows over."

"Maybe we should postpone. We can always go another weekend."

"Nah, I've been up there half a dozen times now. I'll look after you."

***

The drive to the national park boundary took under two hours, and as they neared the spot where they'd leave his SUV, CeCe's unease intensified. Because, despite loving the great outdoors, she was more of a jog-along-the-beach slash surfer-girl.

They traversed the first part of the track without incident, the rain holding off until the hut came into view. Nick's idea of an easy walk didn't match her own. After three hours, her feet ached, and all she wanted was a cup of coffee and a hot bath spiked with a few drops of lavender oil.

As the rain pelted the iron roof with thunderous intent, they played Scrabble, her enthusiasm no match for Nick's. They'd never spent the night together before, and being confined to the small hut—with its wooden bunk beds, potbelly stove, and basic cooking facilities—had her longing for her cozy home above the packing shed and the warmth of her feather quilt.

Her sense of adventure missing in action lately, CeCe heated the curry she'd prepared the night before, and they ate by dull light, the rain still enthusiastic outside. Apart from the two of them, the hut was empty—not surprising given the atrocious weather conditions. And as the evening darkened into night-time, Nick talked nonstop, his attempt at 'conversation' way over her head and so boring it almost hurt her to listen to. Not once did he ask how her business was going or anything else about her life.

At one point, he reminded her of a nutty professor, and she found herself smiling at his silly joke that wasn't even funny. By the time she lay on the top bunk, wrapped up in her sleeping bag with her towel as a pillow, she knew there'd be no other weekends away in the wilderness with Nick the geologist.

Just as she was drifting off into an uncomfortable sleep, she heard, "CeCe?"

"Yes."

"I know we haven't talked much about our relationship…"

CeCe mentally braced herself. What if he wanted to kiss her? Or worse, suggested they have sex, here in the hut, on an already smelly mattress, with an outside toilet and rain that wouldn't let up? *Surely not.*

"Anyway, I've been thinking," he continued, "and I'd like to be free to see other people."

CeCe heaved a silent sigh of relief. Was now the best time to tell him about Luka? But then, what would she say? That she had this guy who she'd hooked up with a couple of times: her bit of fun that didn't want to have fun anymore? "Okay."

He shifted in the bunk below her. "Actually, there's this woman I've met, an archaeologist, but I wanted to talk to you first. I'd still like us to hang out sometimes, but... Anyway, to tell you the truth, I get the feeling you're way out of my league."

"That's not true," she said gently. "But you don't have to explain. I understand. I've kind of met someone as well."

"Okay, good. That's good. I mean, I knew you'd understand, but that's good, really good."

Good. "Night night."

Minutes passed.

"CeCe?"

What this time? "Yes."

"Are you still okay about heading to Ferguson Hut tomorrow? It seems a shame to turn back when we're so close."

The words *shame* and *foolish* competed in her thoughts. CeCe didn't want to carry on, not with the weather so unpredictable. And yet, she also didn't want to disappoint Nick. "Shall we decide in the morning? See what the weather's doing."

"Good plan. The hut's an easy stroll from here. Shouldn't take more than a couple of hours."

Apprehensive, CeCe lay awake for some time, fighting with the lumpy mattress, the racket of the rain, and her thoughts in equal measure. Once she'd been able to sleep anywhere, but looking back, that had been when Anna was alive, when life made more sense. And as was often the case in times of solitude, she thought of Luka—mainly with regret but also with the occasional smile. In her mind, she likened him to a spool of thread, one that sat at the bottom of her mending kit with the unruly loose end.

The uneven fray at the end of a knot.

She eventually drifted off just before dawn, and it was after eight when Nick woke her.

The rain hadn't eased, and from her position on the top bunk, CeCe watched while he shuffled around the cabin— lighting the fire, making porridge. And as she fought to extract herself from her warm sleeping bag, all she could think about was a hot shower and how she longed to go home.

With the rain unrelenting, they stayed put, playing cards, reading, and drinking cups of tea until the sun finally peeked through the clouds around noon.

Earlier, they'd decided to head back as soon as the weather permitted, with CeCe being the main instigator of said plan. But now, with warmth on their faces and heavy cloud drifting eastward, Nick seemed to have other ideas.

"I think we've seen the last of that rain," he said as they stood on the hut's steps. "Why don't we carry on for a bit and see how we go? The waterfalls are spectacular after—"

"Nick." She tightened her hands into fists at her sides. "We agreed. I'm tired and hardly slept last night. I shouldn't have come. I'm only holding you back."

"No, you're not, and it's an easy trek from here. Mostly flat. We'll be there in a couple of hours."

CeCe adjusted the straps digging into her shoulders, looked at Nick and sighed, his enthusiasm and too-broad smile starting to get on her nerves. He'd had all the right words back in Clifton Falls, but now they were out in the bush, she doubted those survival skills he'd boasted about.

"Come on, where's your sense of adventure," he coaxed. "You can do this. And if it's too much, we'll turn back. It's all downhill from this point."

"I'm not sure."

"Hey, no pressure. We've got heaps of time. And if we hunker down at Ferguson tonight, we can stroll back here in the morning, have lunch and be home by dinner time. I'll look after you."

Still unconvinced, she turned and looked back in the direction they'd come, then the other way as she tried to tuck the rain and lumpy mattress away in the back of her mind. Nick was right: according to the map, the walking was easier on this leg of the track, and—encouraged by the sun's warmth—CeCe let his enthusiasm carry her away.

"Okay." As soon as the word left her mouth, her stomach churned. Spending another night in a hut had lost its appeal big time, but she wanted to be a good sport.

This time, Nick's 'couple of hours' almost proved a reality, but as they neared their destination, with native bush to one side and a short but sheer drop to a swift river on the other, the track narrowed dramatically.

CeCe concentrated on following Nick's footsteps as he walked ahead of her. He turned several times, offering his hand in places where the mud was thick and slushy until he stopped at a point where the track was little more than a jagged ledge.

"Looks like the rain's washed out some of the track." He craned his neck for a better view. "Keep close and hold on to those tree roots until we're past the worst of it. Another fifteen minutes, and we'll be there."

Rooted to the spot, CeCe studied the river below, shallow but swift and full of boulders. "Maybe we should turn back."

"We're better off moving forward at this point." Nick glanced up. "By the look of that sky, it's going to rain again tonight. Come on. I'm starving."

CeCe grabbed her water bottle and gulped a few mouthfuls before returning it to the side pocket of her backpack. She followed him, one clammy hand clenching tree roots on the bank to her left and the other aiding her balance as gray clouds rumbled above.

She was just about to grab another tree root when she stumbled. "Nick!"

As she grasped wildly for his outstretched hand, CeCe's foot slipped beneath her, and before she realized what was happening, she'd plunged down the cliff face and into the ice-cold water below.

IN LIMBO

Her headlamp turned to low, CeCe stared over at the stove. Not that there was any point. Even if there had been a glint of an ember in the potbelly, she wouldn't be able to see it through the cast-iron door. With her phone flat and her watch lost somewhere on the floor beneath the bunk, she had no idea of the time but guessed it must be around midnight, meaning Nick had been gone almost seven hours.

Without a fire, the hut offered no protection from the cold, but at least she was dry. Desperate to pee, CeCe struggled out of bed and squatted over the plastic-lined bucket Nick had left for her. She didn't need an X-ray to know she'd broken her collarbone but hadn't realized how painful a break of that type would be.

With CeCe shaken, sore, and sporting a laceration to her thigh that bled like crazy, it had taken them a good hour to get from the river to the hut. Nick carried her most of the way, leaving his pack where she'd fallen. It wasn't until he returned for it later that he realized he'd left his personal locator beacon on the back seat of his car.

When he'd set off to find help, it had still been light. Daylight saving time started almost a month ago, so at least that worked in his favor. He should have traveled the worst of the track before night fell, with only the last couple of hours descending into darkness. Unable to bear the thought of being left alone, she'd pleaded with him not to go at first. But as Nick lay out his argument in front of her, she knew he had to leave before dark. If he didn't go while the rain held off, they might end up trapped there for days.

Returning to her sleeping bag on the bottom bunk, CeCe started to shake, the laceration throbbing to the rhythm of her heartbeat and the pain from her collarbone making it difficult to move. Irrational thoughts flooded her mind as her body tensed. What if Nick hadn't made it out? The rain had gained in intensity now, and with the rivers already swollen, he could easily slip and injure himself just as she had that afternoon.

With her pack ripped from her shoulders and floating downstream to who knows where, Nick had dressed her in his dry clothes before leaving to seek help. Although it was the first time he'd ever seen her close to naked, there had been no trepidation on her part. Nudity ceases to be an issue when you're in pain and a fellow human is doing their best for you. You grin and bear it. Because, what other choice do you have?

Tears welling in her eyes, CeCe swallowed hard. In an attempt to distract herself, she imagined she was with Molly in Burger Shack, eating fries sprinkled with herb salt and drinking an ice-cold strawberry shake while they checked out their social media and talked about boys.

Now that Molly lived in Auckland, they hadn't seen each other since her visit to Lime Tree Hill months before. Sure, they texted all the time, but it wasn't the same as a friendly hug and a burger.

Outside, the wind howled in time to the rain hammering the tin roof. If she concentrated on the sound, would it soothe her to sleep like those white noise apps? She closed her eyes and focused on the rhythm of her breath. But instead of drifting off, she thought of Luka. How she'd once ached for him and how she'd never told him her true feelings. She'd loved him, even if he hadn't loved her in return.

While CeCe had once thought she knew him pretty well, now she couldn't even begin to figure him out. She inhaled a ragged breath and began to sing:

"Will you dance with me? Hold me like I'm precious? Be my only man?

Will you hear me, dare me, catch me when I fall head over heels?

My heart is in your hands..."

Her voice could barely form the words, and the song was more of a croak than a tune. She wondered what her sisters and Mitch and Tayla were doing. Whether anyone missed her. Her father would be furious when he found out Nick left his personal locator beacon in his SUV and that hers had floated down the river, tucked into the side pocket of her backpack.

As CeCe's mind churned, her thoughts returned to Luka. How they'd met. The ease of conversation as they watched the sunrise over Sandwater Bay. The way he'd held her like she was precious...heard her, dared her.

And then, the days spent sitting in his class as if they were strangers, in denial of the pleasure they'd once brought one another.

The way he'd dropped her when she fell.

Drifting in and out of a fretful sleep, CeCe awoke with a jolt every time she moved. Nick had given her two painkillers, plus a honey sandwich and a banana before he left, but now her stomach rumbled with hunger, and everything hurt a whole lot more than it had a couple of hours ago.

She tried to sit up so she could take more meds, but as she steadied herself on the side of the bunk, nausea swirled in her gut, and an overwhelming sense of dread washed over her.

How much longer?

CeCe imagined she heard voices approaching outside. Maybe hunters who'd trekked into the national park seeking refuge from the weather, or perhaps another group in search of warmth and shelter.

But no one came. Only the rain.

If only she had a flat rock.

Anna—she'd write—*I'm lying here in limbo, crushing on a guy I've known for a long time. He's an equestrian, dressed in white jodhpurs and black leather, riding a horse as inky as a moonless midnight.*

His name is Luka. Remember? Hot Chopper Guy? I told you about him once or twice. He used to see me but then pretended that he didn't see me at all. And now...

40

ROCK FALL

Woken from a deep sleep, Luka fumbled for his phone on the nightstand, picked it up, and answered the call. "O'Leary."

"Luka, it's Ray."

"Ray?" Luka closed his eyes, his head sinking back into the pillow. It felt like he'd only just gone to sleep, and he desperately needed a pee. "What time is it?"

"Four fifteen."

"You have to be kidding me. What's up?"

"We have a female, early twenties, slipped down a rock face and into the river up in the Winston Valley late yesterday afternoon. She has a suspected fractured collarbone, one major and a few minor lacerations."

He reached for the lamp switch and turned it on, squinting as his eyes adjusted to the light. "What? What the hell was she doing up there in this weather?"

"Yeah, I asked her boyfriend the same thing. They stayed in Falls Hut Friday night and trekked up the valley yesterday afternoon once the storm blew over. But things turned to shit just before they reached Ferguson Hut. The guy walked for six hours solid to raise the alarm."

Still rubbing his eyes, Luka let the information sink in. "Didn't they have a PLB?"

"He inadvertently left it in his vehicle. The guy's pretty shaken."

Luka huffed a sigh. "When will these people ever learn?"

"Yep. Anyhow, the boyfriend helped her to the hut, but she's exhausted, and he didn't think she'd make it out on her own. Not with the weather the way it is. It'd be rude not to offer her a ride in the chopper, don't you reckon?"

Now fully awake and more than a little pissed off, Luka shook his head. "That's what we're here for."

"Look, I know you're officially not back until tomorrow, but are you around? Barrett's been up all night, simmering a dodgy curry in that cast-iron gut of his, so he's out for the next twenty-four hours at least. We'll need you to ride shotgun provided you can be here by sunup."

"Yeah, okay. I'm up at Rata River. I'll be there in an hour."

"Thanks, mate. See you soon."

His phone still clutched in his hand, Luka sat on the edge of the bed to gather his thoughts. Some days, he couldn't believe the stupidity of people. However, it wasn't his job to pass judgment. He was merely there to pick up the pieces when their lack of judgment got them into trouble.

Dressed and ready to leave, he looked up when his mother knocked on the bedroom door. "Thought I heard you talking on the phone. Is everything all right?"

"Ray's called me into work." Luka shrugged on his jacket and stuffed his toiletries into his weekender. He zipped it shut. "There's a woman injured up in the National Park. They need a hand."

"But you're still on leave until tomorrow, aren't you?"

"Yeah, but one of the other guys is in bed with suspected food poisoning."

"Do you want some breakfast before you go?"

He bent forward and kissed her on the cheek. "No, I'm good. Thanks for the bed. Sorry I won't be able to join you on the ride today."

His mother followed him out to his SUV. Pulling her robe closer against the coolness of the morning, she looked to the pre-dawn sky. "Looks like the rain's drifting in again, so we might not be going out anyway. Call me later and be safe up there."

Luka climbed into the cab and clicked his seatbelt into place. "I will."

Vanessa went to close the driver's door, then stopped. "And don't worry, she'll be fine. Just treat her with care and remember—everyone makes mistakes."

He hesitated at his mother's advice. Who was she referring to? The woman waiting to be rescued, or someone else?

Luka pulled up outside the Search and Rescue office next to the fire station right on five thirty. Although a city, Clifton Falls SAR still relied on a large contingent of volunteers, and that Luka was on the permanent payroll never ceased to amaze him. He was fortunate enough to be doing a job he loved, and that was a plus in today's world.

The office was all lit up when he stepped inside. Ray looked over from his desk. "Good morning."

"Yeah, I'm not feeling the 'good' vibe yet." Luka glanced at the National Park map on the wall. "I was half asleep when we talked. You might have to go over it again."

Ray picked up a long pointer. "Looks like she slipped in this area here from what Nick said. He managed to get her to the hut, but I imagine by now she'll be cold and struggling with the pain."

"Nick?"

"The boyfriend. Reckons he knows the area pretty well."

Unconvinced, Luka glanced around. If the guy knew the area, he should also have known not to tackle it in the kind of conditions they'd had over the weekend. "Where is he?"

"We sent him to the ED so they could check him out. The guy's a mess. He wanted to go back up with you, so we thought we'd get him out of the way for a bit. Collins should be here any minute."

"Where's Russo? Isn't he on duty too?"

"Yeah, but I thought you could assist. Use those gentle hands of yours. I'll stay behind."

Luka chuckled. Ray, who'd been his boss for the best part of four years, was always joking about his hands. "Sure."

Matteo Russo strolled in from the break room, a mug of coffee halfway to his lips. "Hey, mate. Ready to go on a scavenger hunt?"

"Yeah, count me in." Luka checked the computer screen on the front desk. "What's the cloud doing? Do you think we'll get a lift soon?"

"It's not looking good." Ray glanced at his watch. "But you guys better suit up just in case. If we get a window, we should take it."

Paramedic Melissa Collins breezed into the office in her usual whirlwind fashion, suited up and ready to go. She looked from Luka to Russo and back again. "Right, come on. Are you guys ready or what? The cloud's about to lift. I can feel it in my bones."

Melissa—a part-time triage nurse in her forties who ran marathons in her spare time, had four kids, and held a black belt in Taekwondo—was a force to be reckoned with. Always level-headed and focused in a crisis, Luka respected her work ethic immensely.

"I just have to change," Luka said.

"Yes, well, hurry up. Why is it the handsome ones who always drag their feet?"

"Hey," Ray said with a grin. "Be nice. He's officially still on leave."

"Yeah, and I have a movie date with my five-year-old this afternoon. I've been dreaming of hot buttered popcorn all week."

Chuckling, Luka happened to glance out the window as a car sped into the parking lot. When he noticed who sat behind the wheel, he took a second look. *Frank Dobson?*

Mitch and Frank were out of the vehicle and through the door before Luka could react.

"Is there any word?" Frank barked as he charged up to the front desk.

Luka frowned at Mitch as the information circling his brain slowly sank in. "What are you guys doing here?"

"It's CeCe," Mitch said. "Nick left some garbled message on my phone about her having an accident up by Ferguson Hut."

As his stomach lurched, Luka looked at Ray, who was already checking his notes. "Sydney Dobson," Ray said. "Are you guys family?"

"I'm her father," Frank replied, "and this is her brother, Mitch."

"CeCe? It's CeCe who's up there?" Luka asked in disbelief. "In this rough weather? What the hell?"

"Okay, so you obviously know this girl too?" Ray said to him.

"Um, yeah." Luka rubbed the back of his neck. "She's an ex-student of mine."

Frank scoffed and was none too quiet about it. "We're joining the search party. When are they heading in?"

"With the rivers the way they are, we've decided to attempt a chopper run first," Ray said, his attention focused on Frank. "If we can pull it off, we'll be in and out within a couple of hours. Ferguson's a twelve-hour turnaround on foot."

Mitch showed his concern. "Shit. I told her not to go this weekend and now look what's happened. Is the weather clear enough to fly?"

"That's what we're about to find out," Luka replied.

"Right. Sun's up, guys," Ray said. "Let's give this a whirl. If you have to pull back, we'll send in a party on foot." He looked at Luka, understanding in his expression. "You up to this, mate?"

Luka swallowed hard. "Yeah, I'm good."

Luka's stomach lurched as they struck another air pocket. It was always the same when he wasn't at the controls, and despite Russo being an experienced pilot, even he struggled to keep his machine smooth in this kind of weather.

In between focusing his mind on the terrain and the cloud bank rolling in from the west, Luka thought of CeCe—injured, cold, and alone in that hut—and his need to protect her hit him in his already unsettled gut.

His mother's words echoed in his head. *Don't worry...treat her with care...everyone makes mistakes.* He closed his eyes and recalled the girl he used to know. That carefree beach babe who'd rocked his world and turned it upside down. When he thought about it, nothing much had changed in that regard.

Russo's voice sounded in his ear. "You doing okay, O'Leary?"

Luka adjusted his mouthpiece. "All good."

Russo glanced back over his shoulder. "How about you, Melissa?"

"I'll be better when we get our soul home," she replied. "It's not looking too good to the west."

Melissa was right. They'd make it in. But would they get out again?

"At least they made it to the hut," Russo said. "I should be able to find a spot nearby to park the beast."

Battling the relentless rain, Russo touched down in a small clearing adjacent to the hut. Luka and Melissa dashed into a freezing cold room, the potbelly stove in the corner providing no heat. CeCe lay on the bottom bunk in the darkness, huddled in a sleeping bag and space blanket, her eyes like saucers as she stared up at him.

"We have to stop meeting like this." Although a stupid cliché, it was the best he could manage as he crouched and reached for her hand.

"Luka?"

"It's okay. We're going to get you out of here as soon as we can. Your dad and Mitch are waiting for you back at the office, and your mum's on her way."

"It hurts." CeCe pressed back into the mattress and squeezed her eyes shut. "Ouch."

He put his hand to her forehead. Cool to the touch, which

reassured him. "CeCe, this is Melissa," Luka offered by way of introduction. "She's one of the best on our team, so you're in good hands."

"How are you bearing up, sweetheart?" Melissa unzipped the sleeping bag and checked CeCe's vitals. She pointed to the blood-soaked pants.

CeCe's teeth chattered. "It's cold...hurts."

"Hang in there." Luka pulled a pair of scissors out of his bag and cut along the seam line of the pants. He frowned when he noticed a bandage on her thigh.

"We'll have you out of here before you know it. Okay?" he repeated as he carefully peeled the dressing from the laceration. "Melissa's just going to give you something for the pain."

CeCe went rigid. "No. I hate needles."

"Me too," Melissa soothed while Luka pulled antiseptic, a syringe, and bandages out of the bag. "Can you tell me what day it is, CeCe?" She swabbed a spot on CeCe's thigh and plunged the needle home.

"Ouch." Her breathing quickened. "That hurt. Sunday. Where's Nick? Is he okay?"

"He's safe and well. Do you know where you are, sweetheart?"

"Middle of nowhere," she muttered. "I know where I'd rather be."

Melissa dressed CeCe's thigh with Luka acting as her assistant. "Yeah? Anywhere special?" she asked.

"Sandwater Bay," CeCe whispered and looked up at Luka. "Nude surfing."

Luka smiled. He wished they were there too. Walking through the shallows hand in hand. Eating breakfast in the back of the Kombi. Having sex at sunset.

Melissa chuckled. "Yeah? Can't say I've ever tried that."

"You should. Best feeling ever. But you need a...a watchdog."

Russo's voice filled Luka's radio. "You ready to roll? Over."

"Almost. We have a laceration to the left thigh that we're sticking a Band-Aid on. Over."

"Copy that. Don't muck around. Mist's rolling in thick and fast. Think I might let you take the controls on the way back. I hate flying through this pea-soup crap. Over."

"Roger that. We'll be there as soon as we can. Over."

"Right, CeCe," Melissa said as she finished securing the bandage. "This young man will escort you to your pumpkin carriage that awaits outside. You happy with that?"

CeCe nodded, and when Luka caught her eye, she smiled at him like he remembered from his dreams. He leaned in closer. "This will hurt a little, but I've got you. Okay?"

"Okay," she whispered. "I'm sorry. I wanted to turn back."

He helped her sit up. Even with twigs in her hair and her face splattered in mud, she looked beautiful. "Don't worry. We all make mistakes." Luka slipped one arm under her and scooped her up. "Let's get out of here."

41

SEA OF FACES

Fluorescent lighting blazed overhead in the Emergency Department of Clifton Falls General Hospital. CeCe had been waiting almost an hour but still hadn't seen a doctor. She closed her eyes, trying not to think of what might have been.

The rescue flight, through shrouds of mist and heavy rain, had been the most terrifying experience of her life. Every time they hit an air pocket, her stomach lurched, and despite the injection, pain still pinched her tight.

But the entire time they were in the air, she'd been unable to take her eyes off Luka at the controls.

Now, lying on the gurney while waiting to be seen, she ached all over. Luka, Melisa, and Russo had been amazing, totally professional and in control. But when they dropped her off, Luka didn't stay, not for more than a few minutes anyway. And as he'd disappeared into a sea of faces—her parents, Mitch, Tayla, and the nurses on duty—he hadn't even said goodbye.

Maybe it was for the best. She'd fallen in love with him the last time he'd rescued her, and now wasn't the time for history to repeat itself.

Seated in a gray plastic chair to her right, her mother held CeCe's hand, and across the room, her father paced, as he did in times of crisis.

"Why don't you go get yourself a coffee?" Andrea said to her husband.

He stopped pacing. "I still can't get my head around this. That Nick should have his PLB rammed up his backside, so he doesn't forget it next time."

CeCe lifted her head off the pillow. "Dad! That's a terrible thing to say. It wasn't Nick's fault. I should have insisted we stay home. But I didn't."

"Then there's that Luka fella," Frank continued as if he hadn't heard her. "Making eyes at you like you're his." He huffed. "Telling everyone you're an 'ex-student.' As if. I'm getting too old for this crap."

CeCe and her mother shared a knowing smile. Her dad could be a loose cannon, but she still loved him to pieces. Being the youngest, she'd always been his little girl. When she was in her early teens, she had followed him all over the orchard, fascinated by the growing process and eager to learn the ropes.

As was the case in many father-daughter relationships, they'd often butted heads during her teenage years, especially when it came to her riding around in fast cars with boys. But despite this, he'd always been there: playing taxi driver, slipping her extra pocket money when she needed it, and helping to pick up the pieces of her grieving heart when she'd lost her best friend.

After Anna died, they'd sometimes swapped rooms—Frank in hers and CeCe tucked up next to her mother in the master bedroom's king-size bed, sobbing herself to sleep.

"What's taking them so long?" Her father's question

intruded into CeCe's thoughts. She wished Luka were still there, holding her hand, telling her everything would be all right.

"Why don't you get yourself a coffee and something to eat?" Andrea repeated. "I'll text you if the doctor comes."

"Yeah, okay." He rubbed the back of his neck. "Hospitals do my damn head in. The entire health system needs a serious overhaul."

As they watched her father walk away, CeCe managed a small chuckle. "How do you live with him?"

Her mother winked. "He's a cuddly kitty when we're alone." She raised a brow. "Romantic, too."

"Okay, Mum. TMI. Let's keep things PG, shall we?"

"We do have a love life, you know." Her mother chuckled as she stood. "Right, I'm going to stretch my legs and get some chocolate from the vending machine. I'll be back in a sec."

As her mother left the cubicle, CeCe closed her eyes, and memories of the night in the hut flooded her thoughts. The biting cold, the eerie silence, and the shadows in the darkness. It was one of those 'if only' situations that return to haunt you whenever you're alone after making a foolish mistake. While it would have been so easy to blame Nick, CeCe had no interest in playing the blame game. She'd chosen to go with him, even if it had been under persuasion.

After a day filled with examinations and X-rays, they transferred CeCe to a ward for overnight observation, the suspected fracture to her collarbone confirmed, and the thigh laceration stitched and dressed again.

CeCe was drifting off for a late afternoon nap when she heard, "What on earth have you been up to now?"

She opened her eyes to see her cousin standing before her, sporting a wide grin and a beautiful baby-blue cashmere sweater. "Molly! What are you doing here?"

"I heard you went for a stroll in the national park and ended up in a dead-end gully." Molly kissed her on the cheek. "You okay?"

"Yeah. But I lost my new backpack—it cost me over three hundred dollars."

"I'd say that's the least of your worries. What were you guys thinking, out in that atrocious weather? You could have got yourself killed."

"I know. It was all kinds of stupid. But I'm fine. And guess who rescued me?"

Molly pulled up a seat and flicked her hair back over her shoulder. She thought for a moment until it dawned on her. "No way! Hot Chopper Guy?"

"It was like the rabbit-hole incident all over again, but on steroids."

"This is just too good. Tell me everything."

They discharged CeCe the following morning. Back at her parents' house, her mother couldn't stop fussing, and as CeCe lay on the sofa in the sunroom that afternoon—full of a home-cooked lunch—the events of the weekend seemed somehow less significant.

Nick had arrived at the hospital before she'd even seen the doctor, offering apologies and bearing gifts. She'd assured him he had nothing to apologize for but was thankful his comment about the archaeologist meant she could gracefully bow out of their platonic relationship. Nick was a nice guy, full of enthusiasm and with a genuine interest in the world around him, but he wasn't the guy for her.

CeCe picked up the paperback Luka gave her all those years

before and opened it to the first chapter. Despite reading it the week after he'd left Tulloch Point, she wanted to read it again. It still surprised her that he'd read the one she'd given him, even if he had made light of it the morning after they last slept together.

Judging a book by its first line had long been a habit of CeCe's. When she worked at the library, she'd often opened books at random to peek at chapter one. First lines fascinated her, and David Baldacci had some great first liners. It was time to lose herself in the pages once again.

Turned out, her body had other ideas.

CeCe stirred at the sound of a vehicle in the driveway. She sat up and rubbed her eyes, then glanced out the window.

Luka.

While butterflies danced to some brassy tune in her stomach, she ran her fingers through her hair, a natural reaction to the anticipation of his presence. She heard her mother welcome him into the kitchen, then chit-chat back and forth, his deep voice planted in memories from her past.

Her mother came into the sunroom and moved to fluff up CeCe's pillows. "Look who's here. Shall I make you both a cup of tea?"

He stood not two feet away—looking all kinds of awkward but still impossibly handsome in a black shirt and faded Levi's —a huge bunch of flowers in his hand. "Thanks, but not for me."

"CeCe?"

"No, I'm good too, thanks, Mum."

Luka stepped forward as Andrea left the room, the flowers held loose in his grip. He placed them on the table next to her and sat in the adjacent chair. "How are you feeling?"

She set the book down next to the flowers, the effect of his presence immediate as she tried to play it cool. "Good, thanks to you."

He glanced at the cover and smiled but offered no verbal recognition. "I was only doing my job."

"That's what you said last time." She wanted to add 'and look how that turned out,' but Luka wasn't here to be flirted with.

"What did they say about the leg?"

"Oh, the cut's long, but not too deep. They were impressed by Melissa's handiwork."

She hated this—the small talk of ex-lovers turned acquaintances who share an unforgotten story, the strain in her voice as it struggled against the memories. He nodded and held her gaze, perhaps thinking back to the night of the benefit dinner, when they'd whispered lovers' words into the darkness and the world seemed to steady its course for a few hours.

Will you dance with me? Hold me like I'm precious?

He stood and crossed to the window, her gaze following his every step. "This is a great spot," he said as he glanced back at her over his shoulder.

"It is. Mum and Dad love living in Clifton Falls. Dad's planting herbs to jump on 'the organics bandwagon' as he calls it."

CeCe leaned back and closed her eyes briefly. While she'd be forever grateful to him, she was exhausted and couldn't cope with small talk. She wanted him to sit beside her, hold her hand and tell her about the books he'd read recently, just like he used to.

As if sensing her unease, he turned to face her. "Anyway, I'd better go. It's my day off, so I'm on my way to Mum and Dad's for dinner. I'm pleased you're on the mend."

"Thanks." CeCe thought back to when she met Vanessa and

Liam at Mitch's birthday party and then again at the gala. Luka was similar to his mother in his manner, but apart from his eye color, he most resembled his father. "They seem like good people, your parents."

"They are. We're lucky, aren't we, to have such strong family support?"

She nodded her agreement. That was another thing they had in common: supportive families. Luka stilled, unspoken words perching on the tip of his tongue perhaps, but that stillness lasted mere seconds before his restlessness returned.

There was so much she wanted to say to him—share her regrets and the promises she'd made to herself as she lay on that bottom bunk in the cold, dark hut. But he seemed eager to leave, and she had no right to ask him to stay. "Thank you for the beautiful flowers, and thanks for holding back on the lecture."

He gave a shrug. "You might want to add another PLB to your Christmas list."

"No need. I won't be repeating that experience again. Give me the beach any day."

CeCe caught his quick frown. Apparently, she'd mentioned nude surfing to Melissa, back at the hut, but that part of Sunday was hazy. Was his mind returning to Sandwater Bay too? What else had she said that day?

When Luka slipped his hands into his pockets, CeCe raised her head and held his gaze. The anticipated kiss goodbye on her cheek didn't eventuate, and she mentally admonished herself for expecting it. They weren't friends. Not anymore. "Anyway, take care."

"You too." CeCe went to stand, but he stopped her with more polite words. *Please don't get up. I'll see myself out. Bye…*

THE YURT

CeCe drove down the Eastern Pacific Highway and into Carter Bay Road. She wasn't familiar with the area, and as she traveled north in search of Luka's property, the number of homes along the route surprised her.

No mailbox stood at his gate, just a rustic post with *sixty-two* carved into its wood and stained in black. She looked out the windscreen to where a late-model SUV sat parked in front of a yurt.

As she followed the treelined driveway across the field, CeCe took a calming breath. To the right of a shelterbelt, a large contemporary house nestled into the hillside as if it belonged. And on the lot next door, row upon row of green strawberry plants sat atop their raised beds.

CeCe cut the engine and stilled for a moment. She'd texted him almost a week ago to ask if she could visit, and while she knew a proper thank you was long overdue, her stomach still tightened with nerves.

A knock on her side window startled her from her thoughts. Luka stood at the car door, dressed in a black linen shirt and light blue jeans, his usually short hair slightly longer and hanging over his forehead as usual. When he opened her door, she grabbed her bag and the container from her passenger seat and tried to still her unease.

He leaned over, his hand on the doorframe. "Hi. Are you coming in?"

She looked up, lifted her sunglasses into her hair, and nodded. "I guess that's why I'm here."

"How's the collarbone?"

"Good, thanks. But my shoulder's still pretty weak."

CeCe stepped from the car and followed him up the steps and into the yurt, her sight coming to rest on the spines of the roof structure for a moment. "This is cool. It's a lot bigger than it looks from the outside."

"Yeah. I like having plenty of room." He gestured to a pair of chairs flanking a large TV. "Have a seat."

"And you have a new vehicle?"

"Yeah, I thought it was about time."

She offered him the container. "For you...as a thank you. Apple cake."

Luka accepted the gift with both hands. Today wasn't the first time she'd made him apple cake, and she wondered if he remembered the last time. "Thanks." He moved to the counter and put the cake down. "Would you like some?"

"No. I'm fine. I'd love a green tea, though."

As Luka flicked the kettle on, CeCe studied the interior. It was moderately messy, with clothes lying in piles on the bed and several books stacked on the floor. After their last visit at her parents' place, she'd expected to feel more relaxed in his presence, but her skin prickled and heat pooled between her thighs even at the sight of him.

Luka placed two mugs of tea on a small antique bronze table between the chairs and took the seat adjacent to hers.

"How long have you lived in the yurt?"

He sipped his drink. "A few weeks—it's just until I move into the main house. It helps to be onsite at the moment."

"So, this land is yours?"

"Yes, I bought it last year. You would have seen the house as you drove in. All going well, I should be moving in next week."

"Just in time for Christmas. Did you design it?"

"Me, no. William Cook from CookHouse Projects is an old friend of Mum's. He and his wife, Jessa, worked on it together. They're an amazing team."

CeCe couldn't help but notice how he'd crossed one foot over the other, his toes perfectly pedicured. "Do you think you'll stay here long term? In Clifton Falls, I mean."

"Sure. I'd planned to go to the States in the new year, but that's not a happening thing with the border restrictions. I know I could still go, but..."

CeCe sipped, then wrapped both hands around her mug, its warmth welcome. "Anyway, I wanted to thank you for the rescue. I realize you were just doing your job, but... We shouldn't have been up there with the weather closing in, and that dubious decision caused you guys a whole lot of unnecessary stress."

"Yeah. Maybe your boyfriend should have known better. But hey, we all push the boundaries sometimes. I guess luck wasn't on your side that weekend."

They lapsed into silence. It was gracious of Luka to flash the luck card when CeCe knew only too well it was hers and Nick's stupidity that put everyone in danger. "He's not my boyfriend, I told you that, remember? He's seeing an archaeologist."

Luka grinned. "An archaeologist? In Clifton Falls?"

CeCe found herself smiling with him. "Her specialty is seventeenth-century Māori artifacts. The subject fascinates him."

"Really? Although, being part Māori, I can see the appeal." He hesitated. "And what about you?"

"Me?"

"Are you seeing anyone?"

She shook her head. "A broken collarbone and hot dates don't really mix."

He smiled into his mug before taking a sip. "No, guess they don't."

She wanted to ask him the same question but couldn't bring herself to do so. It was none of her business. Not anymore. CeCe picked up her bag from the floor and pulled out a wrapped package. She offered it over the table. "I almost forget this."

"For me as well?" He unwrapped the hardcover autobiography and flipped it over to read the back blurb, a soft grin in place. "Thanks, I've been wanting to read this for ages."

"It's a signed copy."

Luka looked up in surprise. "How did you manage that?"

"Ally's in the music business, so she knows a guy who knows a girl."

He opened it to the title page and read the inscription: "'To Chopper Guy. Enjoy the read.'" He lifted from his seat to kiss her on the cheek, then sat back down again. "That's awesome. Thank you so much."

CeCe steadied her breath. "No problem. I couldn't think of what else to get you."

"I love reading, you know that." Luka set the gift on the table. "Mum said you've booked in some riding lessons."

"Well, our group has. It's not for a while yet. I have to wait until I'm properly healed."

He nodded. His gaze held hers as she spoke, and she wanted to reach over and kiss him. And not on the cheek.

"There's three of us so far," she continued, trying to shift that last thought. "All from that day at Station Winery. The other two can already ride, but they want to brush up on their skills."

"Let me guess, Jaz and Tracy?"

CeCe flashed him a grin and nodded. Jaz was dying to go to the Rata River Equestrian Center, hoping she'd get another peek at Luka in his jodhpurs. She'd considered buying her boyfriend a pair for dress-ups, but as he had at least fifty pounds on Luka, mostly in the form of a beer gut, Jaz didn't think they'd have the same appeal.

"They were hilarious that day," he said. "But kind of scary too."

"Yeah, they're heaps of fun."

"Text me when you're going. If I'm free, maybe I could come with you."

As if. "I don't think so."

He looked puzzled. "Why not?"

"You know why not, Mr. Good-at-Everything. You make me nervous."

"Is that really how you see me? As a smug all-rounder?"

"Not necessarily smug. It's just..." CeCe hesitated. She knew what she wanted to say but struggled to phrase it. "Maybe it's a teacher-student throwback. That 'air of authority' vibe you have going on."

Luka regarded her over the rim of his mug before setting it down. "I stopped thinking of you as my student a long time ago, CeCe." His tone and use of her name sent a shiver down her spine, and strangely enough, reminded her of the days spent in his classroom. "Besides, there are some things I'm totally useless at."

"Name one."

"Tennis. I can't hit a tennis ball to save myself. Maybe you could give me some lessons when your shoulder's back to full strength."

"How do you know I play tennis?"

"I watched you once. Coaching the juniors after class. Your tennis skills were legendary around the school. But you gave it up for a while?"

"Yes. After Anna died." CeCe realized she hadn't thought of Anna as much lately. Perhaps time healed after all. "She was the better player, in my opinion, but I could still hold my own. We played together all the time—until Dillon came between us."

He nodded. "Yep, I understand. I picked a fight with a friend over a girl once. I was fourteen and thought we'd be in love forever."

CeCe tried to imagine Luka as a fighter and failed. "No way."

"It's true. Broke my little finger." He held it up so she could see the bend. "And you've met my mother—she's all about peace, love, and mung beans. She was furious."

"Well, you can hardly blame her." CeCe sat forward in her chair. "Anyway, I should let you get back to your day."

They both stood and walked to the door. As they stepped onto the gravel driveway, she turned to look at him. "Thank you for the tea."

"My pleasure. And thanks for the cake and book."

CeCe glanced away, stalling, and when she looked back, a thickness constricted her throat.

"What are you doing here? Really?" Luka asked, a frown settling on his forehead.

Tears threatened, but she was determined not to let them fall. "I came to say thank you." She swallowed hard. "As I said. But..."

He reached for her hand. "Hey, it's okay."

"Is it? Up there in that hut, all alone with nothing but my crazy thoughts for company, you were on my mind. A lot. And then, there you were, kind and gentle and...well, I felt so small and insignificant. Like my dreams were unimportant and that all the hours I'd poured into my business had stopped me from seeing the big picture. Robbed me of my emotional focus.

"And now, I have no clue what life's about. Why are we here? To run on an endless treadmill, trying to keep up while we pretend everything's okay?" She swiped her eyes with the back of her hand and sniffed.

"I was so scared, Luka. Scared I'd never see you again, or that if I did, you'd be like this—aloof and indifferent—and that makes me so terribly sad. Sadder than the day you left Tulloch Point—the day you stood on your driveway and told me I shouldn't be there."

She rummaged in her bag for a tissue and pulled it free. Wiped her eyes. "And I wish we could go back to Sandwater Bay, eat burgers and fries out of a brown paper bag, and swim naked in the river. I wish we could live like there's no tomorrow and love like there is."

"CeCe, it's okay," he repeated, so softly she hardly heard him.

She looked up at him and dropped her sunglasses into place. "No, it's not okay. And it never will be."

"Hey, come here." He reached for her, but she pulled away, climbed into her car, and drove off.

Luka stayed in CeCe's head on the drive home, and as she turned left into Lime Tree Hill's driveway, she failed to stem the tears.

Other than Pixie, who rushed to her side as soon as she walked through the bottom door, the packing shed was empty.

Tayla had texted earlier to say she'd left some moussaka in the oven, and as she climbed the stairs, a wave of garlic greeted her. Now she was on maternity leave, Tayla's nesting instincts had increased tenfold, and it made CeCe smile for the first time that day.

CeCe turned on the TV and flicked through to her favorite music channel. Then, with her hands covered in oven gloves, she removed the small casserole dish and set it on the cooktop. She grabbed a fork from the drawer and took a small mouthful, but when the heat of it burned her tongue, she left it to cool, planning to return to it later.

Although just after seven, all CeCe wanted was to crawl into bed. She shuffled into the bathroom and filled the tub as Pixie fussed around her. Lying in a hot bath minutes later, she picked up her phone, unlocked it, and scanned her texts.

Luka: I don't mean to be aloof and indifferent. It's a self-protection thing.

She thought about this for a moment. He wanted to protect himself from her; that was the crux of it.

CeCe: I get that. Guess I was trying to do the same. But that doesn't seem so important anymore.

Luka: Well, maybe that's your answer. Only you can work out what's important to you.

The hand holding her phone draped over the rim of the tub, she lay her head back as a Gone West song drifted down the hallway. The water cooled, and she went through the motions—drying off, brushing her teeth, and her skincare routine—longing for this day to be over.

CeCe climbed into a cold bed and picked up her e-reader, but put it back down again, her energy spent. Even so, sleep took the long way around, and when she eventually drifted off, there was nothing deep about it.

When she entered the kitchen the following morning, the moussaka still sat on the counter.

43

THE FITZROY

The Fitzroy was full to bursting when CeCe and Tracy walked into the pub for the bi-monthly Business After Dark quiz night. Three other members of their team had already grabbed a table and were waiting for the quizmaster to arrive.

After ordering a drink at the bar, they took a seat with the others. CeCe looked toward the door as a group of guys pushed their way through the crowd. She recognized one as a friend of Mitch's and when he lifted his chin in recognition and offered a smile, she returned the gesture.

She was about to look away when Luka appeared at the back of the group, smiling at the woman beside him as she stepped closer to whisper something in his ear. CeCe sipped her lime and soda, trying to ignore the heat flushing her cheeks at the sight of him.

As teams of players filled the tables, CeCe flicked her sight toward the bar, watching Luka interact with the woman. Smiles and laughter moved freely between them, and at one point, she struggled to tear her eyes away. Before leaving home, the thought of a night out excited her, but she'd never expected to run into Hot Chopper Guy at the Fitzroy. Wouldn't have thought he was the pub-quiz type.

Distracted, she didn't noticed Jaz slipping into the seat beside her until she spoke. "Sorry I'm late, everyone." She looked at CeCe. "Thanks for filling in."

"My pleasure. I love quiz nights. Haven't been to one since I was at uni."

CeCe looked up and caught Luka's gaze. She froze. The acknowledgment he offered could hardly be called a smile, but at least he didn't frown or ignore her. She watched him settle at a table with his team, now wishing she'd refused when Jaz pleaded her to fill in for the night, while at the same time musing about how hot Luka looked in tight black jeans and a cinnamon-colored linen shirt.

As they waited, CeCe recalled her emotional outburst the day she visited him at the yurt. The contact she'd expected in the following days hadn't eventuated, and seeing him now with the blonde in the white jeans and midriff-revealing top, she understood why.

Eyes fixed on the quizmaster as he perched on a high stool behind the mic, CeCe picked up her pencil, relieved that Luka wasn't in her line of sight and admonishing herself for her sudden burst of jealousy. She had no claim over him. He could see who he liked.

"Welcome to quiz night at the Fitzroy, people. Let's start the ball rolling with a ten pointer in 'who said it first?'"

"I love these." Tracy clapped her hands, and CeCe grinned at her enthusiasm.

The quizmaster read from the paper in his hand as the question appeared on the flat screen behind him. "According to popular opinion, who was the first person to coin the phrase, 'send him packing'?"

As he repeated the question, Jaz whispered, "That would be Shakespeare. It's from Henry the Fourth."

Still smiling, CeCe shook her head at the irony.

If she'd hoped to ignore Luka for the rest of the evening, she was out of luck. When she returned from the restroom at half-time, she found Luka at their table, flashing his charm between Jaz and Tracy as he got reacquainted with them.

CeCe wanted to return to the restroom before he noticed her, but when the quiz master shuffled up to the mic, she had no choice but to slip back into her seat and say, "Luka. How are you?"

"Well, thanks, CeCe." He held her gaze with those sexy eyes, and as much as she wanted to look away, she couldn't until he did so first. "Right, I'd better rejoin my team. Nice seeing you both again, ladies."

"You too, Luka," Jaz said as Tracy smiled up at him.

The three of them watched him return to his table, and when Jaz caught CeCe's eye, she arched her brows and whispered, "He's keen."

"Pity you're taken then," CeCe whispered back as she picked up her pencil and doodled on the paper in front of her.

"I don't mean me, Little Miss Innocent."

"He said three words to me, and coolly."

"Yeah, that's what I mean. He's keen."

"Listen up, people," the quiz master said into the mic. "Seventies music for five easy points. What was Fleetwood Mac's biggest-selling album?"

CeCe glanced over at the woman sitting shoulder to shoulder with Luka, wrote *Rumours* on her answer sheet, and pushed it into the middle of the table for the others to see.

The following day, Luka knocked and popped his head around Mitch's office door. "Hey, mate. Any idea where CeCe is? I tried her lab, but it's locked."

"So you're not here to join me in a beer then? That's a shame." Mitch shut the lid of his computer and stood to greet him. "She's down at the store with Jay, setting up her product display. It's going on sale tomorrow."

Luka nodded. "Okay. I might go see if she's still there. Raincheck on the beer, though."

They walked into the packing shed and out onto the driveway. "Are you going to tell me what's up with you and my sister?"

Puffs of gray cloud partially blocked the sun, holding the promise of rain. Luka pulled his aviators out of his shirt pocket and put them on. "No. Because I don't know myself."

"She's been pretty unsettled since the hut incident but seems to be slowly picking herself up again."

Luka nodded. He'd seen that for himself when she visited him at the yurt, but she'd looked okay at the Fitzroy. Distant, but okay. "That's to be expected after what she went through."

"Yeah. She keeps saying she's fine, so I guess we just have to be there for her."

Luka opened the door of his SUV, his jaw clenching as he recalled the scene in the hut. CeCe cold and scared as the mist did its best to swallow their attempt to fly her back to safety.

Mitch checked his watch. "Right, I'd better get home for dinner. Maybe you could persuade CeCe to knock off early. She's working way too many hours."

Luka chuckled. His days of persuading CeCe to do anything were long gone. "Or not. Say hi to Tayla for me."

"Will do."

Luka drove from the packing shed to the farm gate store and parked beside the building. Jay's Vespa was nowhere to be seen, and as he climbed from the cab, he spotted CeCe through the window—earbuds in and her head canted to one side as she studied her handiwork.

With the store now closed, he knocked on the main door, then again in an attempt to attract her attention. The corners of her mouth twitched when she realized it was him. A good sign.

She unlocked the door and opened it, then removed her earbuds. "You know we're closed, right? But I guess I could put a carton of milk and a loaf of sourdough on your tab."

Her smile had an immediate effect. He wanted to reach down and adjust his jeans around the heat settling in his groin. "I don't need milk or bread."

CeCe broke the hold of his gaze and nodded. She turned away and rearranged the jars of Botanical Ce skincare on the endcap in front of her. "What do you think of my display?"

"It looks great. I bet it's a good feeling, making it this far."

"Yeah, I'm happy with it. I just hope we sell some."

"I'm sure you will." He picked up a jar, studied the label, and put it back again. "Do you have plans for dinner?"

CeCe checked her watch. "Um…I didn't realize it was so late. I haven't thought that far ahead."

"We could drive to Little Brown Barn and share some tapas."

She didn't even pause to consider it. "You know what? I'm exhausted. I might just stroll up the hill and make myself an egg on toast."

A void of silence stretched between them. She'd brushed him off again, albeit gently. Luka followed her out the door and waited while she locked it behind her. Despite the rain clouds, it was a beautiful evening: calm and warm, its gray light softening the tiredness in her expression. "Hop in. I'll drive you."

CeCe didn't refuse. They drove up the long driveway without speaking until he pulled into a park outside the packing shed.

"Thanks for the ride. Are you on your way up to Rata River? I have a gift pack for your mum in the lab. I can run in and get it."

He lowered his window and cut the engine. "Not tonight. I came to see you."

"Me?"

Luka shifted in his seat to face her. "We're not together, CeCe."

"And never were," she muttered.

"I'm not talking about us. I mean Zoe, from the pub." He didn't expand on his explanation. It was a matter-of-fact statement that needed no further clarification.

"Even if you were, it's none of my business who you choose to spend your time with."

"It will always be your business." Luka spoke the words softly but with purpose. "Our history will make sure of that. And no matter how many times you keep telling yourself you're too busy for a relationship, we both know that's one of life's greatest excuses. You don't want me to move on, but you can't admit it to either of us."

CeCe huffed and shook her head. "How do you know what I want?"

"Because underneath that feigned indifference and your 'I'm too busy for a complication' mantra, your body language betrays you."

She turned away and stared out the passenger window. "You're just like Tom."

Luka ran his fingers through his hair and sighed. "Who's Tom?"

"The guy in the book you gave me. He sent Eleanor mixed messages all the time."

"And you think that's what I've been doing? Sending mixed messages?"

CeCe looked his way. "You said you didn't want me, yet here you are."

"That's not what I said, and you know it. But to be clear—I told you I didn't want casual, but instead of addressing that, you take off for the weekend with that idiot geologist to what... make me jealous?"

"Do you hear yourself, Luka? I've never tried to make you jealous. Why would I? Nick is just a friend."

"Yeah? Some friend he turned out to be."

CeCe folded her arms over her chest. "Some days, I really don't like you very much."

"Just some days?"

Luka's question went unanswered. He expected her to open the door and take off inside, but she leaned her head back against the headrest and sighed.

"Some days, I can handle, but if it's most days, we're in trouble. I don't want to share you with other men, and I won't sit here and pretend otherwise."

"And what about the women you've been with?"

Her words echoed around the cab of his SUV. "That's no longer relevant. And for the record, yes, I was pissed when I found out you'd gone into the national park with Nick—and I'm not just referring to your blatant disregard for the weather conditions. So please don't pretend you're confused. You're a discerning woman, and this 'I have no idea what's going on' bullshit doesn't suit you. But I'm not going to chase you, CeCe. If you want me, you know what to do."

"Really?"

"And as for the book, Eleanor sent mixed messages of her own."

"Yes, well, she had cause."

"Don't we all?"

CeCe reached for the door handle. "Okay, this is one of those days where you're really pissing me off." She jumped from the cab and shut the door before he had time to react.

"Hey, CeCe?" Luka called after her as she headed for the packing shed. She turned. "Where's my goodnight kiss?"

CeCe showed him her middle finger and stormed off.

44

CHOPPER GUY

After sleeping badly, CeCe stirred just before dawn, her shoulders tense and sweat trickling between her naked breasts. She lay in bed until long after Ned's rooster started its racket, worrying about her sales targets and what she should—and shouldn't—have said to Luka two days before.

After a long hot shower, she picked up her phone to check her texts as she strolled through to her bedroom.

Luka: You still pissed at me, or is it one of those other days?
CeCe: Depends.
Luka: OK. Can you spare a couple of hours after lunch? I'd like to take you somewhere.

CeCe dropped her phone on the bed, amused and curious at the same time. She'd verbally kicked and screamed at him the last time they saw one another, and now he wanted to 'take her somewhere'? She decided to keep their interaction light.

CeCe: Like on a date?

Luka: Do I detect a good mood, or did I miss the sarcasm in cyber translation?

CeCe: The translation was just fine.

Luka: Great. I'll pick you up at Mitch and Tayla's @ 1. Bring a jacket.

CeCe: Why Mitch and Tayla's?

Luka: It's just more convenient.

As she worked through the morning, CeCe attempted to focus on packing orders and checking payments through her online store. Unable to concentrate, she stopped work at eleven thirty, ate some lunch, and changed for their Sunday drive or whatever it was Luka had planned. Maybe he wanted to talk some more about the space he was giving her.

Eye roll to that.

The stroll through the tree rows to her brother's place helped her unwind, and as she approached the gate leading to the homestead, she knew what she had to do. Enjoy their friendship for what it was and embrace that ex-lovers truce they'd both committed to.

Tayla greeted her at the back door and joined her on the veranda to wait for Luka's arrival. CeCe checked her watch and scratched her palms with her fingertips as nerves got the better of her.

"You seem a little on edge." Tayla picked up her knitting needles and cast on several stitches from a soft pink skein of wool.

"I am bit. Luka has that effect on me. Crazy, isn't it?" CeCe looked out over the orchard to gather her thoughts. Maybe it was time for her to learn how to knit. Something to take her mind off her work…and other things. "Before the disastrous hut sleepover, I worried that if I let him back into my life, I'd lose the essence of who I was. I thought we could have some fun with no commitment, but Luka decided that wasn't his thing."

"Did that surprise you?"

She shrugged. "It's hard to know how much of yourself to give sometimes, and…how much to take from the other person. Does that make sense?"

"Sure. Maybe he wants more than you're prepared to give."

"He kind of said as much, but…who would know?"

CeCe glanced up at the noise of a helicopter overhead, and as it drew closer, she shielded her eyes with her hand to watch it fly over.

"He's here," Tayla said with a grin as it landed in the field adjacent to their house.

CeCe stood, her eyes round as she watched the blades slow. "What do you mean?"

"Luka."

"What?" She turned to Tayla. "No way! He's come to collect me in a chopper?"

"Looks like it. It's not the first time he's parked on our hay paddock. Anyway, off you go. And keep an open mind."

"But—"

Tayla kept knitting and smiled. "Don't overthink it. Just enjoy the afternoon."

"What do you think you're doing?" she yelled as Luka jumped the fence and strolled toward her, his aviators shielding his eyes against the sunlight.

He grinned. "I told you. I want to take you somewhere."

"Yes, but…"

Luka offered his hand. "Come on."

Looking back at Tayla, she hesitated.

"You'll be fine," he soothed. "I promise."

"Have fun, you two." Tayla waved and walked back inside, leaving CeCe alone with Luka.

Head down and jacket pulled close across her chest, CeCe followed him to the helicopter, the same one he'd flown at Station Winery. Once on board, he handed her a headset before fitting his own.

She held on tight to the sides of her seat as they lifted off, that usual nervousness in her stomach refusing to settle. "Where are we going?"

He headed out over Petrie Bay, then inland to the west. "Up to the national park. It's magic on a beautiful day."

"Did your boss say it was okay?"

"I'm not working today."

"Then how come you have the use of a chopper?"

"This is mine, not SAR's."

What? "You own your own chopper? How did I not know this?"

"There are lots of things you don't know about me." He flashed her a cocky grin, and as they flew over the rugged terrain of the park, her hands relaxed at her sides. Luka was right: it was amazing on a beautiful day—lush and green against the blue sky.

Luka landed in the same spot as Russo had, adjacent to the hut that had protected her from the elements all those weeks ago. She looked at him and frowned as the blades above spun to a slow turn. "I can't go inside."

"That's up to you. I know you were scared, but this hut kept you safe. Imagine how much worse it would have been if you were stuck where you fell." He offered his hand once more. "Coming?"

Rooted to the spot, CeCe looked at the hut, then back at Luka. "Will you stay with me?"

"Always. Come on."

The door stood ajar when they reached the hut, and CeCe hesitated once again before stepping across the threshold. She looked around. The room was larger than she recalled and tidy, as if someone had given it a going-over with a broom and a bucket of hot, soapy water. Although it didn't smell as bad as it had that night, there was still a mustiness about the space, like too many people had slept in there with unwashed socks on.

CeCe sat on the same bottom bunk, her arms folded against one another. "I lost my watch under this bunk. It's funny what comes back to you. I loved that watch. It was a Garmin—kept reminding me when to move. By the time you turned up, I'd forgotten all about it."

Luka dropped to his knees and searched under the slats. "Looks like you might have to ask Santa for a new one."

"Yes, I guess I will." She trailed a finger along the end of the bunk and dropped her shoulders. "Thank you for bringing me here. You're right. It doesn't seem so scary in the sunlight."

"I'm glad. It's such an amazing place—I mean the park, not the hut. I didn't want one unpleasant experience to taint your memories of it. My father always says it's good to tie up the loose ends of your life."

CeCe nodded. Since the rescue, she'd tried to banish her time in this hut from her thoughts, but whenever vivid images surfaced, that's exactly what the memories felt like. Frayed loose ends. "That's good advice."

"Are you ready to go?"

She swallowed hard, determined not to cry in front of him. "May I have a minute?"

"Sure, I'll just be outside," he said gently.

Standing in the middle of the confined space, CeCe failed to stop a few tears from falling. She swiped her cheeks with the back of both hands, and just like last time, wished she had a rock. "Thanks, Anna," she whispered. "If it was you looking after me that night, thank you so much."

Luka looked up as she walked toward him. He opened his arms, and as she slipped into his embrace, it felt like coming home. They held one another in comfortable silence for several moments until she pulled back and gazed up at him. "You really are a kind man, Luka O'Leary."

"Yeah?" He put on his aviators and smiled. "Come on, let's fly over the falls on the way home."

Home.

45

KOMBI GIRL

The moment she saw the Kombi, all shiny and new, CeCe couldn't stop grinning. She'd scraped and saved for years to get it to this point. First, they'd had to remove all the rust, then rebuild the engine, next came the interior, and lastly, the paint job.

She'd kept the original teal green color, teaming it with off-white leather seating. Given its state when they started the restoration, CeCe had expected it to come out no more than okay. But standing beside it now with the guys who'd rebuilt it, she couldn't believe how amazing it looked.

"Isn't she special?" The younger of the two men beamed with pride.

"Wow, I can't believe it turned out so well."

"She's a beautiful thing," Andy, the older man, said. "We had a bit of a ripple in the paintwork on the left guard, so I had to respray that, but all in all, I'd say it's a success." He handed her the keys. "Here, she's all yours."

"I'm almost too scared to drive it. I hope it starts first time."

"Course it will," Andy said. "It has a totally reconditioned engine. No breaking down on our watch."

She stepped forward and hugged both men in turn. "I can't thank you enough. Mum's going to be blown away."

As she drove through town, CeCe swayed in her seat, singing along to the radio. She finally had her precious Kombi back! Her first stop was her parents' place. In his usual no-nonsense fashion, her father had supervised the restoration from the get-go, and the day her parents told her the Kombi was hers to keep, she'd burst into tears.

CeCe tooted as she pulled to a stop outside the house, and when her mother raced out of the front door, they hugged each other, then drove into town for a Danish and coffee from the patisserie on Seaview Road.

The following day, CeCe wrote a rock note to Anna and launched it into the river at Lime Tree Hill. She recalled driving Anna to Koru Bay the day after she passed her full driver's license. Frank had been worried sick, but Anna's uncle owned a property there, so they'd stayed with him and his family. That night, they ate fresh seafood and sweet potatoes cooked in a firepit, and later, the two friends swam naked in the lagoon under a full moon.

Much later still, they'd slept in the back of the Kombi, on a foam rubber squab she'd found at a yard sale, and woke to the sun streaming through the van's windows as the new day opened its arms.

On their way home, as The Band Perry's 'If I Die Young' played over the radio, Anna turned to CeCe and said, "If I die young, promise me you'll tell Mum and Dad to scatter my ashes over Koru Bay at sunset. It's the most beautiful place on earth."

That was the first and last summer roady they took together.

As she turned into the northern end of Carter Bay Road the next day, CeCe wondered what Luka would say when he saw her restored wheels. They'd made an uneasy peace over the past couple of weeks, sending one another the occasional text, but they'd not been alone since the day he flew her to Ferguson Hut.

Elevated above the city, the house stood proud, all dressed up in glass, cedar, and schist—like a handsome man in a well-cut three-piece suit. CeCe tried to pinpoint what made it stand out from the rest, and as she turned at the post numbered sixty-two, one word sprang to mind. Honesty. The dwelling's exterior displayed no pretension; it lived and breathed the essence of Luka. Calm and authentic. CookHouse Projects had done a fantastic job.

The driveway was empty, so she parked around the back of his garage suddenly nervous that yet again, she'd turned up unannounced. But that was their thing. She'd done it all the time when Luka lived in Tulloch Point.

It added to the anticipation.

The wooden deck was wide and clutter-free; no potted plants or unnecessary furniture. CeCe sat on the lowest step and removed her shoes. Newly laid lawn soft underfoot, she cleared her mind of anxious thoughts. No need to analyze. Not now that she'd made her decision. The sun, relentless earlier, had mellowed as it readied for the evening. It was her favorite time of day as summer left behind a windswept spring.

She lay back and closed her eyes, letting the warmth dance across her eyelids. With her busy schedule lately, she'd almost forgotten how these moments of fresh air, sunlight, and solitude soothed the soul.

At the sound of Luka's SUV on the driveway, CeCe sat up and checked her watch. The twenty minutes spent waiting had done wonders for her state of mind.

As he stepped from the vehicle, his smile hit her head-on, and those flirty butterflies soared in her stomach. Would he always have this effect? That instant 'wow' she whispered under her breath? The thrill at the sight of him?

"Hi. This is a surprise." Luka stepped forward and fished a ring of house keys from his pocket. "Come on in. Would you like a drink?"

She stood and considered him. "Actually, I was on my way to Petrie Bay for a swim, and I wondered if you'd like to come." She dangled the keys with the distinctive peace sign emblem in front of him.

Luka frowned. "You're in the Kombi? No way." He looked around. "Where is it?"

"At the back of your garage, in the shade."

Luka opened the door, and CeCe followed him inside. She'd expected a minimalist space with black and gray accents. But instead, bold color sprung from the walls courtesy of his extensive art collection, and sofas in burnt orange velvet added a comforting warmth to the interior.

He turned to her and smiled. "A double surprise then. The last time I saw the Kombi was when I dropped that CD into your mailbox on my way out of Tulloch Point. It was parked next to a shed at the orchard, and as I drove away, I remember thinking that I might never see it again." He held her gaze. "Does it still have a mattress in the back?"

"Occasionally." Barely suppressing a grin, CeCe checked him over. Fitted dress pants, tan leather shoes, and a white button-down shirt. *Very nice!* "You're looking smart today."

His hands went to the top two buttons of his shirt, and he

undid them. "Yeah? I had to meet with the council about water rights for our road, so I thought I'd better ditch the jeans and try to look respectable."

CeCe nodded. After three summers of drought, the lack of water in Clifton Falls was an issue.

He opened the fridge and grabbed a couple of beers. "Light beer okay, or would you prefer something else?"

"Beer's good." She turned in a slow circle, taking everything in. "This is fabulous. You must love living here."

"Yeah, I'm thrilled with it." Luka rummaged through a drawer, pulled out an opener, and flicked the caps off the bottles. He handed her one, and they clinked the necks together. "Cheers."

CeCe took a swig, then watched as he guzzled almost half the bottle in one go.

"I needed that. It was so hot in the council chambers, and some of those guys are completely useless. Shit, I hate dealing with bureaucratic idiots." He noted her amused expression. "What?"

"Sounds like you're getting cynical in your old age."

"Yeah, maybe you're right. I've been a little on edge lately."

She took another swig of her beer, the cool bitterness hitting the back of her tongue. "Why's that?"

His bottle halfway to his lips, Luka gave a little huff. Was his edge anything to do with her edge? She wanted to make love to him, and he probably wanted to get laid. In the end, it amounted to the same thing, no matter the variance in romanticism.

"Do you have food?" he asked.

"Food?"

He chuckled, then drained the rest of his beer. "To take to the beach?"

"Oh. Yes. In a cooler. In the van."

"Great." He undid the rest of the buttons on his shirt, putting his six-pack on blatant display. CeCe averted her gaze, heat flushing up her neck and face. "I'll just get changed."

In the sanctuary of his bedroom, Luka sat on the edge of his bed and undid his shoes. CeCe was right; he'd let things get to him lately, especially the damn water issues. But when he'd driven along his driveway and noticed her sitting on the deck, that soft smile of hers welcoming him home, he wished it could be like that every afternoon.

With her hair settled in loose waves about her makeup-free face, she reminded him of the old CeCe. She'd discarded the cutoff shorts in favor of a floaty summer dress that skimmed her ankles and hinted at a lack of a bra. But her bracelets, feather earrings, and leather sandals were similar. And when she'd smiled, he'd wanted to kiss the gloss from her lips, then take her to bed and lose himself in her until they both collapsed with *what the hell was that?* exhaustion.

After stuffing shorts, a towel, and a sweater into a bag, he hurriedly swapped his pants and shirt for jeans and a T-shirt. But as he stood at the side window to lower the blind, he stopped still. "No freakin' way!" He grinned from ear to ear. "CeCe?" he yelled down the hallway. "What the fuck?"

He turned when he heard her come up behind him. "You like?"

"How...?" Luka opened the sliding door onto the deck and stepped outside as CeCe followed. "Is it even the same Kombi?"

"Course it is."

One hand stuffed in his pocket, he walked around the vehicle, bending down to rub his other hand over the paintwork in places. "Wow. It looks incredible. Who did this?"

"Andy from that Classic Restore place in the industrial park out by the airport." She opened the passenger door. "Check out the seats."

"And you actually drive it?"

"Says the guy who drives a brand-new SUV and has his own chopper. I'm hardly going to keep it locked away in the garage at Mum and Dad's, am I now?"

He slid open the side door and laughed when he saw the mattress. "Good point."

"Anyway"—she tossed him the keys, and he caught them— "you drive. I'll just change into my bikini. Do you want me to grab your bag and lock the door?"

His mind racing, Luka only registered three words: *bikini, bag,* and *lock.* "Yeah, thanks."

He sat in the driver's seat and ran his hands over the steering wheel, CeCe all but forgotten as soon as she disappeared inside. Luka studied the dash, inserted the key in the ignition, and grinned when the Kombi started first time. He shifted into reverse, and as he backed around the house to the front door, he laughed at the sound of *Magical Mystery Tour* streaming through the speakers and the faint whiff of lavender from the tiny bunch hanging off the rearview mirror.

CeCe stood on the deck, a look of pure joy lighting up her face. Luka rolled the window down farther. "Are you coming, Kombi Girl?"

She pretended to hesitate before leaping onto the driveway. He expected her to open the passenger door and jump inside, but instead, she stuck her head through the driver's side window, cupped his face, and kissed him. "I could get used to this look on you, Chopper Guy. Parked up in the front seat of my Kombi."

"You just kissed me." He leaned out the window and kissed her back.

"Yeah. I thought it was about time I showed up."

WHISKEY OVER ICE

Luka took the back route, past the airport, and turned off at the junction of Five Mile Delta and the Eastern Pacific Highway. From there, Petrie Bay was barely fifteen minutes' drive. With orchards and market gardens along one side of the road and the South Pacific Ocean in the distance on the other, it was CeCe's favorite stretch of coastline.

As they passed Lime Tree Hill, 'Magical Mystery Tour' flowed through the speakers. Luka looked at her and smiled. "This CD's kinda growing on me."

"Yeah? Someone left it in my mailbox, gosh, almost five years ago now." She smiled as she recalled arriving home that Tuesday after Easter to find a small package from Luka on her nightstand with the CD and her sarong inside. The first time she'd played the title track, she'd lain on her bed and cried.

The day had been a scorcher, with no breeze and a burned-off sky, and waves spoke in whispers as they approached a parking spot at the northern end of the bay. She'd never seen it so calm. Out enjoying the perfect conditions, kids frolicked in the breakers, and along the shoreline, families gathered for picnics.

They sat and watched the roll of the surf until Luka turned side-on in his seat. "Thank you. I really needed this today."

"How come?"

"I thought we'd lost our way."

His words wrapped around her like an old friend's embrace. He leaned forward, his breath warm on her neck, and kissed her, one hand on the steering wheel and the other along the back of her seat. CeCe relaxed into his touch, and as his tongue swept her mouth with impressive style, her shoulders loosened.

Luka pulled back and smiled. "Shall we go for that swim?"

"I think we'd better. I'm suddenly feeling all hot and sweaty."

His chuckle followed CeCe out the door. Beside the van, she tugged her dress over her head and stood before him in her bikini.

He stared. "That color really suits you."

"Thanks. I just bought it today." She tightened the straps at her neck. "I'm not normally a fan of bright green, but the sales assistant talked me into it." She watched him, those moody eyes intense as always. "Are you coming in?"

A playful look flashed across his face. "In where?"

She leaned forward and helped him out of his T-shirt. "The water, remember?"

He grabbed her around the waist with both hands. "Maybe we should just head back to my place and park the Kombi in the shade."

"No way." She stepped back. "Get those jeans off, Chopper Guy, before I take them off for you."

CeCe turned and headed for the water. By the time he caught up with her, she was already knee-deep in the surf. He swept her up and carried her as he waded through the breakers. And when he set her on her feet, she could feel his hardness as their bodies molded together.

Saltwater on their lips and sun in their hair, they kissed. And as Luka wrapped her in his arms, his gaze searched hers. "I never stopped caring about you, CeCe, and as much as I tried to in the past, I now have no desire to get over you."

He released her and drifted away on the ebb of the tide until he was out of reach. Just like their first time together at Sandwater Bay, CeCe floated through the swell and watched him swim toward the horizon, his stroke relaxed but powerful.

CeCe closed her eyes and drifted on her back, letting the waves lift and lower her as she recalled those Tulloch Point days. So much had happened in the years they'd been apart, but as the sun gradually lost its strength and a light breeze rippled across the bay, those years ceased to be of importance. By his own admission, Luka had no desire to get over her, just as she had no desire to get over him.

Their next step could only be forward.

Floating to her feet, she felt his gaze, and she turned to watch him swimming toward her, the easy freestyle from before traded for breaststroke. As he drew closer, she swam to meet him. Her arms encircled his neck as she wrapped her legs around his waist. "Hey, Chopper Guy. You hungry?"

The urgency of his kiss took her by surprise. "Yep. Very hungry." He bent down and sucked the curve above her collarbone as his hands cupped her breasts.

"Luka!"

He drew back, flashing her a huge grin. "What?"

"We're on a public beach."

He looked toward the shore, squinting against the setting sun. "And it looks like we have company."

CeCe followed his line of sight to see Mitch and Tayla's SUV pulling up beside the Kombi. When Tayla waved through the open car window, CeCe waved back.

She jumped onto Luka's back as they waded into shore and whispered, "Guess that quickie in the Kombi will have to wait for another time."

He burst out laughing. "Did you actually just say that, or am I dreaming?"

"You're not dreaming."

They stayed at the beach for a couple of hours, sharing food and stories with Mitch and Tayla. On the way home, they drove with the windows down, the breeze lifting Luka's hair from his forehead, his foot tapping time to a Sam Smith song on the radio.

When CeCe stopped outside his front door and cut the engine, they both stared straight ahead, the sky still light in shades of pink and pearl gray along the horizon.

Knowing the ball was in his court, CeCe sat in silence as Luka turned to her. She didn't want to leave but if he wanted her to stay, and she was almost certain he did, he had to offer the invitation.

He leaned over and brushed a kiss across her lips. An *unfinished business* kiss that teased and offered a gentle hint of suggestion. "Are you coming in for a nightcap?"

She smiled. "Do you have any whiskey?"

"Sure."

"I feel like a whiskey right now for some reason."

He nodded. "Sounds like a plan."

Luka held her hand as they took the wide steps to the front door. Despite the warmth of the evening, CeCe shivered as he unlocked it, and as he led her into the dark foyer and switched on the lamp, a sudden desire to slow things down surprised her.

He turned to her. "Ice?"

"Sorry?"

They reached the living room, his lazy smile warming her insides. "In your whiskey? Do you want ice?"

"Oh, yes. Thanks." She looked around. In the corner, a Christmas tree sat in a hessian sack. Decorated in white, silver, and gold, it seemed almost too traditional for his taste. "Do you mind if I have a shower first? I'm all sandy."

"What, alone?"

"If that's okay?"

"Of course. Use my en suite. The towels on the rail are fresh."

"Thanks. I'll just grab some stuff from the van."

While it would have been nice to shower with him, that could wait. After all, what was an epic love affair without anticipation? And just knowing that Luka was in the kitchen, pouring her a whiskey over ice as he imagined her naked in his shower, made her ache for him with a strength that couldn't be denied.

Taking her time, CeCe washed her hair and let the water soothe her. She thought of the whiskey waiting for her on the end table by the sofa, how a few sips would heighten her senses and loosen her inhibitions. Because now that she'd stepped up, even though they'd slept together only a few weeks before, she still felt a little apprehensive. Perhaps he did too.

CeCe cut the water and grabbed a couple of towels off the rail. With one wrapped around her hair and the other loose at her hips, she stood in front of the mirror and wondered if he'd noticed the difference between the CeCe of today and her eighteen-year-old self. The fuller curves and breasts.

The dress had been a last-minute idea before leaving home.

After all, with no need for a bra or underwear, it seemed perfect for the occasion. And as she shimmied into the Valentina original, CeCe fantasized about a shirtless Luka clad in those white jodhpurs and black boots. After fastening the choker collar around her neck, she freed her hair from its bath-towel turban and checked her reflection again.

Her hair drying into curls, stilettos on, and red lipstick and mascara in place, she fished in her bag for the wrapped box she'd carried with her for over a week.

As CeCe left his bedroom, a cover version of Coldplay's 'Fix Me' floated along the hallway. She longed to go to him, to slip her arms around his waist from behind and rest her head between his shoulder blades as they swayed to the beat.

In the living room, the whiskey sat exactly where she'd imagined it would, the song played a little louder, and the Christmas tree lights twinkled in the corner. Luka sat in one of two leather chairs that flanked the fireplace, whiskey in hand, his head back and eyes closed.

CeCe tiptoed across the room to place the gift underneath the tree before picking up her drink. The first sip burned its way down, and at the sound of the ice clinking in her glass, Luka opened his eyes.

Stared.

Shook his head.

Formed a lazy smile.

"Well, just look at you."

47

RED LIPSTICK BOW

Luka could scarcely believe his eyes. That dress—with its submissive straps and form-fitting style—had haunted him for weeks. Now here she was. All wrapped up in those silver heels and sporting a red lipstick bow: the perfect Christmas gift.

"I thought I should dress for the occasion."

He stood and stepped toward her. "And what occasion would that be?"

CeCe sipped her drink and glanced up at him through heavy lashes. "I don't believe I need to elaborate." She raised her head and met his gaze. "But I will say this. I've given the whole 'existence of pheromones' theory much thought over the years."

He suppressed a smile. "Is that so?"

"Uh-huh. And I've come to the conclusion that, while there's ongoing scientific debate, in my opinion, their existence is highly probable. In fact, if pushed, I might even use the term *absolutely* probable."

Luka took her glass and set it down next to his on the side table. He inhaled deeply and nuzzled into her neck, his lips finding their way from choker to earlobe as she tilted her head to one side. "I think you're probably right," he whispered. "Because, damn, I've missed the scent of you. So, so much."

CeCe drew back and grinned. "Same."

The music changed to Bic Runga's 'Sway.' Luka held her gaze as she moved with the melody, and as her breasts pressed against his chest, he stiffened in response. This girl—with her theory on pheromones, sexy-as dress, and full, red lips—had shown up. No more polite lies, no commitment issues, no baggage. Just the two of them, and a fresh dose of honesty.

"Do you know how many times I've imagined fucking you again in this dress?"

Her flirty smile had him stiffening even more, which amused him. They hadn't even made it to the bedroom yet. Then again, she'd always had that effect.

"No, but I might also have imagined us having sex while you have your white jodhpurs around your thighs and your black boots on."

He chuckled at the thought. "Yeah? I'm not sure that would work."

CeCe tilted her head a little more, inviting easier access, her light fragrance flirting with his senses as her breath hitched. He'd tried to remember the scent of her over the years and failed. Now it seemed so familiar, he couldn't understand why it had ever left him.

"Why not?"

Luka smoothed his hands down her dress until they reached her butt. He squeezed lightly. "Because I don't like restrictions when I'm having sex."

Her expression shifted from playful to serious, her breathing less controlled. "In that case, you should take me to your bed."

"Not to the Kombi?"

"Not tonight."

Despite wanting to lift her so she could wrap her legs around his waist, he knew the dress wouldn't rise to that occasion, so instead, he took her hand and led the way, L.A.B.'s 'In the Air' playing in the background.

There had been many times lately when Luka had imagined pushing her up against the wall and taking her hard and fast as he had after the benefit dinner, but as she sat on the bed and lifted each foot so he could remove her shoes, the reverence of the moment hit him head-on. This was their second chance, and he didn't want to mess it up. He loved her and had no doubt she loved him back. And for that very reason, he'd take it slow.

CeCe placed her hands on his shoulders and kissed him, the taste of whiskey fresh on her tongue. He grasped hold of the hem of his shirt and pulled it over his head. When she bent down and sucked on his nipple, Luka's back arched, and he went from stiff to rock-hard in an instant.

"Ah, I remember that," she said.

Panting now, so ready for her. "What?"

"Your breasts are supersensitive."

He chuckled. "I don't have breasts. I have pecs."

CeCe trailed her fingertips over them. "And they're magnificent." While maintaining eye contact, she rubbed him through the denim of his jeans and was none too gentle about it. "In fact, you're magnificent all over. But we need to speed things up, Chopper Guy, because I'm about to combust just from looking at you."

Struggling to release his fly, Luka forgot all about the reverence of the moment. As usual for their first time of the evening, CeCe didn't want it slow. She wanted lust scorching the air between them. She slipped off the bed and stood at his side, her hands unclipping the fasteners that held the choker to the straps of her dress.

Her smile widening, she turned her back to him and glanced over her shoulder, lifting her hair off her neck. "Can you unzip me?"

Luka obliged, his hands clumsy and unsteady in the simple task, and as her naked back came into view, he felt as if he were unwrapping a gift. One he'd been wanting forever. She wore no bra, and when he peeled the dress over her hips, he discovered she'd worn no panties either.

Their clothes pooling in a heap on the floor, they kissed with hungry lips, his fingers wrapped inside the choker and her nails digging into his back. CeCe pushed him backward onto the bed and straddled him. "Condom?"

His mind blank, he stared up at her, naked everywhere except for that choker. "Shit, um…" *Did he have condoms? Of course he did!* Luka pointed to the nightstand. "Top drawer."

She leaned over, her breasts rubbing against his chest, and as she moved back, he placed his hands behind his head and watched. "That choker is so damn sexy on you."

"I'm glad you like it."

She lowered herself onto him, a slight hesitation on her brow as he lifted his butt off the bed. And as they kissed and started to move, he struggled to maintain control.

"Slow down," he commanded. "Or I'm going to come."

CeCe gripped his shoulders, frowning down at him while slowing her pace. "And you think I'm not?"

Luka's head sank into the pillows, eyes closed as he forced a "Shit, CeCe," through gritted teeth. He rolled her onto her back and pulled out. "Not just yet, you're not."

She shook her head, panting hard and cupping her breasts as he sat back on his haunches. "You're not playing fair."

"Course I am." He eased into her, then withdrew.

"Do that again."

He laughed and did as instructed. "So bossy. Again?"

"Yes...please!"

CeCe collapsed onto the bed, the choker still around her neck and a hint of red lipstick staining her lips. "Wow, that feels so much better," she murmured.

"What the hell *was* that?"

She lifted her head to look at him and kissed him on the cheek. "Red-hot sex. That's what it was."

"But I planned to take it slow. To worship you. Show you how much I'd missed you."

"Oops. Sorry. I didn't really get that vibe." CeCe giggled. "Okay, let's go make some banana on toast, and then maybe—"

"Banana on toast?"

"Best energy food ever." CeCe lifted a brow and beamed a naughty smile. "You know how walnuts look like a brain, so they're supposed to be good for your mental abilities? Well, bananas—"

He chuckled. "Yeah, I get your point."

She jumped out of bed and picked up his T-shirt from the floor. And as Luka watched her put it on, he wanted to tell her how much he loved her.

But that could wait.

"Come on, you, get up. I'm starving."

***

Dawn's first light streamed through the bedroom's double doors as CeCe stirred. They lay on their backs, legs tangled together under the top sheet and hands entwined, in one of the most comfortable beds she'd ever slept in.

After their snack, they'd had sex once again. Long and slow and reverent. When it was over, and Luka held her with care, his fingers drawing lazy circles around her belly button, she'd wanted to tell him how much she loved him. But that declaration held weight, a heaviness that deserved the perfect occasion.

Luka opened his eyes and smiled. "Are you in work mode already? I can almost hear your brain cogs turning."

"No. I've given myself the day off."

He wrapped her in his arms. "Good for you."

"But I do have a question."

"Yeah?"

"So, this girl you can't stop thinking about—the 'sexy as F' ex—tell me about her."

He pecked her on the cheek. "Losing her was my 'if you love someone,' moment. Seemed like a good idea at the time, but it's been five years, and I thought we'd never get a second chance."

CeCe looked up at him. "I have one of those too."

"What? A sexy as F ex?"

"Yep. He rides a black horse and flies a chopper. He can be a bit moody at times—sends mixed messages and likes to be in control. But what's one or two flaws between friends?"

"Mixed messages, huh? Maybe he wants you to define your feelings, so he knows exactly where you both stand."

"I suspect he already knows where I stand. After all, I don't let just anyone drive my Kombi."

"Yeah, there is that."

She snuggled closer. "So, you loved her then, this ex? Loved her enough to set her free?"

He sighed. "I didn't realize it then, but looking back, I did love you in my own way. You were my gorgeous, carefree surfer girl. So different to any woman I'd met before…or since."

"I wanted to say it," she whispered. "That last day, back in Tulloch Point, I almost did."

"But the timing was off?"

"Most definitely."

Luka sat up and crossed his legs, the planes of his chest covered in goose bumps and a slight smile playing about his lips. He took her hand and kissed it. "I do love you. Very much."

CeCe's free hand went to her lips. "Oh my gosh, I think I'm gonna cry."

He pulled her into a hug and kissed the top of her head. "Hey, it's okay. Let's go eat breakfast."

"But I haven't said it back."

"I can wait." Luka rose naked from the bed and walked across the room and into his closet. At the sight of him, she smiled, tears forgotten.

That butt…cut to perfection.

48

GIVING GIFTS

Phone in hand, Luka stood at the window overlooking the lawn and watched the rain pelt the earth. He'd planned to sow the grass from scratch, but with the house behind schedule, he'd run out of time, so had settled for ready-lawn.

He loved it when CeCe stayed over, and on nights like this, when she insisted on spending time alone so she could catch up on her business, he found it difficult to sleep without her.

Luka: Come over. I want to open my present.
CeCe: I told you, not until Xmas day. Are you coming to Mum and Dads for Xmas lunch?
Luka: Yes. If you stay the night with me beforehand.
CeCe: I've stayed almost every night for the past two weeks.
Luka: And the sex just keeps getting better and better.
CeCe: *blush blush*.

Luka walked across the room and picked up her gift to him —a box wrapped in navy blue paper and finished with a silver bow—and gave it a shake before setting it back under the tree. Sitting beside it was his gift to her. He'd thought about what to get her for weeks. CeCe was unimpressed by wealth and ostentation, that much he knew. She usually wore earrings made from shells or feathers, and that blue butterfly still graced her neck whenever she rocked up in jeans and a T-shirt at the weekends.

Although that black choker outfit of hers remained a favorite look, he loved her floaty beach dresses and cut off shorts too. No matter which way one looked at her, physically or spiritually, the simplicity of her manner and the depth of her soul made CeCe a beautiful person, inside and out.

How had he got so lucky?

His phone chimed with an incoming text.

CeCe: I'll stay. That way we can wake up together on Xmas morning. We'll eat pancakes with blueberries and maple syrup.
Luka: Sounds good. You realize what this means?
CeCe: No, what?
Luka: We're a proper couple now. Spending Xmas day together. Lunch with your folks, dinner with mine.
CeCe: Damn! Let's just go surfing instead.
Luka: Not this year.
CeCe: Goodnight Chopper Guy.
Luka: Night.

It amused Luka how so much had changed lately. Frank Dobson had even offered him a whiskey when he and CeCe visited them the week before. They'd talked choppers and horses and organics, and when they bid her parents farewell, Frank's handshake had been firm and accompanied by a smile.

Last weekend, he'd given CeCe a riding lesson, and it

hadn't gone well. He doubted she'd ever feel comfortable in the saddle. But she'd been a good sport about it, even when Spartan, usually a placid old fella, took off at speed.

Afterward, with his parents and twin brothers away for the night, they'd had hot, messy sex on a chair in his old bedroom; Luka with his jodhpurs around his thighs, and CeCe dressed in nothing but a smile and a blue butterfly.

Luka opened the fridge and peered inside, feeling restless. It wasn't a beer kind of night, but he grabbed one anyway and flicked off the top. Just as he was about to take a swig, his phone chimed again.

CeCe: What are you doing?
Luka: Nothing much. I'm about to have a beer and turn on Netflix. You?

When his doorbell rang, he put down his beer and phone on the side table. His brow creasing in a frown, he stepped into the foyer and peered through the peephole, surprised to see a mass of dark curly hair. Luka opened his front door. "What are you doing here?"

"You invited me."

He scooped CeCe up and carried her inside, and as he set her on her feet, his lips found her neck as usual. "Does that mean I can open my present?"

"Not the one under the tree."

Thanks to Tayla going into labor just before lunch and delivering a baby girl nine hours later, their Christmas Eve didn't quite go as planned. The entire family congregated at the hospital, and CeCe and Luka finally made it home around ten, elated but exhausted.

The Christmas tree lights bathed the living room in a dreamy glow, and as he held her in his arms and kissed her, Luka's tension drained away. "Let's open our presents before we go to bed."

"Okay."

They grabbed their presents from under the tree and sat beside one another on the wide hearth of the fireplace.

"May I go first?" CeCe asked. "I have something I want to say."

"Sure."

She handed him the box. "I had no idea what to get the man with everything. So before going to sleep a few nights ago, I put it out to the universe."

Luka shook his head and grinned. "Some days, you sound alarmingly like my mother."

"Anyway, I love you with every single breath, and as soon as I decided, I knew I'd chosen the perfect gift."

He kissed her, his arms loose around her neck. "Thank you." His hands worked the bow and then the paper. The flat box inside looked like it might contain a wallet or cuff links. But when he opened it and saw the peace symbol, he smiled at her and shook his head. "A key?"

She smiled back. "Yes, to the Kombi. I want to share it with you."

Luka's eyes widened. "Seriously?"

"Seriously."

"I don't know what to say. Can I sleep in it when you get moody?"

"Sure. That's what it's there for. But I don't get moody too often."

He chuckled and handed her his gift. It was a similar size to hers, and it amused him how they were on the same wavelength. CeCe tore away the paper without restraint and peered into the box, her expression unreadable. She frowned. "A key as well? What's it for?"

"This house. I want to share it with you. You can sleep in it when I'm in the Kombi—and any other night you choose."

Her frown deepened. "You're asking me to move in?"

"Not tonight, obviously, but maybe on Boxing Day."

"But that's the day after tomorrow."

"Yeah, I know. I thought it was about time." He smoothed a lock of hair from her face. "Are you keen?"

"Can I bring Pixie?"

"Of course."

CeCe flung her arms around his neck. "Then I'm more than keen. But are you sure?"

"Positive. Now, let's go to bed."

"But we haven't had any dinner. Well, only those horrible falafel wraps at the hospital."

He laughed. "Okay. I'll pop some bread in the toaster while you peel and slice the bananas."

She leaned forward and whispered, "Have I ever told you you're sexy as fuck, my ex-teacher?"

Luka picked her up, tossed her over his shoulder, and carried her through to the bedroom. "No. Never."

"Put me down." She giggled. "What about our toast?"

"It can wait."

EPILOGUE

Dearest Anna,

Sorry it's been so long. Life's been crazy here on earth-side, so I have a lot to tell you. I went to the river yesterday and found the largest, flattest rock I could carry. I hope it's big enough for all the words I've been saving for you. I might have to fill both sides.

Luka and I are officially a couple after exchanging key rings on Christmas Eve. I gave him a key to the Kombi, and he gave me one to his house. He set me free, and I came back to him. I'm so happy I did. It's been six months now, and each day we find out new things about one another. He calls me his sexy as f@#k ex-girlfriend when we're alone, but I still like Hot Chopper Guy for him.

I moved in with him between Christmas and New Year. It's a neat place to live. Spacious and light and restful, and I feel at peace here. Luka's even putting in a tennis court for when I get the strength back in my shoulder. He wants me to teach him how to play.

If someone asked me to describe the feeling of my new home, I could sum it up in one word: serene. Just like that little church at Koro Bay when we spent the weekend with your uncle's family.

What a great trip that was. Remember that Sia song, 'Chandelier,' we sang on the way? Whenever I hear it— even now—I think of you and that trip. Over the past few months, Luka and I have been on two road trips to Sandwater Bay. Not only is it our special place, but it's also where I feel especially close to you.

Travis got married. Did you know that? His wife is lovely, and while he's still a bit of a jerk, I'm pleased for him. They have a café and make amazing vegan treats out of chickpeas and tahini and pulled 'pork' sliders using banana skins (I kid you not). You'd love it.

Molly's relationships continue to go from good to really awful in the space of a long blink. She meets guys at gigs and falls head over heels. But they never last. It's sad for her because I know how much she wants to settle down and have kids. That might sound old-fashioned, but it's not a bad thing.

Speaking of kids, Mitch and Tayla welcomed a baby girl on Christmas Eve. Her name is Storm Ivy Harrington, and she's just beautiful as you can imagine. Liz is pregnant again with a baby boy and due in the Northern autumn. She and Ally still live in London. I miss them terribly, but the chances of either of my sisters ever living in New Zealand again are slim to none.

And do you remember Levi Hokianga, that little shit of a kid that lived next door to the orchard and always got detentions? Anyway, he's in law school now. Who would have thought that one up? He's turned out to be a really neat guy. Then again, I always did have a soft spot for him.

So, life is good. I love my Chopper Guy, the Kombi is all shiny and new, and my family's well. Also, I started a new business—my own range of organic skincare. It's called Botanical Ce. It's been so much work, and some days in the beginning, I wondered what I'd gotten myself into, but now sales are growing so rapidly, I can hardly keep up.

My one wish is that you could be here to share in my happiness and volley a few tennis balls back and forth. I miss you so much, Anna. Every single day.

I have to sign off now before I start blubbering. We're going up to the falls for a picnic in the Kombi later, and I will throw this into the veil. Promise me you'll catch it.

All my love,
C. xoxo

The End

Thanks for spending time with Luka and CeCe. Book Three in the Reluctant Kiss series is out now, so if you'd like to stay in Clifton Falls to find out what happened to Molly Parker and the musician who once held her heart, then download *The Last Autograph* today.

"Curiosity takes us places we seldom imagine going."

"...I absolutely loved this charming story. It had more twists than I expected, which kept me hooked from start to finish."
5 Stars!
Goodreads Reviewer.

Download *The Last Autograph* today.

Available at Amazon stores worldwide.

Or, if you are curious about Luka's parents, Liam and Vanessa O'Leary, *Field of the White Snow* is also available on Amazon. Although it can be read as a standalone, to avoid spoilers you might want to read *The Watershed* first.

Field of the White Snow

A perfect companion to *The Watershed.*

So much more than a coming-of-age story, *Field of the White*

Snow follows the life of Vanessa Blinkly and Liam O'Leary, the son of her mother's employer, as they come to terms with the circumstances
that brought them together.

All they needed were forty-eight sunsets.

Buy Now @ Amazon.com

———

MANY THANKS

Hi there,

As you may have guessed, I'm a Kiwi, so I often write about Kiwi characters living in Kiwi locations. And down here in New Zealand, some things are a little back to front and upside down compared to where you may live.

The school year goes from February to December, we have a summer Christmas, not a winter one, autumn is in April, spring in September, and kiwis (the fruit) are called just that—kiwifruit. We also drive on the left side of the road, and the legal drinking age is eighteen.

Kiwis love the great outdoors and national parks cover large parts of New Zealand. In these parks, small and not so small huts provide warmth and shelter for trampers (hikers). So, when you visit New Zealand, you can go and stay in a hut just like CeCe and Nick did. Just watch out for the bed bugs. Kidding!

And, Kiwi authors love reviews, so if you enjoyed this book, please consider leaving a short review/star rating on Amazon and/or Goodreads. Your reviews matter, and I appreciate your time.

Cheers, (Kiwi speak for *best, kind regards, sincerely, have a great day, etc.)*

Frances.

ACKNOWLEDGMENTS

People often ask me where I get the ideas for my books. A few years ago, my friend's son taught for a year after completing his science degree, but soon left teaching to pursue other goals. When we were at a dinner party one evening, he jokingly suggested I write a book about a chemistry teacher, and that's where this story originated.

Apart from my family, I have many people to thank. My editors: Liz Dempsey, The Error Eliminator, for your attention to detail. I couldn't do this without you, Liz. Samantha Burton, who helped develop the story with her usual enthusiasm. To Steven Novak, from Novak Illustration, for the cover completion; it's great to work with you as always.

Thanks also to my beta readers: Jane, Laura, Carole B, Phil, and Kate G-S. Your feedback was, as always, highly valuable. And to Kate and Marjorie for your encouragement over our writing-group lunches.

The members of the Otago chapter of Romance Writers of NZ, you guys are a great support. I'm privileged and humbled to have you in my writing life, and I thoroughly enjoyed the wilderness retreat with some of you recently.

To RM for the information on rescues in the New Zealand bush, National Park huts, and PLBs.

To Kevin, thanks always for your enthusiasm.

To Grant, my lifelong friend who joined Romance Writers

of New Zealand the year after me and sadly passed away in December 2020 before his written words were ever published. I dedicate this book to you, my friend, with much love.

Last, but by no means least, to my readers. My heartfelt thanks for taking the time out of your busy lives to read my novels. If you enjoyed *Reluctant Chemistry,* please consider leaving a review on your book retailer's site and sharing the title with your romance-reading friends. Happy reading,

Frances

ABOUT THE AUTHOR

Frances Cowie hails from a picturesque lakeside town nestled below the Southern Alps of New Zealand, where she writes romantic women's fiction and contemporary romance HEAs, all with a dash of spice.

A keen baker, Frances has a passion for apple desserts and Whittaker's coconut chocolate.

For more information, including sneak peeks at upcoming projects, visit Frances online at:

www.francescowie.com

ALSO BY FRANCES COWIE

Clifton Falls Companion Novels

The Train Station – A Clifton Falls Novella

The Watershed

Field of the White Snow

An Imagined Kiss – The London Series

The List Maker

How About Thursday

Hampton Lane

A Reluctant Kiss – The South Pacific Series

Lime Tree Hill

Reluctant Chemistry

The Last Autograph

For an ordered book list, including content information, please log on
to my website at:

www.francescowie.com